Beth Bradley 2.0

- Emma Ernst -

ISBN: 9798536411988 (paperback)

For Ada

TABLE OF CONTENTS

-1-

JULY

The night started out like a regular Tuesday evening. Chad came home from work after picking up Zoe, our five-year-old daughter, from science camp. I heard them come in, heard Zoe throw her backpack on the floor and Chad put his keys on the side table. Zoe ran into the kitchen, her ponytail swinging from side to side as I took a lasagna out of the oven.

"Mommy!" she said.

"Zoe! How was your day?" I said as she gave me a gigantic hug. Zoe was small for her age but gave mighty hugs.

"It was so great! I learned about the planets in the solar system."

Chad followed Zoe in and gave me a kiss on the cheek. "You know, when Mommy and I were your age, there were nine planets."

"Really? What happened to the last planet?" Zoe was always asking questions; she was an extremely curious kid.

"They decided it didn't meet the planet standards anymore," Chad said. Chad was really into science and watched a lot of nature shows. It came in handy with Zoe's numerous questions. The two of them spent hours looking at books about animals and the Earth together.

"What does that mean?" Zoe asked.

"Hmm." Chad tilted his head to the side. "I'm not exactly sure."

"This weekend, we'll go to the library and get a book about Pluto," I offered. "Time for dinner. Zoe, can you set the table?"

Zoe set the table as I served the lasagna. Family dinner was my favorite part of the day. With life as hectic and chaotic as ours, I cherished the time all three of us could be together. Life was busy. Zoe was involved in a number of activities, including soccer and gymnastics. Chad played softball on Sundays and had a poker night with his friends every other Friday night, and I had my monthly book club. It was so nice when we could all just be together.

"That was really good," Chad said, pointing to his plate. "Possibly your best ever." He looked across the table and smiled at me. He still wore his work clothes and looked even more handsome than the day I'd met him. His sandy blond hair was a little shorter than usual, but it suited his round face, and the burgundy shirt he wore brought out his hazel eyes.

He got up from the table and kissed me on the forehead. I smiled thinking about how happy I was. Last weekend at our annual block party, we were all snuggled up watching a movie outside. Chad rubbed my shoulders, while Zoe lay her head in my lap. It was pure bliss.

If only I had known.

After dinner, I got Zoe ready for her bath while Chad cleaned up. I read Zoe two of her favorite stories and kissed her good night. When I came downstairs, Chad was in our living room, sitting on the couch. He had just turned the lamp on, rather than the over-head light, so the room looked dark. He'd poured himself a glass of scotch and was scrolling through his phone.

"Do you want to watch something?" I asked.

"Actually, can we talk?" He took a sip of his drink.

"Sure. Just let me grab a drink." I went to the kitchen and got a glass of wine. I sat down on the couch next him. I figured he wanted to talk about going to the beach before the summer was over, or maybe he was trying to put another boys' fishing trip on the calendar.

"So, what's up?" I asked.

He took a deep breath. "I feel like things are off between us. We just aren't connecting."

A knot started to form in my stomach. Chad normally didn't bring up this kind of stuff. The last time we'd had an intense talk was three years ago, when Chad and Zoe got into a car accident. They were coming back from picking up dinner, and he got rear-ended. The back of the car was crushed. Zoe was just two, and while she only had a few bumps and bruises, I became extremely overprotective. The first few weeks after that accident, I wouldn't let Chad drive her anywhere. He finally talked me out of that for logistical reasons, but I was constantly checking up on him. It got out of hand, and I decided to see a therapist. We talked about my control issues, and how I needed to trust more. I thought that, not only was I making a lot of progress, but we, as a family, had been doing better.

I didn't speak. I wanted to let him continue, to see where this was going. I took a sip of wine and put my glass on the side table. I gave Chad my full attention.

"Okay," I said. I wasn't sure if I was supposed to answer, or if he had more to say.

"And we barely have sex."

"What are you talking about? We have sex all the time. Like once a week. Given our busy schedules, that's pretty good."

"Yes, but when we do, if feels like you're just crossing it off your list. It doesn't feel like you want to do it, it's just an obligation."

I jerked back in surprise at the accusation. I felt like we had a pretty good sex life considering we were two working adults with a five-year-old. Sex might have been something I mentally checked off my to-do list, but at least I was trying. I believed sex was important for couples, but at this stage in my life, it wasn't necessarily on the top of my list. But at least it made it to the list.

"Okay, well, then let's find ways to have more sex. We can have more date nights, and now that Zoe is old enough for sleepovers, maybe we can go away, rekindle our flame."

"I don't know, Beth. We've just lost our spark." He took a deep breath and then another drink of his scotch. His eyes darted from mine, and he was just staring at the half-empty glass.

I put my hand in his and looked into his eyes. "I know this was hard to bring up. I'm glad you did. Let's talk about ways to make us connect again."

"I'm not sure that's possible. The spark has been gone for a while, and since your promotion at work, I just don't feel like you're making time for me. I don't know where my place is anymore."

A year ago, I'd been promoted to director of the analytics department at my company, Market Insight. I had been working there since college and had worked extremely hard to get my promotion. It had come with a nice bump in my salary and a lot more responsibility. At first there were some additional late nights, but I was lucky to work for a company that really valued a work-life balance, so I was able to work from home two days a week. After a few months, I was back in a groove and the late nights were more sporadic.

"Your place is right here, as my husband, as Zoe's father," I said. "We can work this out. I know we can."

I wasn't sure where this conversation was going, but I was glad that Chad was bringing it up. If he was unhappy, then, together, maybe we could make a change. My family and my marriage were important, and I wanted to do everything necessary to keep them together and moving in the right direction. We could work this out, find our special spark again. I didn't want to lose my family. I didn't want to lose Chad. This was just a bump in the road that we would work through together and come out stronger than ever.

I put my hand on his arm. It made me sad to know that Chad had felt this way and hadn't told me. My heart clenched. Did he really feel that way? Was I a bad wife, someone who didn't even see when their partner was unhappy? I made a mental note to do better. To really engage and make time.

He stared into my eyes and inhaled deeply. He shifted his focus back to his glass. I expected him to say, "Thanks, I think I just needed to hear you say that. I agree, we should take some time to talk about this and figure it out."

I wasn't at all ready for what he *actually* said.

"The thing is…" There was another long, deep pause. He rubbed his face with his hands. "I've been having an affair. With Courtney, from work. We've been together for three years. I love her, and I want to be with her."

My heart sank. I couldn't believe the words coming out of my husband's mouth. Did he really just say what I thought he'd said? He'd been cheating on me for *three years*?

Dizziness swept over me. I couldn't believe this was happening. Who was this man sitting next to me? This had to be some sort of sick joke.

I sat there in silence, the words hanging there between us. I stared at a picture of Chad and me kissing in the moonlight. We had gotten it as a five-year wedding anniversary gift from my parents. Time felt like it stood still. The knot in my stomach worsened, I couldn't breathe. It started to feel like someone was ripping out my heart and stomping on it. A wave of feelings came over me all at once. I was hurt. I was in denial. I was in disbelief. I couldn't believe he was just going to throw away everything, the life we had together, just like that. He wasn't even going to try? Just a few minutes ago, I thought I was a bad wife, started to doubt myself. But *he* was the one who had messed up.

He continued on. "We've rented a house a few miles away, so it will be easy for Zoe. Courtney has kids, too; they get along with Zoe."

"Are you fucking serious? I can't believe this."

Chad just sat there with a blank look on his face.

"What about Zoe?" I asked.

"What about Zoe?"

"You're just going to pluck her out of this home, with both of her parents, and put her in another one, with strangers? You're destroying her world, you know."

"Zoe will be fine. She gets along with Courtney's kids. She knows them; they aren't strangers. You should see them play together. It's cute."

My blood started to boil. My face burned and I just didn't know what to say. Was this for real? Not only was the man who'd promised to love me in good times and in bad cheating on me, but he'd already found a place to live with his paramour and had introduced her and her kids to Zoe. This was an absolute nightmare.

"You seriously introduced her to them without me knowing? That's fucked up."

"What does it matter?" he said.

"It matters plenty. I am her mother and I deserve to know who she spends time with."

"I told you we were with a friend—that's all you needed to know."

My blood continued to boil. I couldn't believe his betrayal. I couldn't believe this was happening. I put my head in my hands and rubbed my temples to try to calm down. It was something I always did when I was stressed. I took a few deep breaths and stared again at our picture on the wall. The knot in my stomach was getting worse.

"But I don't want her in a broken home. She deserves better than that."

"It's better than being in a home where the parents don't love each other."

I took another deep breath. Tears started to stream down my face. "But I *do* love you."

I wiped away the tears. "Why didn't you tell me this sooner? We could have worked on it. We could have gone to see a counselor together. We could have worked on our problems."

Chad shifted on the couch, refusing to look in my direction. I didn't know what to do. I wanted to hold onto him, to tell him we could make this work, we could figure it out, that he didn't have to leave. But on the other hand, I was so angry at him! For lying, for cheating, for ripping apart our family. My family meant everything to me! And I thought it meant everything to Chad, too.

I started to feel sick and ran into the bathroom. After throwing up, I went to the sink and splashed water on my face. I stared at my reflection in the mirror. Why didn't Chad love me anymore? Why was he leaving? Why didn't he fight for me? Why didn't he fight for our family? Our problems weren't any different than other couples'. And if he was that upset, why hadn't he said something? After the accident, I had suggested that he go with me to counseling, but he'd refused. I'd thought it would be good for us to talk to someone about communication, our weak point. We usually brushed things under the rug, and I wanted to have tools in our wheelhouse so we could have productive conversations. But Chad refused, he didn't think therapy was going to help him. I thought he was afraid of discussing his feelings in front of a stranger. Looking back, it was probably because he had already started his affair with Courtney, and he was probably terrified it would come out.

I came out of the bathroom. Chad had poured himself a second drink. I plopped down on the coach and crossed my arms.

"So, all those times you were at a happy hour, or working late, you were with her?"

"Not always." He shrugged. "Look, after the accident you changed. You got crazy, and I just needed someone to talk to, and Courtney was there."

"That's such bullshit, and you know it. I admit, I got scared after the accident, but that's because our baby could have been hurt."

"But she wasn't. And you stopped trusting me with our daughter. How do you think that made me feel? I felt inadequate, like I wasn't cutting it as a dad. Courtney was there to pick me up. You didn't see I was hurting."

"I'm sorry. I know that was a hard time for both of us, which is why I saw a therapist. I asked you to come with me, but you said it was my problem to solve."

"It *was* your problem. You were the one who went nuts."

"That's not fair."

He just sat there, silently.

"And then, since the promotion, I feel like it's back to everything being about you. I just don't feel valued or appreciated. Courtney values me."

"I value you. Where is that even coming from?"

"You don't. I work hard, too, you know."

"I know you work hard." I had always been the breadwinner in the family, and that was never a point of contention for us. Chad joked about having a sugar mama. But since my promotion, there was a clear gap in our salaries. I never thought anything of it because we were a team, and while I might bring in more money, we were in this family together.

"And you're always yelling at me for staying out late, or spending too much time in the yard. You don't know what it takes to make our yard look like it does. You never compliment me on that."

"Seriously! I had every right to yell at you for staying out late. You were sleeping with someone else!"

"But you didn't know that."

I couldn't believe Chad felt this way, that our fighting justified him having an affair, falling in love with another woman, and leaving me. This was not the man I thought I'd married.

"So, this is my fault? You're unbelievable. If you were so unhappy, you should have said something, not lied to me. But I guess I wasn't worth it to you."

He opened his mouth to say something, but I had had enough. "I can't believe you've been lying to my face for the past three years. You are not the man I thought you were. Even now, you can't even admit that you're wrong. You think that your actions are justified?" I stopped for a minute considering my next move. I might regret it later, but I didn't have to take it.

"Get the hell out," I demanded.

He slowly set down his scotch, then walked to the front door. He looked back at me. "I'm sorry, but this is just how I feel."

He closed the door behind him.

I got up, snatched the closest thing I could find, a children's book, and threw it at the door.

Returning to the couch, I sank down. My lips were wet. When had I started crying again?

I wasn't sure what to do next. A good thirty minutes later, I was still staring at that picture. Twix, our cat, snuggled up next to me, purring loudly.

I finally gained enough strength to get off the couch and head up to bed. As I climbed the stairs, I passed pictures of our family on the wall. The time we went to the pumpkin patch and Zoe tried to lift the biggest pumpkin. The first time we took Zoe to a Nationals game. I paused at a picture of us from last fall. Chad was raking the leaves, but Zoe couldn't resist jumping into the big pile he'd made. Together, the three of us played in the leaves, running and jumping. We managed to sneak in a selfie. Leaves were everywhere, but our smiles were genuine. It was one of those moments that just randomly happen but that you remember forever.

And it was all a lie.

I stared at Chad's face, trying to see if there were any signs that he was thinking about Courtney, thinking about leaving me.

When I checked on her, Zoe slept soundly with the monkey she'd had since she was two tucked under her arm. She took it everywhere with her. I kissed her on the forehead and just sat there for a while, watching her sweet face. I didn't know what this news meant for her, but I knew it wasn't going to be an easy road.

I headed into the bathroom, washed my face, brushed my teeth, and climbed into bed. The bed felt empty and cold. Sleeping alone wasn't something I wanted to get used to. I turned off the light and tried to sleep, but I couldn't. My heart ached unbearably. The last few hours just kept going through my head. The hurtful things Chad

had said. Trying to make this *my* fault, telling me he didn't love me. I couldn't believe this was my life, that this was really happening.

That my husband was leaving me and my family was being torn apart.

When I woke up the next morning, Twix was curled up next to me. I rolled over and felt the emptiness in the bed. I jolted awake. It hadn't been a dream. Last night had really happened. My husband of ten years really had left me for another woman.

I stared at the ceiling. The pain in my heart was still there. I took a deep breath. *Why doesn't he love me anymore?* Tears formed in my eyes. Was this really my life?

I stared at the clock. 6:30. I threw on some workout clothes, went down to the kitchen, and poured myself a coffee. The events of last night played on repeat in my head. It didn't make any sense. For the past three years, Chad had been lying to my face. How could I have been so oblivious? I realized that it would be impossible for me to get any work done today, so I sent an email to my boss telling her that I wasn't feeling well. I had a mountain of work, but it would have to wait.

At seven, I went to wake up Zoe.

"Rise and shine, sweetie," I said as I opened her curtains. I wanted to ask her about Courtney, but knew better. I still couldn't believe he'd introduced our daughter to his girlfriend and her kids before I even knew they existed. Chad and I were going to have to talk to Zoe together, but she had to suspect something was up. People never gave kids enough credit—they're more intuitive than we think.

"Five more minutes. I'm so sleepy." She pulled the rainbow comforter over her head.

"Nope! It's time to get up. You don't want to be late."

"Okay, okay." She reluctantly got out of bed and headed to the bathroom.

After dropping Zoe off at camp, I marched across the street to my best friend Camila's house. Camila and her husband Sebastian moved onto Highland Avenue shortly after we did. They owned a restaurant, La Caverna. Camila was, by far, one of the most caring people I had ever met, a natural host, who effortlessly put the needs of others ahead of hers.

About a month after they' moved in, Camila and Sebastian invited Chad and I over for dinner. The two of them went all out with a full four-course meal. After the dishes were put away, Camila and I started belting '80s ballads at the top of our lungs and have been best friends ever since.

Our families were extremely close as well. Camila and Sebastian had two boys, Julian and Arlo. Julian was four months younger than Zoe, and Arlo just turned one in June. Since the kids were so close in age, our two families spent lots of time together, taking beach trips, going to wineries, picking apples, and other fun stuff. Zoe and Julian had a blast playing together and were inseparable. Camila and I joked about becoming future in-laws and all the funny stories we'd tell at their wedding. Arlo was the happiest baby, and Zoe loved making him smile. One night she was jumping off the couches, and Arlo was in stiches. Camila said she hadn't heard Arlo laugh that hard ever.

When she opened the door, Camila had clearly just come out of the shower—she still had her bathrobe on, and her long brown hair dripped down her shoulders and neck. One look at my red and puffy eyes, and she dragged me into the house.

"Beth? What's wrong?"

I just fell into her arms and sobbed. "He left me," I said, choking on the words.

"Who left? What are you talking about?"

"Chad."

"What?"

She pushed me upright and led me into her kitchen. Usually, I loved Camila's bright, cheery, appliance-packed kitchen, but today it was lost on me. I sat on one of the stools at the counter.

"Here, have some coffee, and start from the beginning." She handed over a steaming mug.

As I drank, I filled her in on the details.

"Man, I'm so sorry, Beth. I did *not* see this coming."

"I know. I mean things have been weird since the accident, and then with my promotion, but still, who just walks out on their wife and child?"

"A coward, that's who. If he was lonely, he should have told you."

Tears seeped out of my eyes.

Camila put her hand on my shoulder. "Have you eaten? I'll make you breakfast."

"I don't have much of an appetite."

"You need to eat."

Camila whipped up some chocolate chip pancakes, with homemade whipped cream on top. Camila was a whiz in the kitchen, impressing me with how she made it look so easy and natural. Camila and Sebastian were born entertainers and were always inviting people over for parties at their house. At least twice a month, we'd be over for an impromptu get-together. Chad and Sebastian talked about sports and lawn care, as Camila and I gabbed over a bottle of wine while the kids played.

But that was back when I thought we were a happy family.

"How can you resist this?" Camila handed me a plate and grabbed forks and napkins.

I took a bite. She was right. Her pancakes were delicious, and the chocolate chips hit the spot.

"Thanks," I said.

I took another bite, but I had no appetite, even for yummy chocolate chip pancakes.

"I'm just so heartbroken. How could he do this? How could he stop loving me?" I put my hands in my head, rubbed my face, and took a deep breath. Tears formed in my eyes again.

Camila came over and rubbed my back.

"Honey, I'm sorry. I don't know what to tell you, and I don't know how to make this better. But I'm here, you know that."

The look in Camila's huge brown eyes told me that she empathized, even if she didn't quite get it.

"I know. Thanks. There's just so much to process. He's been lying to me for three years. He already has a new home with a new family."

I started to cry again. Camila handed me a tissue.

"And then there's the future to think about. Can I stay in the house? How do I make it as a single mom?" I sighed heavily. "What am I going to do?" I asked as I plopped my head in my hands.

"You're going to take this one day at time. Step one is to get through today."

I rubbed my temples and took a deep breath. "I don't even think that's possible. I just want to curl up in a ball and cry."

"Well, I think that's allowed," Camila said with a smile. "What are you doing tonight? You should come by La Caverna, with Rachel and Jennifer. I'm sure Avery can babysit."

Rachel and Jennifer also lived on Highland Avenue. Rachel and her husband, Travis, lived next door to me. They had two kids: Jake, who was in middle school, and Avery, who was in high school. Rachel and Travis were both accountants at top firms, and their children were extremely smart, but also very kind. Avery loved to babysit, and Jake was like a big brother to Zoe.

Jennifer and *her* husband, Michael, lived two doors down from Camila and Sebastian. They had twin boys, Nicholas and Tyler, who were three years older than Zoe and Julian. Both Jennifer and Michael played sports in college, and they remained extremely athletic and active as a family. They rode bikes in the neighborhood or played tennis at the park. Jennifer and I ran together once a week, too. She was faster than me, but I liked that she was a good motivator. The four of us were a tight-knit group, and we'd even dubbed ourselves the "Ladies of Highland Avenue."

"I don't know if I'm up for going out," I said.

Camila refilled my coffee. "I understand, but it will be good for you. I'll make you a deal. You can curl up in a ball and cry all day if you promise to come out tonight. I think there needs to be a limit on endless crying."

It was true that I didn't necessarily want to be by myself, and it *would* be nice to be surrounded by friends.

"Okay, but no promises that I'll have fun."

"I'm not asking you to have fun. I just don't want you to be alone. Look, Beth, I'm sorry. I really am. You don't deserve this. But I'm here for you. If you need to cry, if you need to yell, if you need to dance." Camila started twirling in the kitchen. That was Camila, she seemed to always know what to say to make you feel better.

"I'm going to take you up on that, I promise. But, right now, I'm going to head home. My brain and heart hurt."

"I'll be here if you need anything. Here, take these pancakes and promise me you'll eat them." She put the pancakes and whipped cream in a Tupperware.

"I'm so glad you live across the street." I gave her a giant hug.

I finished up my coffee and headed back across the street. I got through the front door and headed right for the couch. Twix jumped on my lap and started to purr. She head-butted me, wanting me to pet her. Curling up in a ball and crying had sounded so good when I was at Camila's house, but I found that, once I sat down, there were no tears left. I couldn't decide if I was sadder about Chad leaving, or angry about all the lying. I guess there was no reason why I couldn't be both.

Getting restless, I decided to take walk.

I found myself heading toward the park a few blocks away. It was a park that we all frequented. Zoe had even had her second birthday party there. They had tennis courts, a playground, a huge field for softball or soccer, and even a little wooded path. I was headed toward the path when I saw a familiar face. My friend, Noah, was out with his dog, Rusty. Noah lived in the town houses behind Highland Avenue.

We had met at the park three years ago. Zoe and I were playing monster, and I was chasing her around. She didn't watch where she was going and ran right into Noah, who was playing fetch with Rusty. I apologized, but Noah understood, having a little boy himself. Noah and I kept running into each other at the park. Sometimes he was with Rusty and his son, Caleb, and other times it was just him and Rusty. Our friendly nods and smiles had turned into the typical conversations about the weather. We exchanged pleasantries like "Nice day" or "Looks like rain." Eventually the weather talk turned into more, and we became close friends. He was actually the one who'd encouraged me to go for the promotion at work. Zoe was also a big fan of Noah's—well, probably more Rusty's. Zoe desperately wanted a dog. Noah showed Zoe how Rusty liked to be petted and let her play fetch with him.

"Look who it is, Rusty," Noah said, giving me a hug hello.

Of course, I started to cry again.

"Whoa, Beth. What's wrong?"

I was pretty sure I'd never cried in front of Noah, and embarrassment washed over me.

"Everything," I moaned.

"What do you mean? Is Zoe okay?"

When I had originally told him about the accident, he'd been extremely sympathetic.

"Yeah, Zoe is fine," I said.

"Then what's wrong?"

"Chad is…leaving me." I could barely get the words out.

"What? What happened? Want to walk?" he asked.

"Yes, that sounds nice."

We started down the path together, and I told him about the previous night.

"I'm sorry, Beth. That really sucks." He put his arm on my shoulder.

We got to the big field, and Noah threw a ball for Rusty to fetch.

"I feel like my life is over," I sighed.

"Look, I know you may feel like this is the end. But take it from me, you *will* get through this. Remember my divorce? I was a wreck. But time does help, and things do get better. You'll see."

Noah's divorce had been finalized six months ago. When I first met him, he'd seemed like he was in a happy marriage. But as our relationship grew, he started to tell me how unhappy he was, and how he and his now ex-wife, Erica, fought all the time. He didn't know what to do, but he knew that the fighting was starting to cause issues for Caleb, who was seven at the time. Caleb had started getting quieter, and his teachers pointed out that he wasn't participating in class anymore. Noah and Erica decided that divorce was the right choice. However, the divorce had been extremely messy. Erica wanted full custody of Caleb and had asked for an exorbitant amount of money.

During that time, Noah had clearly been in a dark place. Fear of losing his son—and all his money—made him moody, and he drank a lot. But as soon as his papers were signed and everything was settled, it was like something snapped. He was happier and he took up his old love, swimming, again. It was like this huge weight was lifted off him.

And, six months later, he was better than ever.

"Thanks. It's just so much. I don't even know where to begin."

"Just take it one day at a time."

"That's what Camila said."

"Well, she's right. And let me know if you need anything. I can give you some tips on getting through the battles, not that you're there yet."

I didn't even want to think about all the decisions that Chad and I were going to have to make. I was still coming to terms with the fact that he was leaving me to be with someone else. Sure, I didn't want to be with a man who cheated, but instead of coming to me and trying to make our marriage work, he'd gone to her. I felt like my heart had been ripped out, broken into pieces, and then stomped on. How could this be happening to me? It didn't feel like my life.

"Thanks."

Noah gave me a hug. "You're going to be okay. It's going to be okay. Just trust me," he said.

I wanted to trust Noah. I really wanted to believe that this was going to be okay. But, at that moment, it all felt hopeless.

"What's for dinner? I'm starving!" Zoe sat at the counter, her little legs dangling from the chair.

"Chicken tacos," I replied.

"Yummy! My favorite." She licked her lips.

"I'm going to brown the meat. Do you want to help get the tomatoes and corn?"

"Yes!"

"Thanks. And then can you set the table?"

"Sure! Is Daddy coming home for dinner tonight?"

I hadn't heard from Chad all day, except for a quick text telling me that he would arrange a time to get his stuff later. I asked about clothes and essentials in the meantime, but he simply replied that it had already been taken care of. I ran to his closet and when I noticed some of his shirts gone, I screamed. He had even started the process of moving out without telling me.

"No, he had to," I struggled to think of an excuse, "help a friend with something." I responded with a fake smile. The day had been taxing, and the last thing I wanted to do was lose it in front of Zoe.

I felt terrible lying to my daughter, but I knew that this was a conversation Chad and I had to have together. Even though he'd gone behind my back by introducing Zoe to Courtney, I still needed to play fair. I watched Zoe carefully putting the plates on the placemats. My gut clenched, thinking what shared custody would mean.

Obviously, Zoe would have time with Chad, which meant that I wouldn't be able to have dinner with her every night. I started to cry.

Zoe looked over at me. "Are you okay, Mommy?"

"Oh, yes. I just got something in my eye," Wiping the tears away, I tried to change the subject. "How was camp, sweet pea?"

"It was good. We learned more about the Earth, and how gravity helps us from getting dizzy, since the Earth spins around. I also made a picture of the Earth out of felt." She ran over and reached into her backpack and showed me the felt Earth. Even though she insisted she was going to be an artist when she grew up, she'd unfortunately inherited my inability to do anything remotely artistic.

"Oh wow! That's really cool," I said, as I put it on the fridge next to her other art projects. "So, I'm going out with Ms. Rachel and Ms. Jennifer tonight, and Avery is going to come over and babysit!"

"Yes!" Zoe exclaimed. Zoe loved when Avery babysat her.

After we'd cleaned up dinner, Avery came by. Zoe was already getting some games out for the two of them to play.

"One popsicle, and don't forget to brush your teeth," I said. I gave her a big hug and kiss. "I love you more than anything."

"Love you, too," she exclaimed as I closed the door.

La Caverna was a Spanish restaurant known for its cocktails, especially Sebastian's famous sangria. Since it was in the neighborhood, it was the perfect go-to spot for most of our evenings out. Even though it was a Wednesday night, the place was packed. Sebastian was manning the bar, making sure our glasses were always full, and

Camila occasionally had to step away to greet guests and check in on tables, but she was still able to hang out.

"Let's slash his tires," Jennifer said. She was always one for getting even, and she wasn't taking the news about Chad well. She was the mama bear of the group, and if you crossed one of us, you didn't want to know what she'd do. Last year, a boy pushed Nicholas down at the bus stop. His mom didn't do anything, and Jennifer was furious, especially because the boy refused to apologize. Two days later, Jennifer showed up at the bus stop and handed the mom *How To Raise Considerate Kids*. "Here, I thought you could use this," she'd said, and then she'd just smiled and walked away.

"Or TP his house." She continued plotting her revenge.

"I don't even know where he is right now. How could he have this all planned out already? I mean, he has a *house*! Like, this didn't just happen yesterday. Who rents a house with their girlfriend before officially leaving their wife?"

"I'm sorry, Beth. This totally sucks," Camila said, her tone sympathetic as she reached over and put her hand on mine.

The words, "I want to be with her," were still ringing in my ears. How could I have been so naïve? How could I have not seen the warning signs? He'd been lying to me for three years, and I hadn't even known. The more I thought about him and this mystery woman, the sicker I felt.

"Did you know Courtney at all?" Rachel asked as she munched on some chips and salsa.

"It's funny, I never heard him mention her. He occasionally talks about other girls he works with, but never her. I did some digging this afternoon and found out she works in a different department. Her ex-husband stopped appearing in her Instagram pictures a few months ago. Seems like they've both been unfaithful."

"You should meet her ex-husband," Rachel said.

"Yeah, you two have a lot in common," Jennifer added. "Maybe he can let you in on her weaknesses, and we can use that for ammo."

"Okay, let's not go overboard. And what am I going to say, 'So your ex and my ex screwed us both over, want to grab a drink?'" I did wonder about him, but I had other things to think about.

I twisted the sangria glass in my hand; even the taste of Sebastian's famous drink couldn't cheer me up today.

"I just feel like a fool. Three years, and I had no idea."

"None of us did," said Camila. "You two always seemed so happy together."

Jennifer put a hand on my back. "I know this sucks, Beth, but you'll get through this. I promise."

Tears started to roll down my cheeks. Would I ever be able to stop crying unexpectedly?

"Why didn't he fight for me? Why didn't he fight for our family?"

"I don't know," Jennifer said.

"Like, what does this Courtney woman have that I don't? I just feel like I'm not good enough. And it's a terrible feeling."

"You *are* good enough. No, you're *better* than good enough," Camila said.

"He's such an idiot. There's no way this Courtney girl is better than you," Rachel declared.

"Chad thought she was."

I put my face in my hand and looked down at the bar. It was decorated with blue Spanish tiles. I started to get lost in the patterns.

"Look, I know you don't want to hear this now, but you deserve better. You don't want to be with someone like that," Rachel said as she motioned to Sebastian for another plate of chorizo and Manchego cheese.

"That's easy for you to say, your husband worships you," Jennifer replied.

It was true. Rachel and Travis had an amazing marriage. They made it look so easy. Travis made sure to always make Rachel happy, no matter what. He was the type of guy that gave her jewelry just because, and he always took out the trash. Last year for her fortieth birthday, he planned an amazing getaway to South America. Every detail was planned with the motto, "What would Rachel want?" He was the type of husband that the other husbands on the street teased, but really, I think they were just jealous they didn't know their wives quite as well as Travis knew Rachel.

"He doesn't worship me," Rachel argued. "He just gets me."

"Please. You still walk hand in hand down the street like you two love birds are in your twenties," said Jennifer. "I think I saw you yesterday with your hand in his back pocket. Michael is lucky if he gets a pat on the back."

"Same with Sebastian," said Camila.

Jennifer and Camila clinked their glasses in solidarity. Michael and Sebastian were both great husbands, but they knew they weren't quite Travis' caliber. Even so, they didn't cheat on their wives, which made them grade-A in my book.

"Ugh, I'm so mad at him! What a jerk. I still can't believe he did this to you and Zoe. Men can be so selfish." Jennifer clearly still wanted to find a way to get revenge.

"Ugh, guys, I'm sorry to be such a drag. I just can't believe it."

"You're allowed to be a drag. This crazy life-altering thing happened to you, and we're here to listen," Camila said.

"Thanks, ladies," I said.

"I still can't believe he used the accident as an excuse to start his affair. And that he said you went crazy. I would have been ten times worse if that happened to Nicholas or Tyler. Michael would *still* need my permission to take them in the car, three years later," Jennifer said.

"I know," Rachel chimed in. "But, now that I think about it, I do remember, after it happened, Chad was complaining to Travis. I heard him say something like, 'This is not what I signed up for. She's lost it.' I thought it was just guys venting, but, now that I look back, he should have been way more supportive."

"So much for in good times and bad," Jennifer added.

"What a jerk," Rachel affirmed.

"Here's to that." Camila lifted her glass and took a sip.

"What am I going to do? I thought Chad was the love of my life, but he's stomped all over my heart and torn apart the family I loved so much."

"Like I said, just one day at a time," Camila said. "You're going to get through this. One day, you're going to look back on this moment and realize just how strong you are. You're going to be okay, and you know why? Because you are Beth, and you are awesome. If you weren't awesome, then we wouldn't be friends with you."

My friends all raised their glasses in agreement. I smiled gratefully and hoped Camila was right. I wanted to be able to look back at this moment and see how strong I was. But everything just felt hopeless. My entire life had just been torn apart, and I hadn't seen it coming. It was hard to see past this moment, to see a future where I could feel optimistic again. Right now, all I could think of was the fact that I wasn't loveable, that I wasn't worth fighting for. That being with Zoe and me wasn't enough for Chad.

"You need a rebound guy," Rachel piped up.

"What? Too soon!" I protested.

"I don't know. He cheated on you! Go out and get some. That guy over there is a cute." Rachel pointed to a guy at the bar that couldn't have been older than twenty-five.

"He's a pup! No way he'd be interested in me. I'm a thirty-eight-year-old single mom," I said.

"Please! You're hot, Beth, and you know it," Jennifer said.

I wasn't the type of girl who turned heads, but I did get occasional smiles and looks. I was a dedicated runner, so I had very toned legs and a slim, muscular body. My best feature, by far, was my sparkling blue eyes. On our first date, Chad told me he kept getting lost in them.

"I'm just not ready yet."

"Well, if you need a wingman, I'm your girl," Rachel said.

Sebastian came by and asked if we wanted another round.

"We should call it a night. It's been a weird twenty-four hours," I said.

The night ended as we walked home from the restaurant. It was the dog days of summer, which meant hot and humid. I entered my house, a bit sticky from the walk home, and took a deep breath. Sure, I was going to be okay. Sure, I deserved better. But it was still all so much to take in. I couldn't believe that this was my life. It was a long road ahead, and I knew that. But, as Noah and the ladies said, I just needed to take it one step at a time, and the first step had been to get through today.

And I had.

-2-

AUGUST

The past two weeks had been extremely difficult. I was still trying to make sense of everything that had happened. I was constantly searching my brain for any clues I'd missed that would have indicated that Chad was having an affair. But, at the time, everything had an explanation.

There was that one night, about six months ago, when Chad said he was going out with some friends from softball. As I was putting Zoe to bed, she complained that her tummy hurt. I had felt her forehead and noticed she was warm. Curling up next to her in her bed, I rubbed her back while she listened to her lullabies. Suddenly, she threw up all over the place, including on her monkey. She was inconsolable. I put her in the bath and threw the sheets and monkey in the laundry. I texted Chad to let him know that Zoe had thrown up and wasn't feeling well.

After I got Zoe out of the bath and into some fresh pajamas, I checked my phone and saw there'd been no response from Chad. He usually had his phone on him, and I thought he'd want to check in and see how she was doing. Zoe wouldn't sleep without her monkey, so we just laid in my bed, waiting for the laundry to finish. She said her tummy hurt again, so I grabbed a trash can. Just in time, too, because out came more vomit. I rubbed her back and held her hair out of the way. Zoe didn't get sick that often, and it hurt me to see her in so much pain.

Still, there was no text from Chad. I sent him another one, giving him an update. I was a little worried that something had happened to him, but I didn't give it much thought because I was focusing on Zoe.

Three hours later, Zoe was finally asleep. I looked at the clock, it was almost 2:00 a.m. I lay there, stroking Zoe's long blond hair, when I heard Chad stumble in downstairs. I went to the kitchen, where Chad stood at the sink, filling a glass of water.

"Where were you?" I asked sharply.

"What's with the tone? I was out with friends," he said.

"It's Tuesday night, it's two in the morning, you're super drunk, and you reek of cigarettes. And I've been texting you that Zoe's sick," I replied. I was furious that he was in this state. While I was dealing with our sick child, he'd been out doing who knows what. He couldn't even be bothered to check his phone.

"Well, not much I could have done. You usually take care of these things. And stop with the attitude. I'll come home when I want to."

"Are you serious?" I tried not to yell. I didn't want to wake up Zoe, but I was fuming. "I've been home caring for our sick daughter, and you can't even check in with me over text message."

"Ugh, stop it. You're always giving me a hard time about going out an' enjoying myself. I don't do this when you have book club or go out with the ladies."

"I'm not out until two o'clock. And I check my phone for emergencies."

"Well, my phone died. And what does it matter what time I come home? Being out is being out."

I burned with anger, but I was too exhausted. I didn't have it in me to fight.

"Whatever. I'm too worn out for this." I went back upstairs and lay down with Zoe. I couldn't sleep. My heart kept pulsing. I couldn't seem to calm down.

Chad slept in the guest room that night. At the time, I couldn't see past my anger and irritation with him for not caring about Zoe and for not trying to help. In hindsight, he was probably out with Courtney that night, which was why he didn't check his phone.

The next day, I'd stayed home with Zoe. We snuggled on the couch and watched movies. Chad came home with flowers and cookies—his way of apologizing. I put the flowers in a vase, and we all cuddled up on the couch. He never actually *said* he was sorry for the night before. Looking back, we probably should have talked about that night, why he felt the need to be out so late, why I felt like everything was on my shoulders. But we never did.

Now, when I wasn't racking my brain for clues of an affair, I remembered the good times, and I tried to figure out why they hadn't been good enough for Chad. We'd been married for ten years, and we dated three years before that, so Chad had played an integral part in one-third of my life. We had so many happy memories together!

Chad and I met playing intramural soccer, and I'd instantly fallen head over heels in love with him. The thought of being with him made me giddy with excitement. Every time I saw him, I lit up. We were the couple that couldn't keep their hands off each other. On our second date, we sat in the back booth of a bar, making out like teenagers.

A year after we started dating, we took a trip down to Hilton Head Island. It had been an amazing trip. We stayed at a posh hotel right on the beach and played golf and tennis in the mornings. We took long strolls down the beach, talking about life and the future. We stayed up late drinking wine on the balcony, listening to the ocean waves, talking about our hopes and dreams. It was after that trip that I knew I wanted to be with Chad for the rest of my life. Everything about us meshed. At that moment in time, we were on the same page and had the same roadmap for where we wanted to go in life. It seemed to me that Chad was my soulmate.

And up until two weeks ago, I'd still thought he was. I thought the life we were building was the same as the one we had discussed on the beach so many years ago. Sure, we had taken a few detours, but in my mind, we were still headed in the right direction. We had amazing friends, good jobs, a beautiful daughter, and we had each other. What I didn't realize was that Chad also had a girlfriend and another view of where he wanted his life to go. And, unfortunately, it no longer included me.

So, overall, the past two weeks had been an emotional roller coaster, and I struggled to navigate the ups and downs of processing that my marriage was over, and that I was going to have to start fresh. A week after Chad dropped his bomb, he arranged a time to get some of his stuff while I was at work. All day I tried to focus on work, but I kept getting distracted. I tried to prepare myself for what it would be like to come home and not see Chad's stuff in the house. He told me he was just going to get a few things, as we still needed to figure out the specifics of who was keeping what. But I knew that his closet would be bare, and the University of Minnesota poster he'd had since college wouldn't be hanging on the wall of the office. That night, after Zoe went to bed, I sat in his empty closet, listening to Fleetwood Mac. I felt a sting of melancholy and confusion as I stared into the open space. Luckily, my friends were right across the street and constantly checked to make sure I was okay.

On the first night that Zoe was at Chad's, I didn't want to be alone. Camila had to work, but Jennifer and Rachel were both free for drinks.

Jennifer was the first to arrive. "Hey, Beth. I brought some wine." Jennifer handed over a bottle of zinfandel.

"Thanks. Come on in," I said.

I headed to the kitchen to open the bottle as Twix came to greet Jennifer.

"Rachel should be here soon," I yelled to her.

As if on cue, I heard a knock as Rachel opened the door. "I'm here with snacks!" she proclaimed.

"Great!" I poured three glasses of wine, and we headed into the living room.

On my way in, I tripped over one of Zoe's toys. "Ugh, I told her to pick these up!" There were two naked Barbies on the floor, with their clothes in a big pile.

"Just be glad you didn't step on a Lego." Jennifer grimaced.

"Oh yeah, those hurt like a bitch," Rachel added.

I gave them their wine, and Rachel laid out cheese and crackers.

"Thanks for coming over, ladies. The thought of being alone started making me feel depressed. And thanks for bringing wine and cheese. I looked in the cupboards yesterday and realized I desperately need to hit the grocery store."

"No problem," Jennifer said. "I needed to get out of the house. Michael and the boys were playing basketball. I swear, I need to move the net away from my bedroom window. There's no way for me to relax."

"I saw them out there playing. It looked like Tyler was crushing Nicholas," Rachel commented.

"Yeah, they're both so competitive. But that just means that, tomorrow, Nicholas will want revenge."

"I wonder where they get it," I said in jest.

Michael and Jennifer had constant competitions between each other about mundane things, like who could empty the dishwasher the fastest, or who could fold a pile of clothes first.

"I know we're to blame for this behavior," Jennifer said, giving a little shrug and taking a drink of wine.

"Speaking of competitive, how is Avery's swimming going?" Jennifer asked. Avery was doing an elite summer swimming program for high school students around the D.C. metro area, which included Virginia, D.C., and Maryland.

"Pretty good. But we've been traveling all over the area. It's exhausting. We drive for three hours just for Avery to swim in three races that each last less than two minutes. But she's having a ball." Rachel shrugged. "Her meets sometimes interfere with Jake's baseball schedule, but Travis and I just split duties. It's hard running around with all of these activities."

"I know what you mean," Jennifer interjected. "The boys are doing swimming, baseball, lacrosse, plus camp. I feel like I'm just a chauffeur. It's tough."

"Suburban mom problems, right?" I asked.

I was envious of my friends, that tight schedules was the hardest thing they had to deal with. True, I knew the nightmare of a calendar, and I only had *one* child, who wasn't in as many activities. But those were the problems of old Beth, and they seemed so trivial compared to new Beth's problems.

Jennifer got up to use the bathroom and came back asking for toilet paper.

I ran downstairs to get some. When I handed her the roll, I noticed how dirty the bathroom was. Then I looked around and noticed how dirty the whole house was. I couldn't remember the last time I'd cleaned it.

"Oh my gosh, I'm so sorry. I didn't realize the state of the house," I said. Embarrassment brought a flush to my face. My friends' houses were *always* clean. Even when they were messy, they still kind of sparkled.

"You don't have to clean up for us," Rachel reassured me.

"I know, but I just realized I haven't cleaned the house since Chad left. It's a disaster."

"Well, you've had a lot on your plate," Jennifer said.

"It's just all so overwhelming." I put my hands in my face and let out a deep breath. Jennifer and Rachel came over and sat next to me, one on each side.

"Between work and taking care of Zoe, it's hard to find time. Not to mention I'm just emotionally exhausted. I don't have the energy for things like cleaning. I either just want to curl up and cry or throw things."

"I'm down for throwing things," Jennifer noted with a smile.

"And the lawn. I need to figure that out; Chad always took care of it." We lived on a sizable lot, and Chad had taken a lot of pride in making sure the grass and garden were always in pristine condition. It was like all the husbands had this unspoken competition about who had the nicest lawn, and Chad took it very seriously. But I think he was the only one who cared so much.

"I don't think I even know how to work the hedger. Plus, Chad and I haven't even begun to talk finances. I want to stay in the house, but I hadn't been planning on paying the mortgage on a single income."

I took another deep breath. There was so much on the to-do list, and I had little motivation to do it. I was so heartbroken that even the smallest task seemed daunting. It was hard to get out of bed, let alone do anything else. I pulled myself together when Zoe was around; I didn't want her to see me like this. But that took so much effort.

"I just feel like I'm drowning."

Jennifer put her hand on mine. "Beth, you just had a major life change. You can give yourself a break. The lawn is fine, and so is the house. Sure, it's not perfect, but nobody's is."

"That's easy for you to say. Your house always looks great, and you both have husbands who didn't leave you and have time to mow the lawn," I said. I was trying not to be rude, but neither of them had to run a household by themselves—they had partners, partners who hadn't just up and left them.

Jennifer just sat silently for a minute. I could tell she didn't know what to say.

Soon, though, she reverted to mama bear mode. "I'm going to kill him for what he did to you. This isn't fair," she said.

"Well, don't kill him. Zoe still needs a dad," I said.

"Okay, well, I'm going to do *something*. You don't deserve this, and he needs to hurt as much as you do," she said.

I did hurt—I hurt like I never thought possible. My heart ached, and I felt sick to my stomach all the time.

"You're going to figure this out," Rachel said. "And we'll help. If you need us to watch Zoe while you take care of some things, we can. We're here for you."

"And I'm sure Michael can show you how to work the mower and the hedger," Jennifer added.

"Thanks, guys," I said. "Zoe's with Chad this weekend, so that'll give me some time to take care of things. I just need to find a new routine, a new single-mom routine."

"You've got this, Beth," Rachel said.

"And I'm still seeking revenge against Chad," Jennifer added.

I had the best friends ever.

"So, how's your first weekend without Zoe going?" Camila asked.

It was a hot August night, and we were having drinks on her deck while Arlo and Julian played in the backyard. Jennifer and Rachel had told Camila about our conversation the other night, and how I felt like I was drowning. She felt bad, and didn't want me to be alone, so she'd invited me over for dinner the next night.

"It's going, I guess. I thought a weekend to myself was going to be good. I had a long list of things to do, but last night I was just so exhausted. I opened a bottle of wine and cuddled with Twix on the couch. I watched some new show on Netflix. I don't even think I was actually watching it, because I couldn't tell you what it was about."

Arlo was watching Julian go down the slide. Each time, Julian would make a funny face, and Arlo would laugh hysterically. At that moment, I started to think about Zoe, and wondered what she was doing with Chad. What was he making her for dinner? Was she also playing with Willow and Wyatt, Courtney's kids, in her new backyard, or were they with their dad this weekend? I'd imagine they wanted the kids to be together, but I wasn't sure what Courtney and her ex's custody schedule looked like. I wondered if Zoe missed me, or if she was having too much fun. I wondered what her new room looked like.

"Beth?" she said.

"Oh sorry, I was just thinking about Zoe. I miss her." I took a sip of wine. Three nights in a row without her was going to be tough.

"I know you do." Camila gave me an understanding look. "This schedule is going to take some getting used to."

Chad and I had agreed that he would have Zoe Wednesdays nights and every other weekend. I wanted all my nights with Zoe, and for Chad to have to bring her back to my house on school nights. But my divorce lawyer assured me that our agreement was pretty standard, and I would enjoy the time once I got used to it.

I took a deep sigh and another sip of my wine. "I don't want to get used to it. I want to go back to being a family."

"I know you do. So, what did you do today?" she inquired, trying to change the subject.

"I was hoping to sleep in, but, of course, I couldn't sleep. My mind kept racing, so I was up at 7:30. I decided to pull myself out of bed and forced myself to go on a run. I did two miles and it felt pretty good."

"Good for you. Exercise is so good for mental health. If anything, it gets the heart pumping and clears your mind."

"Yeah, I felt pretty good after it. It wasn't my best run, but I felt like I'd done something positive. After that, I made myself a to-do list for the weekend. I was able to knock out about a third of it today, including going to the grocery store and cleaning the house."

"Two very important tasks. Are you feeling better about things?"

"I'm feeling better about the cleanliness of my house, but that's about it. There's still so much. Tomorrow I'm going to tackle the yard. Michael said he'd help me figure things out. I don't think I even know how to start the mower."

"You're a smart cookie, I'm sure you'll figure it out," she said. "But that's nice of Michael to help you. It's okay to feel like you're drowning, I get that. But that doesn't mean you have to make it to shore by yourself. It's okay to ask someone to throw you a rope."

Camila was right. If I was going to do this single-mom thing, I'd have to rely on my friends, and not just to listen to me complain while drinking wine. They were there to really help me, but I needed to make sure I asked.

"Are you processing everything, Chad-wise?" she asked, pouring me another glass of wine.

"Oh man, I'm all over the place. During my run, I thought about asking Chad if he'd reconsider. Whether we could just work this out together. I want the chance to fight for our marriage and see if we can get our spark back."

"I can see you wanting to work this out, Beth. Your family is important to you. It always has been. But he *moved in* with her. I don't think there's much left to fight for."

"I know, but I just miss him. I just keep thinking that maybe this is just a mid-life crisis, and he'll see the light, and see how we just need to work this out."

"But you'd never be able to trust him again after all the lying he did. You don't want to be in a relationship without trust. That's not going to be good for Zoe."

"I know. I just wish it didn't have to be this way. I wish that I could have fixed us, that he could have been happy with me. That he would have fought for me. I just can't help but think, why wasn't I enough? Why doesn't he love me?" A sob rose in my throat. Camila came over and put her hand in mine.

"I know it's hard for you to see this now. But it's not about you. You are enough, you're amazing. He's a coward. Afraid to admit his faults. It takes a strong person to say, 'Something's not working, and I might need to fix myself.' And now it's clear that Chad isn't that person. He didn't want to look in the mirror. Instead, he took the low road and blamed you for a problem he was a part of. He didn't want to put in the work, and that's not your fault. This isn't your fault. This sucks. It totally does. You just got the wind knocked out of you, and you don't deserve it. But you will come out of this on the other side, stronger. And you will see that, while it's hard to admit now, you couldn't have fixed your relationship, and you're better off not in it."

I took a deep breath and wiped the tears from my eyes. I wanted to believe Camila. I wanted to believe that this wasn't about me, and I was better off without him, but I just couldn't yet. Chad was my future, but I wasn't his. And I blamed myself for that. For not being enough for him.

"Come on, I think the chicken is ready," she said as we headed inside to eat. "You're looking thin, are you eating?"

"I haven't had much of an appetite."

"Well, you've come to the right place," Camila replied. "My spicy chicken with lentils is hard to resist."

After dinner, Avery came by to watch Julian and Arlo. On Saturday nights, Sebastian and Camila swapped who went to the restaurant first, while the other made dinner for the kids. Then, usually Avery or another kid from the neighborhood watched Julian and Arlo after they went to bed, so both Sebastian and Camila could be at the restaurant. Last summer, they'd hired a new manager who always worked Sundays so that they could have a mandatory family dinner. Balancing a restaurant and family was tricky, but Sebastian and Camila made it work.

When I got home, I cracked open a bottle of wine and turned on the TV. I felt so sad and so alone. I felt like a person without a family. A wife without a husband, a mom without a child.

I finished my wine and headed upstairs to bed. I still slept on my side. I don't know why I didn't use the full bed. Maybe it was my subconscious hoping that Chad would come back if I left room for him. That I'd get my family back.

But Camila was right. There was no more marriage to fight for. I just wasn't ready to accept the reality that he was gone. That Chad had decided to love someone that wasn't me.

Before Chad left, my mornings had been busy. I'd get up at 5:45 and head into the shower while he and Zoe slept. I'd drink my coffee, blow dry my hair, and get ready for work. Then, around seven, I'd wake Zoe up, get her breakfast ready, and get her dressed for school or camp. We'd be out the door by 7:45 sharp, so that I could get to work on time. Now when I woke up, I mentally had to think about what day it was. Whether or not Zoe was with me, or with Chad.

The alarm clock still went off at 5:45 every day, but today it was Monday morning, and Zoe was still with Chad. I reminded myself that I really didn't need to get up, but I couldn't go back to sleep. Instead, I just stared into space and thought about how my life had changed. The heaviness of my situation was still weighing on me. This wasn't the life I wanted; this wasn't the life I'd chosen for myself.

I had missed Zoe all weekend, but I was excited to see her that afternoon. I got into the office early, since I knew I would have to leave at 4:30 on the dot if I didn't want to be late for camp pickup. Luckily, work was hectic, which took my mind off things for a while. I'd told my boss about Chad leaving. She was shocked and very sympathetic. I assured her that my work wouldn't slip, but she let me know that I could take some time if I needed it. Time was the last thing I needed. Time was just me in my head thinking about my life falling apart. I had to stay busy, and work was definitely helping.

"Can we make cookies?" Zoe asked on our drive home that afternoon. I loved baking with Zoe. We had a lot of fun in the kitchen together, making brownies, cookies, and muffins. It was something the two of us had done together ever since she was two. She enjoyed the mixing and pouring, and she was starting to perfect cracking eggs, though we still did it in a separate bowl, just in case there were shells.

"Sure, we can! I've been in the mood for some chocolate chip cookies."

When we got home, Zoe rushed into the kitchen and grabbed our aprons off the hooks. They'd been a Mother's Day gift last year from Zoe. Mine was blue, my favorite color, with a cake on it that said "Mommy." Zoe's was purple, her favorite color, with a cupcake on it that said "Zoe." She'd been so excited for me to open the gifts on Mother's Day. I wondered if next Mother's Day, Zoe would be going with Chad to get gifts for Courtney, instead of for me.

I tried to shake off that thought. It was my time with Zoe, and I wanted to focus on mother-daughter fun.

"Thanks, Zoe. Can you get the eggs? I'll get the rest of the stuff."

I put all the ingredients on the counter and turned on some music.

"How do you feel about living with Daddy and Courtney in one house and Mommy in another house?" I asked as I helped her pour the flour.

A week after Chad told me that he was leaving, we talked with Zoe together about Chad moving out. She was sad that we were not going to be together, but she said she was excited about having two rooms. I figured the change hadn't really hit her yet, so I wanted to make sure she knew she could always talk to me about how she was feeling. I had even bought her a story about having two homes. It reiterated that, even though moms and dads don't always live together, they never stop loving their kids, and that this situation was just something that was different and special. She seemed to like the story.

"It's okay, I guess. I miss you when I'm not with you."

"I miss you, too. But I'm sure you had a good time with Daddy."

"And Courtney and Willow and Wyatt. They are so much fun."

Of course, how could I forget her insta-family? I'd forgotten that she had met them before all of this. I wondered how well she knew them. Zoe had never mentioned Willow, Wyatt, or Courtney before Chad's bombshell, but then I thought back to the company picnics that Chad had taken Zoe to. His work always did the picnics in the summer on a Friday. For some reason, I always had a work conflict, but Chad never pressed me to take the day off. He assured me that he and Zoe would be fine. Now, I knew the real reason; he didn't want me and Courtney to meet.

Then, last April, Chad said he was helping a friend from work whose kids played softball. I'd already agreed to meet up for drinks with coworkers, so he said he'd take Zoe. Later, he'd said that Zoe had had so much fun watching the game, that he and the coworker had grabbed dinner with the kids afterward. I didn't bother asking who the coworker was. I just assumed it was one of his male friends, so it didn't seem odd when he asked to take her again the following week. Now I realized that it had probably been Courtney and her kids. Looking back, I felt stupid for not seeing it. But everything had had an explanation.

I got out the mixer and gave it to Zoe.

"Daddy bought us a new bounce house. It's so great. Last night, Willow and I bounced all night in it."

Typical Chad, trying to buy his daughter's affection. Sure, your mom and dad don't live together, and you don't realize that your life is never going to be the same, but here is a bounce house. Mommy doesn't have a bounce house.

I put on my happy face. I never wanted Zoe to know how upset I was with her dad, or that I didn't like Courtney, so I made a silent promise to always have a happy face when Zoe talked about her other life. But, deep inside, I was reeling thinking about the fact that my daughter had been with her new family, while I sat on the couch, in the dark, drinking a bottle of wine.

"That's great! I'm glad you like it over there."

"These cookies are going to be tasty!" Zoe said, grabbing the bag of chocolate chips. "Can I have one chocolate chip, Mommy? Just to make sure they're okay?"

Zoe always made me laugh. She was a very polite kid, but she could reason her way into anything, especially if it involved chocolate.

"Just one."

She gave me a smile, her dimples showing. She knew I couldn't resist that face.

"Okay, two, but give me two also." I held out my hand.

"You're the best mommy ever!" She handed each of us two chocolate chips, and we agreed that they were okay. She poured half the bag into the bowl and started mixing them in. "Let's give some of our cookies to Mr. Gregory," Zoe suggested.

"Good idea, sweetie. He'd love that."

"I can also draw him a picture," she said.

"That's very thoughtful."

Gregory was our elderly neighbor who lived next door. His wife had passed away a few years ago, and we often brought him dinners or sweets. Zoe told me that she felt good making Gregory pictures, because she didn't want him to be sad that he was alone. I was proud of my daughter for thinking about other people and doing things that make other people happy, I and was glad it was something we could share.

This single-parent thing wasn't easy, but, luckily, I had a great kid, and we always had fun together. But it was sad to think about how I'd have to share my time with Chad. I wouldn't always be able to give her a hug when she needed one. If she had a bad day at school, but then went to Chad's, I wouldn't be there to listen to her problems and help her figure them out. In fact, she might confide in Courtney. Ever since the day she was born, I'd wanted to be there for her, and Chad was taking that away from me. I didn't want to share her, but my lawyer advised me that it'd be difficult to get primary custody. She told me I'd spend a fortune in court, and I'd probably lose. It'd be easier for me to try to work things out with Chad. I knew that Chad needed to be in her life, but it just wasn't fair to me. None of this was fair.

After dinner, we wrapped up the cookies for Gregory, along with Zoe's picture, and took them next door. Zoe ran up the stairs to his porch and rang the doorbell.

A few moments later, Gregory answered the door. "Well, if it isn't two of my favorite neighbors."

"Hi, Mr. Gregory! We made you cookies and a picture," Zoe said excitedly as she handed him the package.

"Well, don't these look tasty. I was just finishing dinner, so I'll save one for dessert. And, boy, this picture is fantastic. I'll put it on my fridge. Thanks, Zoe."

"You're welcome," she said with a smile.

"How are you doing, dear?" Gregory asked me. He'd heard from Camila that Chad had left.

"Hanging in there, I guess."

"Well, if you need anything, you know where to find me."

"Thanks, Gregory."

"Have a good night, Mr. Gregory," Zoe said.

"You, too, Zoe! And thanks again for the cookies and picture."

After bath time, I read Zoe two stories. She picked out a story about mermaids that we'd read ten times before, and a new one about dinosaurs.

"I had a fun night with you, Mommy," she said.

"I had a lot of fun, too." I kissed her on the head.

"Good night, Mommy. I love you."

"Good night, sweat pea," I said as I shut the door.

Sharing Zoe wasn't going to be easy, but I was just going to have to make the most of the time we had together.

Downstairs, I poured myself a glass of wine, settled on the couch, and thumbed through a magazine. I thought about what Zoe had said, about having fun with Courtney and her kids. I wanted her to have fun, and I wanted her to be happy. But the one thing that I really had a hard time accepting was the fact that my daughter had another mom figure in her life. It was the toughest pill to swallow. Chad's betrayal was hard, but Courtney had also betrayed me. It was one thing for her to sleep with my husband behind my back, but it was a whole other thing to spend time with my kid, without me knowing. And then there was the fact that they'd found a place to live and hadn't even discussed it with me. It was all so infuriating.

Sure, their personal life was probably none of my business, but I had a right to know who my kid was going to live with, and *where* she was going to live. Chad should have told me about Courtney and introduced us before Zoe met her, and certainly before they were all living together under one roof. Courtney was also a mom; she should have known better. Wouldn't she have wanted to know, if the roles were reversed? How would she have liked it if her ex-husband moved in with some woman without her knowing?

I felt a sudden urge to meet Courtney. I had a right to know who was living with my daughter. I texted Camila, Jennifer, and Rachel to see what they thought.

> Me: *Thinking I should meet Courtney. After all, she does live with Zoe.*
>
> Camila: *Yes, you need to meet her, if anything to just know what she is like.*
>
> Rachel: *And to see if you are prettier than her.*
>
> Jennifer: *Or, if you could beat her in a fight.*

With everyone's blessing, I sat down and wrote Courtney an email, asking if she would be open to meeting. I didn't have her personal account, so I used her company email address that I had found on their website. I took a deep breath and hit send. There was no going back.

The next morning, I woke up in a panic. Did I really email Chad's girlfriend asking her to meet? Was I ready for this? To come face to face with the woman who ruined my life? I grabbed my phone and saw that Courtney had already responded to my email. She suggested meeting on Wednesday, since Zoe would be with Chad that day, at a cafe close by.

I arrived ten minutes early. I didn't want to look like I'd put in too much effort, so I wore a casual summer dress, but I made sure to blow out my hair beforehand. My palms were sweaty, and I couldn't stop fidgeting.

At exactly 5:30, Courtney walked in the door. She wore two-inch heels and a tight dress. She carried a designer handbag, which looked like it cost more than my entire ensemble. She ordered a tea at the counter and sat down. Her perfectly manicured nails made me feel a little intimidated. This woman was the exact opposite of me. I was more girl next door, down to earth, while she looked like she belonged on Rodeo Drive.

When I set up the meeting, I'd told Courtney that I only wanted to talk to about Zoe. I had no interest in hearing about her affair with my husband. She sat down and gave me a smile. The awkwardness was palpable, but I tried to be brave.

"Thanks for meeting me. Since you and Zoe live together part of the time, I thought it'd be good to meet you."

"I agree," she said. She kept rubbing the tips of her fingers together and her eyes were darting everywhere. I'm sure she never thought she'd be having coffee with me, but here we were.

"I just want to ask a few questions. This won't take long."

I had prepared a list of questions ahead of time. I stared at my paper, silently I told myself I could do this. She was here in front of me. I needed to be strong and get through this.

"Okay," I squeaked.

I took a small sip of my water and continued.

"Do you smoke?" I inquired.

"No." she said sharply.

"Do drugs?"

"No."

"How often do you drink?"

"A few glasses a night," Courtney took a drink of her tea and folded her arms. "You know, I'm a mom. I know how to take care of kids," she continued on. "Zoe is fine with me and Chad, we aren't party animals, we are adults."

"I know you are a mom," my voice started to quiver. "Which is why I don't know how you could agree to sign a lease with somebody who had a child, without talking to that child's mother first."

"I didn't see an issue. Zoe's with her dad, that should be good enough."

"So, you are never alone with Zoe? He never runs to the store, or grabs dinner, without Zoe."

"No, I didn't say that," she huffed.

We sat in silence. I had only made it to question three, and the rest of the questions seemed pointless now. All I really wanted to do was meet Courtney, see what she was like, see who Chad thought was better than me.

"Look," she said. "I love Zoe, she is a great kid."

"I know she's a great kid" I interjected.

I stared into Courtney's eyes. Did this woman really tell me that she loved my kid? Did she really feel like that would be appropriate? Did she think I would be relieved to hear this?

"I'm not trying to replace you," she said.

That was exactly what she was doing. This woman had my husband, my daughter, she had everything. I was left with nothing. A great pang gripped my heart and my eyes were prickling with tears.

I got up from my chair, stood tall, and said, "But I will always be Zoe's mother. Thank you for meeting me."

I walked straight out of the cafe and into my car. I turned on the radio and cried. After I let it all out, I drove home.

I pulled into the driveway and saw Camila was on her porch. She came over with a glass of wine and a big hug.

"That was so hard," I told her.

"I know, but you were so brave to do that. To face that woman, so you could feel comfortable with Zoe being there."

"I don't know if it accomplished anything. It just made me feel worse, I think."

"Why?"

"She was so polished. Like, is that why Chad left me? Because I wasn't elegant enough?"

"No, Chad left you because he's a coward and a jackass."

"I wish he loved me still. I wish it didn't hurt so bad."

"I know you do. You planned your life with him, you had a child with him. You don't deserve this."

"Am I fool for wanting him back?"

"No, you're not a fool. You trusted him to love you in good times and in bad. And you kept up your end of the bargain, which is why you're a good person. And it's why you want things to have worked out. Because you were ready for bad times, and you wanted to work through them, but he won't."

"I'm weak."

"You are the strongest person I know, Beth. You've been thrown a curveball, and you're handling it with grace."

I looked down and realized we had gone through the entire bottle.

Camila put the bottle in the recycling. "You're going to get through this. I know you will."

"Thanks." As I started to leave Camila's, I noticed Twix sitting on Camila's porch waiting for me. Twix was an inside-outside cat and very loyal. Zoe and I joked that she was our "dog-cat" because she followed us around the neighborhood and waited for us to come home. She'd made it as far as the park a few times.

"Oh, Twix, you'll never leave me," I said as she rubbed against my legs, purring.

She replied with a big, "MEOW."

"Let's go," I said, and she trotted behind me across the street.

When I got home, I was emotionally drained, but not tired. I had trouble falling asleep, partly due to it being so hot, but also because of the thoughts that raced in my mind.

I went downstairs and grabbed a bottle of wine, then put on some music. I noticed the photo albums I kept under the TV. I was one of the few people who still printed out pictures, I was sure, but I loved the idea of an album. I loved flipping through pages, reliving time gone by.

I opened the cabinet and grabbed an album from before Chad and I were married. It was filled with pictures of happy times we'd had together, going to baseball games, our trip to Maine, our annual camping trip with friends Chad had gone to college with. We'd stopped the trips after everyone moved on and had kids. Chad had lost touch with a lot of those people.

I flipped through the pages, thinking, if only I could go back in time and tell twenty-six-year-old me that he wouldn't be worth the trouble, that he'd only break my heart.

I put that album back, poured another glass, and opened our wedding album. I remembered there'd been a big football game that day, and Chad and his groomsmen were running late, because the game had gone into overtime. As if a football game had been more important than our wedding. But being the planner I was, I'd expected there would be a few bumps, and we were able to get back on track.

Chad and I danced all night, and I felt like I was on walking on air. It was one of the happiest days of my life (finding out I was pregnant, and the day Zoe was born also topped the list). I paused at the picture of Chad and I saying our vows.

I started to cry, but then an anger inside of me started to boil. I went into the office and grabbed a Sharpie, pulled the picture out of the album, and wrote in big black letters "LIAR."

I took another picture out and did the same thing. "LIAR."

I flipped through the album and found a picture of Chad and I in a candid moment. At the time, this had been my favorite wedding picture. The photographer had caught us in a moment that nobody was supposed to see.

Chad had pulled me away from the dance floor to a private corner. "I am so lucky I found you," he said as he kissed the top of my head. The photographer had captured the butterflies I was feeling.

I took the picture out and went to the kitchen sink. Scrounging a book of matches out of our junk drawer, I lit the photograph on fire and let it burn.

Fuck you, Chad.

-3-

SEPTEMBER

"We're only four games back, and the Mets play the Braves tonight. So if we win, we'll still be in good shape," Rachel said. It was September, and the Nationals had very little chance of making the playoffs, but we still had hope. Rachel and I had bonded over our love for baseball. Travis and Chad were also big fans, and a few times a year we'd take our families to the games. Travis's firm had season tickets right behind the Nationals dugout. Zoe and Jake enjoyed watching the game, eating popcorn, and cheering on the team, while Avery usually stared at her phone, texting her friends.

"I don't know. We were in this same position last year. We were one game back and then we blew it," Travis said, as he gave Rachel a kiss on the head.

Rachel and Travis had invited Zoe and I over for dinner and to watch the game. Travis eagerly showed off his new big-screen TV, which provided optimal viewing for baseball, almost as if you were right on the field with the players. Chad would be so jealous. He'd really wanted a bigger TV, but I'd told him the one we had was fine. I wondered if that was the first thing he'd purchased in his new home with Courtney. I wondered if Courtney had said something like, "You work hard and deserve a big TV." Of course, then, Chad would think to himself, "That's exactly why I left Beth, because she wouldn't let me have a bigger TV. Courtney *gets* me." I knew that wasn't the reason he left, but it was hard to not let my mind go there. I constantly kept score about the petty things that Chad and I fought about, but that I imagined he and Courtney didn't.

I enjoyed my time with Travis and Rachel. They were adorable together, and being with them made you feel like you were in the presence of real love. They always seemed to have each other's back, and they really focused on making each other happy. That they still had bi-monthly date nights impressed me. Last week, Rachel put on her fake smile while Travis took her to the driving range, but she did it because it was his turn to choose their activity. Two years ago, when Rachel's mom was sick, Travis took the kids on afternoon outings to make sure that Rachel had mandatory self-care time. I wished that Chad and I had had that kind of caring relationship—maybe then he wouldn't have cheated on me. But Chad never saw me struggle, let alone thought of ways to help.

"We still have two more months. Anything can happen," I said. "Chad and I have been talking about the Nationals making the World Series for years. Watch this be the year they go."

Chad and I both loved baseball and college football. On our second date, he took me to the Nationals game. He'd been impressed by how much I knew about the team and the strategy behind the game. In the fourth inning, I mentioned that going for a sacrifice bunt was the best call. At that moment, Chad kissed me on the cheek and said, "I never thought I'd find a woman who was into baseball as much as you are. You certainly are amazing." I'd felt giddy and knew this was the beginning of something real.

Baseball continued to be our thing, going to games together, sending each other emails about player updates, like who was injured, or a detailed analysis of someone's hitting slump. It would feel strange if the Nationals made it to the World Series, and I wouldn't be able to share it with Chad. Two years ago, the Nationals made it to the Division Series, so we went to a playoff game. It was the most exhilarating game I'd ever been to. It went into extra innings, and the Nationals won with a walk-off home run. The whole crowd erupted, and there was so much happiness and excitement in the atmosphere. On the way home on the metro, the crowd had erupted into "Let's go, Nationals" chants the entire way home. It had been an electrifying night, an exciting memory to share with Chad. But now I didn't have anyone to reminisce with about being at the most exciting game ever.

"We'd need a miracle, but anything can happen," Rachel said. Always an optimist when it came to the Nationals. "So, what stage are you in today?" she added.

I'd been ping-ponging all over the place emotionally. One day, I'd really hate him and hate what he did to me, and the next day I would think about what I did wrong and if I could fix it. Then, later that same day, I would be thinking that this still must be all a dream. It became difficult for my friends to keep up. Two weeks ago, Camila came over and asked how I was doing. She was using her calming, sympathetic tone, expecting me to cry and need a hug, but at that moment I was so angry, I could scream. Which is what I did to Camila. Well, not exactly, but I snapped at her. She was so taken aback, and I apologized, but we all decided on a system. They would ask what stage I was in, and then I would let them know, so they could plan accordingly. I was hoping for a time where I would just be back to normal, happy Beth, and my friends didn't have to walk on eggshells around me, but there was still just so much to unpack.

"Today is definitely anger, I got all worked up during my run, thinking of all the lies he had told me. Like the time he had gone to a buddies' to play cards, but he texted at 1 am saying he was too drunk to drive home, so he was just going to crash there. Of course, there was no 'buddy.' It was Courtney. At the end of my run, I just screamed at the top of my lungs." I said.

"That asshole. I hate how he treated you. All those late nights, he was just boning his coworker."

"You deserve better, you know that. Nobody deserves to be lied to like that," Travis added while taking a handful of popcorn.

It was nice to have Travis on my side rather than following some "bro code" and sticking up for Chad's actions.

"But then that anger quickly turned into sadness. After my run, I was all fired up. I jumped into the shower still reeling, but I don't even know what happened. All of a sudden, I tasted salt water. I didn't even realize I was crying, and then I broke down into big heaving sobs."

"Was it at least cathartic?" Rachel asked.

"It was. There was a bit of a release which was nice."

"You know what else provides a good release? Sex," Rachel said, giving me a little nudge.

"The best kind of release," Travis added.

After a few drinks with the girls, Rachel often mentioned her very healthy sex life, something we were all amazed by. I was really happy that Rachel and Travis still had that spark in their relationship, that, after all these years, they were able to keep up the romance and intimacy. It wasn't something either of them felt they needed to check off. But, at the same time, I was jealous. I wished that Chad and I had had that. If we had, then maybe he wouldn't have left.

"Okay, we get it. You two are so in love, and you still have great sex," I said, giving them both a silly grin. "I'm just not ready for that."

"You know, if you were a guy, you would have been out all night and have already slept with, like, six twenty-something girls," Travis said.

"That doesn't really solve any of my problems, though. Does it?" I asked.

"True. But it takes your mind off things, and it's a better release than crying in the shower," Rachel said. "Travis, go find someone in your office to make out with Beth. But don't make it sound like she's desperate, or some sort of charity case. My poor friend's husband left her, and she wants someone to play tonsil hockey with."

"I'll send out an all-staff email." Travis made like he was going to jump up and grab his laptop.

"Please don't," I said. "I just don't have a lot of self-confidence these days."

"You need a self-esteem boost. You should go out with Sean. I saw you two talking to each other," Rachel said.

"Yeah, Sean is a great choice," Travis added with a smile.

Sean was our neighborhood UPS delivery guy. Everyone in the neighborhood knew him. He was probably the nicest, friendliest person I had ever met. Whenever he delivered packages, he stopped to say hi and asked about everyone's days. He'd follow up on conversations we'd had weeks before. Last year, I'd briefly mentioned that I was hoping to get a promotion at work. Three weeks later, he had asked me about it. I was impressed with how invested he was in people. He didn't just exchange pleasantries, he *actually* listened. Neighborhood kids were excited when Sean came by, too. He'd played basketball in college, so he'd do a few trick shots if they were outside. Over the past few years, he'd really become a staple in the neighborhood. It didn't hurt that Sean was easy on the eyes. He had movie-star good looks, tall and muscular, with thick brown hair, bright blue eyes, and a playful smile.

Sean and I became more friendly after Zoe was born. I got multiple packages a day, some of them gifts from family and friends, and some from late-night Amazon orders. Since I was home from work on maternity leave, Zoe and I would wait for Sean on the porch when I expected a package. It was nice to have another adult to talk to during the day. Sean loved babies and enjoyed seeing Zoe. His son was just over a year old at the time. When I complained about the late nights, and the crying, and he'd assure me that every moment was worth it. He talked about the first time his son smiled at him, his face lighting up in a way I had never seen before. He was a proud dad, and I could tell he cherished every moment with his son, good or bad.

Two years ago, he shared that he and his wife had split up. He didn't give details, but Rachel was the first to notice when he stopped wearing his wedding ring. I'd always enjoyed talking to Sean, and did find him good-looking, but I'd never thought anything of it, since I thought I was in a happy, healthy marriage.

"I'm not going to date Sean," I said as one of the Natinal's star players struck out.

"Why not? He's the perfect rebound guy. You know him, he's hot, what else do you need?" Rachel smiled slyly.

The Nationals scored a home run, and we did our signature home run dance. We all stood up and clapped, "N-A-T-S, N-A-T-S," and then pumped our fists in the air saying, "Go! Go! Go!" Zoe and Jake loved doing the dance. Avery participated when at home, but she got embarrassed when we did it at the stadium.

"Because he's Sean. And I see him all the time. What if things went south and he stopped delivering all of my packages?" I said.

I knew Sean never would do that, but, still, people had to be cautious about dating someone they had to see every day.

"Or *your* packages, once I told him you were the ones who suggested we date," I added.

"No, I need Sean to deliver my coffee and wine," Rachel protested.

"Okay, not Sean, and not that twenty-five-year-old from La Caverna." Rachel put her finger to her chin as if she was deep in thought. "What about Noah?"

My face grew hot. Rachel was extremely adamant about me finding a rebound guy. "You know we're just friends."

"You can be friends, but now you're both single, so you can be more."

It's true Noah and I got along really well—we'd spend hours chatting at the park, walking Rusty. He was a great listener and always offered good advice, but he wasn't the right guy for a rebound. That could ruin our friendship, which I valued. I was also pretty sure he didn't think of me in that way. However, he had been looking better since he'd started swimming more. I'd noticed his arms and legs were more toned.

"Earth to Beth." Rachel waved a hand to get my attention.

"Sorry, I drifted off."

"Mm hmm, were you thinking of Noah's hot bod, or Sean's?" She gave me a playful smile.

"Neither. I'm not sure if a guy is the right distraction," I said, getting frustrated. "You just don't get it. Sleeping with someone is not going to take away this heartache."

I didn't mean to snap at Rachel. The thought of being with another guy seemed so intimidating. For one, I wasn't over Chad, and a part of me still wanted him back, or at least my family whole again. On the other hand, I had very little self-confidence. Why would some random guy at the bar want me? I appreciated Rachel for trying, and it was nice to be reminded that the possibility was out there, but I just wasn't ready. Rachel just wanted me to be happy, but I knew myself, and that wasn't what I needed.

"I'm just trying to help." Rachel gave me an apologetic look.

"I know, and I appreciate it. I just have to figure out what's right for me."

"Well, there's always wine and baseball, two of my favorite things!" Rachel said.

"This is true, but I can't just drink my sorrows away every night. I need to do something productive with my time."

I looked at my watch and saw it was already nine o'clock. "Okay, Zoe. After this inning, time to go home," I said.

That night, after putting Zoe to bed, I poured myself a glass of wine and finished the game. The Nationals pulled it off in the ninth with a walk-off home run. I put the bottle in the recycling bin and noticed the ever-growing collection of wine bottles. I couldn't continue down this path of a bottle or more of wine every night. I needed to spend my time doing something productive.

I decided not to open another bottle, but instead opened my laptop and googled, "what to do after a divorce." There were a lot of suggestions for self-care and spa days. I was a big fan of my weekly face mask and soak in the tub, but I needed something more.

A few minutes later, I stumbled on an article about volunteering, and how it increased self-confidence and gave you a purpose. Two things I needed. I needed to feel good about myself again, and I also needed something useful to do with my free nights. I used to volunteer a lot in high school and before I got married. I'd wanted to do more of it, but life always seemed to get in the way.

I found a few homeless shelters that served breakfast and dinner, but they were all far away and were either asking for a once-a-week commitment, or their requested volunteer times didn't work out with pick up and drop off at Zoe's school. I needed something once or twice a month, since I still had a lot on my plate with work, taking care of the house, and Zoe.

I kept searching and finally found an after-school center called SOAR: School's Out Afternoon Recreation, for kids from low-income families. The center was only a few miles away, and they were looking for volunteers to help students with homework from five o'clock to six o'clock. That sounded very promising.

Finally, something to possibly look forward to, rather than just endless loneliness.

The next day, Zoe and I ran into Noah at the park. I told him about my idea to volunteer as a tutor.

"That's a great idea, Beth. I've been meaning to find something new to do as well. Do you mind if I join you?"

"Of course not, it'll be fun to do with someone else."

"Can you do airplane, Noah?" Zoe asked. Zoe loved it when Noah picked her up and ran around the park like she was an airplane. I used to be able to do it with her, but after she turned four, she was too heavy for me. Luckily, Noah had lots of practice with Caleb, and didn't mind it at all. I loved to see Zoe smile and laugh as she was hoisted up in the air and spread her arms wide.

"Sure! No problem. As long as your mom watches Rusty."

"I'd be happy to. What do you say, Zoe?"

"Thank you! Thank you! Thank you!"

"Prepare for takeoff," Noah said as he scooped her up and ran around making airplane noises.

Zoe screamed in delight. "Higher! Higher!"

"Uh-oh, turbulence," Noah proclaimed as he started to bounce her around.

As the flight came to an end, Noah slowly put her down.

"Great landing!" Zoe said, as she petted Rusty.

"Thanks!" Noah said, then turned to me, a little breathless from running. "So, tell me more about this place."

"It's actually just a few miles away. Kids whose parents work and can't afford after-school care go there. They provide a snack and an activity, like basketball and dance, when the kids are let out from school, and then they have designated homework time for an hour starting at five o'clock."

"Do they need volunteers for the other activities?" Noah asked.

"I think so. We should find out. There's an orientation next week. I'll send you the link so you can sign up."

A week later, Noah and I went to an orientation about volunteering at SOAR. I'd had no idea this place existed, even though it was only about three miles from my house. Apparently, the center had been around for fifty years. The mission was to give kids a positive sense of community and a place to go after school. It was in a decent-sized building, with a big kitchen, dining area, a few small rooms with books and desks, and a large gymnasium. The person who ran the tutoring program told us that, on any given day, there were about twenty to thirty kids who came by the center after school while their parents worked. Kids were divided up into small groups based on their age, and volunteers could help with homework. For the younger kids, there were also books to read.

The room brimmed with volunteers of all ages. There was a small group of high school students seated in front of us. Something like this probably looked good on a college application. There were also a few older people as well. If Rachel had been here, she'd have been checking around for cute eligible bachelors I could hook up with. Might as well do good *and* get a date.

After the director gave her presentation, we took a quick tour, which ended in the dining room. All the kids had gathered, and there were cupcakes to celebrate anyone with a September birthday. Noah and I went over and started talking to some kids. I met a little girl in a bright purple shirt named Josephina, who was about 9, who told me that her favorite subject was English, and she liked to write stories about unicorns. I was really excited about this opportunity. It would be a good use of my time, and I was glad Noah was doing it with me.

Noah and I decided that we'd go on Wednesday together, and the next week, he picked me up at in his Jeep, and we drove over.

"I'm really glad we're doing this," he said as I climbed into the car.

"Me too. I think it'll be good, make us feel productive, like we're helping the community."

"Okay, what's your one thing to vent about for the day?" Noah inquired.

I told him how uncomfortable I was that Camila, Jennifer, and Rachel were walking on eggshells around me. They were my best friends, so I knew they were just trying to be supportive and that they would do anything for me, but I hated feeling this way. However, I still needed to talk things out. Having also gone through a divorce, Noah understood. So, we made a rule that I was only allowed to complain about one thing a day. We would discuss it together and then move on.

"Chad and I agreed that the schedule we decided on in August would be sufficient. We haven't even begun to talk about holidays, but Thanksgiving isn't for another few months. There's a lot to think about, but I can only handle one fire at a time."

"How do you feel about the schedule becoming more permanent?"

"I miss Zoe when she's over there. And the thought of her with her new family kind of makes my stomach turn."

Zoe had started talking more about her time at Chad's house. She and Willow, who was seven, were really getting along and enjoyed running around outside and playing together. Apparently, Willow had quite the Barbie collection. It seemed like a nice time for Zoe, which I wanted, but the insta-family situation still made me want to vomit in my mouth. It was hard enough accepting that my marriage was over—I didn't want to also accept that my daughter had a new mom figure and siblings. Thinking of Zoe's new family just reminded me how intense Chad and Courtney's relationship was, which just burned even more.

"Well, I can't speak to the insta-family issue, but you will get used to the nights without Zoe. Already you are thinking of productive ways to fill your time. Volunteering is such a good idea and a great step in your journey." Noah gave me a reassuring smile.

"My journey? Now you sound like my therapist."

"Well, I do know how to talk the talk," he said with a shrug.

We got to the center, and Noah and I were assigned to the elementary school kids. I was a little nervous but also eager to help. Another volunteer, David, had already arrived. The three of us talked a little bit, and then four kids came bouncing through the door and threw their backpacks on the desks.

"Hey, David!" a little girl shouted. David was a regular and knew most of the kids. He seemed to be a fan favorite, because they all wanted to work with him.

The girl who I'd met at the orientation sat next to me. "I remember you," she said.

"Josephina, right? Have you written any good stories about unicorns lately?" I asked.

"I'm still working on a magical one named Rainbow Princess, but I'm not done yet."

"I can't wait to read it. What homework do you have today?"

"Social studies. We're learning about the American Revolution." She rolled her eyes.

"Sounds like fun. Let's see what I can do to help you."

Josephina and I read through some passages about George Washington, and I helped her answer some multiple-choice questions about the text. A few of them she got right away. For the ones that she didn't, I helped her use process of elimination to find the answer and then gave her a high five when she picked the correct one.

"You're doing great. These are some tough questions," I said with encouragement.

Noah was great with kids. He was helping Josephina's brother, Christopher, who was in kindergarten. He kept Christopher engaged, even though I could tell the little boy wanted to be somewhere else. After Christopher finished practicing writing the letter E, he and Noah had a dance party. Noah was a terrible dancer, but it was sweet to watch him and this little boy rock out. I smiled broadly at Noah. Something about seeing him interact with Christopher seemed so endearing. Noah was a quality guy, and it was assuring to know there were still some of those out there. His goofy dance moves made me laugh.

Suddenly, I realized that my heart had started to beat a bit faster.

"That's not how you dance!" Josephina exclaimed.

"Oh yeah? Let's see," Noah challenged her.

Josephina started in with some moves, and then suddenly, all of us were having one big dance party. We rocked out, smiling and laughing.

When the song ended, David corralled the group back to the desks. "Okay, back to work, but we can do a dance party the last five minutes, if everyone finishes their homework."

Josephina and I went back to working on her multiplication tables. Before I knew it, David declared that it was time for our last dance party.

During the car ride home, I couldn't stop smiling. Noah and I had really connected with Josephina and Christopher, and we'd had a good time doing it. I already looked forward to going back. Noah had the same feeling.

"That was so much fun. The time just flew by," he said.

"Yeah, it was *really* fun. But you're going to need to work on your dance moves."

"What are you talking about! I'm a great dancer!" Noah did some bopping around in the car to prove it. I just laughed at him and then joined in.

When I got home, the house still felt empty, but I felt better about it. I'd done something good with my time. I felt a surge of happniess.

I sat on the couch and stared at the picture on the wall, the one of me and Chad kissing in the moonlight. I loved that picture, but looking at it made me sad and reminded me of Chad. I got up and took it down.

Looking around the room, I realized that everything in here reminded me of Chad. If I was going to get over him, and start my new life, I was going to have to erase him from this house.

I'd never been much for interior design, so I went on the internet and looked through some ideas to see what I liked. I wasn't sure where to start. My house was reasonably sized—there were three bedrooms, one that was used for an office, plus the kitchen, living room, dining room, and basement. It seemed so daunting to change everything all at once. My mind raced from one room to the next, thinking about ways to change everything. This was supposed to be fun, not overwhelming.

I took a deep breath, and then remembered what Noah and Camila had said right after Chad left, "one day at time." I'd use the same motto for my house. One room at a time.

I decided to start with my bedroom, and then, every weekend that Zoe was with Chad, I'd work on another room.

Jennifer loved shopping, so she agreed to go to Target with me.

"Okay, we're going to start with your bed," she said. "You can't be sleeping on the same sheets that the lying bastard slept on, and you deserve something luxurious, with a nice thread count."

We grabbed a cart and headed to the bedding section. There were so many options to choose from for comforters and sheets. Back when Chad and I got married, we'd registered at Macy's. We went through the entire store, marking things that we wanted. The bedspread had been a big debate. He didn't want something too girly, and I didn't want something plain. We'd compromised on something with light blue and gray stripes.

"This is great, Beth. I'm glad you're doing this," Jennifer said, as she slowly perused the merchandise. "You get to pick out what makes *you* happy, and only you. It's your room, so you should feel good in it."

"What about this one?" I pointed to a pintuck lilac comforter. The set came with throw pillows in purple and gray. "It'll look really nice against my gray wall."

"Oh, I totally agree." Jennifer grabbed the comforter and put it in the cart. "I was going to ask if you wanted to re-paint, but I love that gray."

When Chad and I had moved into the house, the master bedroom was an awful blue. It clashed with our bedding and made me think of the Smurfs. It had to go. Chad didn't care what color we painted it, so I chose a stone gray, which made the room shine when the sun came through the windows.

Jennifer and I picked out some cream-colored Egyptian cotton sheets to go with the comforter set and then moved to picture frames. I'd already taken down all the pictures of Chad, including the ones from our wedding day, but I wanted new frames. The old ones felt tainted.

Before going to Target, I'd found a few pictures that I wanted to put on my nightstand and dresser. One was of Zoe and me from two summers ago when we went for an overnight girls' trip to Dewey Beach. We had a great time playing in the sand and in the water. It was a happy memory. Whenever I looked at the picture, I could still hear the laughter in her voice as we raced away from the gigantic waves crashing on the sand. I also chose a picture of me, Camila, Rachel, and Jennifer one night when we were having drinks at La Caverna. The four of us were sitting at a table, talking and laughing. Sebastian took a candid photo and later said we looked like models and wanted to put the picture on the restaurant's website. I also wanted to feel empowered, so I included a picture of me crossing the finish line of my first 10k.

We kept walking around Target, picking up little knick-knacks to place around my room. I found a wooden sign that said, "The

Best is Yet to Come," and put it in the cart. Maybe a constant reminder that things were going to get better would be something
inspiring to wake up to. Finally, I spotted a picture of a woman
dancing in the rain, while other people looked on from under their
umbrellas. The second I saw the picture, I fell in love with it. I loved
how the woman didn't care that she was getting wet. She was still
going to dance and love every moment of it. She looked like she
didn't have a care in the world. She looked comfortable with who
she was. I wanted to be that woman.

"I think we have everything," Jennifer declared.

"I agree. It'll be good to see it all together, and we can always
come back again."

We headed to the checkout counter.

"What room are you going to do next?" Jennifer asked while we
waited.

"I don't know, maybe the living room? There's still a lot of 'Chad'
in that room."

"So, I take it this means you'll be able to stay in the house?"
Jennifer asked.

"It looks that way. I really don't want to leave. I love that house,
and I love living by you all. The fact that I got that promotion last
year really helps, as I don't think I'd have been able to stay with my
previous salary."

The thought of leaving Highland Avenue depressed me. I'd
do everything possible to stay. I had sat down a few nights ago to
look at my expenses—as of now, I'd be able to afford the mortgage.
However, Chad and I hadn't had the finance discussion yet, and
I wasn't sure what that would mean in terms of alimony or child
support. I made more money than he did, and I wasn't sure if we'd
end up fighting about it. Noah was the only other person I knew

who was divorced, and he'd ended up paying his ex a big chunk of money, though not as much as she'd originally asked for.

I got home and put up my new decorations and made up the bed. It was the first night since Chad told me he was leaving that I looked forward to going to sleep. I climbed in and surveyed my room. The new sheets felt cool and crisp. The purple comforter was calming, and the picture of the woman in the rain made me hopeful. I was delighted with the way my room had turned out. I didn't feel Chad in the room at all—instead, I felt *me*. For the first time in months, I felt like I had made some progress in my healing process.

That night, I decided to take up the entire bed. It was mine, and I was going to enjoy it.

-4-

OCTOBER

Fall was, by far, my favorite season. I loved when the leaves turned colors, there was a crispness in the air, and I could get by wearing jeans and a cute sweater, a classic outfit. Our annual trip to the pumpkin patch was something I looked forward to every year. Ever since Zoe and Julian were babies, our families would take a quintessentially fall trip to Riverrock Farm. The farm had everything: apples and pumpkins to pick, hayrides, animals to feed, face painting, and corn mazes. It was a fall wonderland.

But this year, I was apprehensive about continuing traditions that I'd once shared with Chad. The first time we'd gone to Riverrock Farm, Zoe was almost one. Chad and I held hands while Zoe toddled her way through the pumpkins. I was happy to have our family of three and our best friends there together. The warm sun beamed down on us, and at that moment, everything felt perfect. Every year after that, I looked back on pictures from our first trip and thought about how the kids were growing, their smiles getting wider. It was a magical place, and I didn't want to have to go without Chad. Would it make me sad that he was no longer a part of this tradition, that now we'd have to pick out only two pumpkins instead of three?

I talked to Camila about it, wondering if we should just skip this year. I could always get pumpkins at the grocery store. She reminded me of all the fun Julian and Zoe had there, and what joy it brought us to see their smiling faces. Of course, she was right about that, but it was still a reminder of how much my life had changed in just three short months. It would be difficult seeing the other happy families together, making memories that they'd be able to look back on, and I wasn't sure I wanted to put myself through that. My heart still ached for that life, even though I was slowly coming to terms with the fact that it was over. Camila finally convinced me, though, saying that a change of scenery and connecting with nature would be good for me. She also mentioned the delicious donuts, and I knew I couldn't say no to them.

After Zoe's morning gymnastics class, we drove up, singing our favorite songs in the car. Zoe mostly enjoyed top 40 hits, but I made sure to give her a proper music education, introducing her to music from all decades, especially the '80s and '90s, which were my personal favorites. It was a scenic forty-five-minute drive. Along the twisty roads, the leaves had all turned to red, orange, and brown. It was relaxing and peaceful. We got to the parking lot and looked for Camila and her family.

"Is Julian here yet?" Zoe asked excitedly.

I checked my phone and saw a text from Camila saying they were running late and would be there in ten minutes.

"They'll be here soon! Let's go see the goats. I'll tell them to meet us there." I pulled out some quarters so that I could get some goat food, and we headed down the hill.

"Look, Mommy! A baby goat." Zoe loved babies, especially baby animals. "It's so little. I just want to hug it. Can I feed it?"

I put a quarter in the food machine and got a handful for Zoe. She stuck her hand out and giggled as the goat licked it.

Zoe and I had gone to a farm in Pennsylvania when she was

two. Chad had been camping with his brother, so I decided to take Zoe on an adventure, just the two of us. We stopped off at a farm, and Zoe really wanted to feed the goat, but she was too scared. She kept dropping the food on our side of the fence, and the goat was getting restless. I showed her how to hold her hand out, just close enough so that the goat would come to her. After a few tries, she eventually got the hang of it. She had a huge smile on her face as the goat licked her hand. Every time she was out of food, she'd jump up and ask for more. We spent thirty more minutes and five dollars feeding the goats. We'd had so much fun, Zoe and I, just the two of us. It was the first time I'd traveled with Zoe by myself, and I'd been a little bit nervous, but she turned out to be a great travel companion. She was a go-with-the-flow kind of kid.

After that, we'd taken a lot of mother-daughter trips, always ending up in laughter and fun.

I'd just dispensed another handful of food when we heard "Zoe! Zoe!"

Julian ran down the hill toward us, with Camila, Sebastian, and Arlo coming in behind. Arlo was strapped to Sebastian in a wearable baby carrier. I'd never been able to use one of those with Zoe, but everyone else made it look so easy.

Julian gave Zoe a big hug.

"Sorry we're late. You know how it is getting out of the house with these two," Camila said as she pointed to Julian and Arlo.

"No problem. We were just feeing the goats. Julian, do you want to feed them too?"

"Yes!"

"Yes, what?" Camila gave Julian a stern look.

"Yes, please, Ms. Beth," Julian said.

I grabbed more food and gave a handful each to Julian and Zoe.

They excitedly fed the goats as Arlo screamed in delight. Zoe tried to teach Arlo how to feed the goats, but he was getting restless. It was heartwarming to see her be so patient with Arlo.

"Okay, who's ready to get some pumpkins?" Sebastian asked.

"I am!" Julian and Zoe shouted in unison.

They ran off to get in line for the hayride that would take us to the pumpkin patch. Zoe and Julian sat on their knees, with their hair blowing in the wind, while I entertained Arlo with a game of peek-a-boo. When we got to the patch, Zoe followed Julian on the hunt for the perfect pumpkin.

"Don't get that one, Zoe. You want to find one that's good for carving," I instructed as she tried to pick a pumpkin that was covered in warts.

They kept looking, making their way through the tangled vines, until they each found a pumpkin. Zoe's was tall and narrow, while Julian had found a nice round one.

"Now we need to get you one, Mommy," Zoe said.

"Okay."

She grabbed my hand as we walked and tried to avoid the vines. My mind raced to all the times Chad and I had been in this exact field, holding hands. I thought I'd feel a hint of pain; instead, Zoe's small hand in mine gave me a warm, fuzzy feeling. I was glad that we'd come to the pumpkin patch. Zoe and I were a good team, and we always had fun together, even without Chad. I was determined to show Zoe that the two of us were enough. She didn't seem bothered that Chad wasn't here, so I wasn't going to let it bother me either.

Zoe found a small pumpkin. "This one is cute, Mommy. You should get it," she said.

I did like the small pumpkin, but it wouldn't be easy to carve something so small.

"How about this one?" I said, choosing a perfectly ripe, bright orange pumpkin. It was a little bigger than Zoe's, and she said she liked that mine was the mommy pumpkin and hers was the baby pumpkin.

"I'm going to make mine into a scary face," I said.

"No, Mommy, we need to make nice pumpkins."

I laughed. Zoe always wanted to be good. Two years ago, we'd both been witches for Halloween, and she had insisted we were good witches, not evil witches. Even when I told her stories, she always made sure that the monsters and ghosts were good and helped people.

We walked over to where Camila and Sebastian stood with their pumpkins. Julian showed Zoe the pumpkin he'd picked, and the one he'd picked out for Arlo.

"I'm hungry," Julian exclaimed.

"Me too! Mommy can we have a snack?" Zoe said.

We took the hayride back, holding our pumpkins in our laps, and then walked over to the concession stand to get donuts and hot apple cider. Zoe gobbled down two donuts. Sebastian agreed to take Zoe and Julian through the corn maze and to feed the fish, while Camila and I hung back with our pumpkins and Arlo.

"Thanks for making me come," I said when we were alone. "I'm really having a good time, and so is Zoe."

"I'm glad," Camila said.

"I thought I'd be sad about Chad not being here. Every inch of this place has some sort of memory. Our families have had such good times coming to Riverrock together. It *is* a little weird he's not here. His absence is noted, but not in a sad way. More in a 'this is how it is now' way," I told her.

"Yeah, Sebastian and I talked about that on the ride up here. Our families have done so much together. I know this is hard for you, but it's kind of a loss for us, too. Not that I'm taking away from what you are going through."

"I didn't really even think about that, but you're right."

I hadn't even thought about how this was affecting their lives. Sebastian and Chad had been tight. Of all the husbands in the neighborhood, they were by far the closest. Had Chad processed that he had lost all of his friends on Highland Avenue? Was Courtney worth it?

"I know what he did to you was terrible, and lying to you was horrible, but he also lied to us," Camila continued. "I think about all the times he was over at our house, watching the game, or grilling, and that whole time he was having an affair? Sebastian had no idea. We also feel duped."

"He was a good liar, I guess. Not the best trait to have." I shrugged my shoulders.

"No, not at all. Sorry, I know our feelings aren't your problem."

"No, it's fine." I waved my hand. "It kind of makes me feel better. Like I wasn't the only fool." I gave her a sincere smile.

"How is Zoe doing with everything?" Camila asked as she gave Arlo a bite of banana.

"She seems to be adjusting. She talks about missing Chad at bedtime, but we started doing phone calls to say good night."

"That's good. Keeps them connected."

"Yeah. She talks about Willow and Wyatt a lot, but Zoe doesn't bring up Courtney that much." I asked Zoe about life at Chad's house. Not in a nosy way though. I wanted her to feel that she could tell me anything. I tried not to prod, and I hoped that I showed her how excited I was for her. She would tell me about all the games she and Willow would play, and I tried to engage and share her happiness. I didn't want her to think that I didn't like Wyatt or Willow, and especially Courtney.

"I wonder if, in some way, she knows not to. Like subconsciously," Camila said.

"Yeah, I wonder. I wonder if Courtney ever talks about me?"

"I'm not sure what she'd say. She's the one who did something bad, not you."

"Oh, I know. But maybe something to justify this to Zoe. Like, the decision for Chad to be with Courtney is justified because of something I did."

Camila looked horrified. "I'd hope not. I mean, if she was in your position, she probably wouldn't want to be talked about like that."

"You never know. People who have affairs don't necessarily think about other people's feelings. They are more concerned with their own well-being."

I took another delicious bite of donut. Just then, Zoe and Julian came running back with Sebastian.

"Mommy! Guess what?" Zoe panted, out of breath from running.

"What?" I said, patting my knee and giving her a big smile.

"Julian and I raced on the big slide, and I won twice!"

"You did?" I said. "That sounds like fun."

"It was, and then Mr. Sebastian did the corn maze with us."

"But we got lost," Julian interjected.

"What?" Camila said. "Mr. Sebastian is not very good with directions."

"No, he's not," Julian said, and he and Zoe both laughed.

On the ride home, Zoe fell asleep in the back seat, tuckered out from the busy day. It had been a successful trip to the farm. I was happy I'd gone.

Driving back and looking at the picturesque landscape, I thought about which traditions I wanted to continue, but also what new ones I wanted to create. I thought of all the different adventures Zoe and I could go on together. It made me hopeful for the future. Sure, there were plenty of photo albums of Chad, Zoe, and I having a great time together, but Zoe and I could fill our own albums.

We pulled into the driveway as Zoe woke up. "Can we carve the pumpkins now?" she exclaimed.

"Yes, just let me get in the door."

Zoe ran into the house, and I grabbed the pumpkins. When I got inside, she was already laying out the newspaper on the floor. The actual carving was usually something Chad took care of. But I'd done a search on Amazon and found some stencils and utensils that made it look easy to do. Zoe grabbed the stencils and chose two happy faces for our pumpkins.

I cut the tops off, and Zoe grabbed two spoons to scoop out the seeds. We put them in a big bowl, so we could clean them and make roasted pumpkin seeds with olive oil, salt, and paprika. I loved the way the house smelled when they were baking. It reminded me of my childhood. Growing up, my family had had roasted pumpkin seeds from the beginning of October through the end of November, and it was a tradition that I carried to my family.

"It's so slimy," Zoe said as she separated the seeds from the pumpkin pulp.

"Eek," I said, making a squishy face.

"Can I go trick-or-treating with Wyatt and Willow?" she asked politely.

I froze. Chad and I hadn't talked about how we were going to split Halloween. I wanted to continue our Halloween traditions with Zoe. Every year Rachel, Camila, Jennifer, and I took the kids trick-or-treating, while the husbands stayed home to hand out candy. Then after an hour, we'd all go to Camila's house to drink wine while the kids sorted out their loot and traded Skittles for M&Ms. I just assumed we'd do the same this year. But if Zoe wanted to go with her dad, I couldn't really stop her. It hurt a little that she wanted to spend time with her new family, but I was also glad she was happy with them. In the end, that's all a parent really wants, for their children to be happy.

"Sure. You don't want to trick-or-treat with Julian this year?" I asked her, keeping my voice even so she wouldn't know I was upset.

"Well, I'll see him at school. And Courtney said that we could all be zombies. She'd even make our costumes."

Zoe seemed excited about the idea of being a zombie, and I didn't want to take that away from her just because I didn't want to be alone. I wondered if Chad and Courtney would dress up. The past few years, we'd done the family costume thing. Last year, Zoe was Dorothy from The Wizard of Oz, and Chad and I dressed up as the Tin Man and Scarecrow. Zoe looked adorable in her pigtails, with one of her stuffed dogs in a basket.

"That sounds like fun. I hope you all have a good time," I said.

I was bummed out that I would be spending the holiday without my family. I hadn't really thought about it, but I guess there were many other holidays that we'd have to split. We hadn't even talked about Thanksgiving, New Years', or winter break. There was so much going on, I hadn't had time to think about it. I figured that would be an issue for the future, but the fall had crept up on me.

I made a mental note to talk with Chad about our schedule for the remainder of the year. I couldn't keep kicking this can down the road.

"I hope I get a lot of candy," Zoe said.

"I'm sure you will, but don't eat it all at once." I knew Chad would let her eat as much candy as she wanted, and she'd probably be bouncing off the walls come bedtime.

"Okay, Mommy." Zoe rolled her eyes.

"And don't forget to brush your teeth."

We finished carving our pumpkins and put them on the porch outside. Rachel and Travis had just finished putting up their decorations. Their huge inflatable jack-o-lantern played "Monster Mash." Other houses in the neighborhood were also decked out. Some were scary with graveyards and ghosts, while others had jovial pumpkins and scarecrows. The neighborhood looked festive with the leaves falling on the grass. Our lawn was in dire need of some raking. I thought about getting Zoe to help me but knew that I'd have to schedule in some time for the heavy lifting. I took a deep breath. Another thing to put on the ever-growing to-do list.

"These look great," I said to Zoe, as we surveyed our handiwork.

"They do! I'm glad they aren't scary."

"I had a fun time with you today."

"Me too," Zoe said, giving me a big hug.

The next morning, Jennifer and I went for a run. We always did about four to five miles together on Sundays. I told her about Zoe wanting to go to Chad's for Halloween.

"You should still trick-or-treat with us. It's tradition," she said.

"It's funny you say that. Just yesterday I was thinking about continuing traditions without Chad. I wasn't sure about going to the pumpkin patch, but it turned out to be a great time. I hadn't thought about continuing traditions without *Zoe*."

After Zoe had gone to bed last night, I'd thumbed through the pictures of past Halloweens while sipping my wine. We'd all had so much fun together. My heart ached to think that this year would be different, not just because Chad wouldn't be there, but because I would be alone. I loved my friends, and I loved their kids, but I didn't want to trick-or-treat childless. That sounded depressing. I didn't want to be around all my friends who were happy and able to share this time with their kids and husbands.

"We sure would miss you," Jennifer said.

"I know, but I don't think I'd be much fun. I think being around everyone would just make me sad, and I don't want to be Debbie Downer."

"You'd be with your friends. We'd cheer you up."

"I appreciate it. I really do. But this time I think I need to sit it out. Being with you all will just be a constant reminder of all that I've lost this year."

"Okay, well, if you change your mind, you know where we'll be. What are you going to do instead?" Jennifer asked.

"I don't know. I think I might just hand out candy with Noah. Caleb is with his mom this Halloween. We can be single and child-less together."

"It must be nice to have Noah."

"So, both you and Rachel think I should date him, huh?" I said giving Jennifer a playful look.

"No, not at all. I just think it's nice to have someone who under-stands what it's like to be a single parent. I'm here to listen, always, but I obviously don't know what it's like for you. He does. There's something about being in it together—it's just different."

"That's true. He's a constant reminder that there's a light at the end of the tunnel. And he knows the trials and tribulations of co-parenting."

"What do you mean?" Jennifer asked, looking perplexed.

"Well, Chad and I don't live in the same house anymore, so Zoe has two sets of rules. And while consistency is good, there's nobody there to make sure it happens. Like, we could agree on a bedtime, but that doesn't mean that Chad would stick to that, and I have no way of enforcing it. Like Chad can let Zoe stay up as late as he wants."

Just the other night, Zoe told me that when she was with Chad, he let her and Willow stay up until ten o'clock. I thought it was just a one-time thing, but it turns out that's just her bedtime over there. I called him to ask about it, and he just replied with 'My house, my rules.' I pushed down my frustration with that whole conversation. I tried to reason with him that she needed consistency, and ten o'clock was too late for a five-year-old, especially on a school night. But he wasn't having it. He just told me to stop controlling him and hung up the phone. I was so furious with him. The next day, I sent him an email about coming up with a consistent set of rules and the benefits of sleep for children, but he never responded.

"I asked Noah for any tips he had about co-parenting, and he said that I had to choose my battles. It's difficult not being able to control what goes on at the other house, but he assured me that I'd make myself crazy if I tried. It's good advice, and something I needed to figure out. But still, it was frustrating."

"Well, Michael lets the twins stay up late when I'm with you girls."

"But that's a special treat, and I'm sure you two talk about it after. I have no control. It's unbelievably maddening. Especially when Chad just won't see it my way. He doesn't have to compromise; we aren't married anymore. There's nothing in it for him, so he no longer has to be a partner."

"Like I said, it's good for you to have Noah, because I want to get it, but I just don't," Jennifer said.

Jennifer was right—my friends were trying to be there for me, but sometimes they just didn't get everything I was dealing with. It was easy to talk about the heartbreak, and bash Chad, but that was just the tip of the iceberg. I was essentially starting over at the ripe old age of thirty-eight. I was getting over the man I thought was love of my life, figuring out who I was, and who I wanted to be, all while working, managing a household, and raising a kid. Having Noah was nice—he got it and had been at this longer, so he could provide advice along the way.

"So, I was thinking," Jennifer said, as we passed the playground. "These runs have been good, and I love doing 10Ks, but maybe we should up our game."

"What were you thinking?" I asked.

Every year Jennifer and I signed up for two 10Ks, one in the spring and one in the fall. I'd done the first one with her three years ago. I'd always enjoyed running, and I liked that I felt empowered after a good run. After a race, I felt accomplished. The training wasn't that intense, but there was a euphoric feeling crossing the finish line.

"Do you want to train for a half marathon? There's one in April. We could totally do it. I found a training plan online that will help us figure out how to increase our mileage," Jennifer said.

A half marathon seemed like a lot and would take some dedication. I'd never run more than six miles, and that was only twice a year. I wasn't sure I could do thirteen miles, or would even have time to train for something that much longer.

"I don't know, that's a lot. Are you sure?" I asked, feeling skeptical.

"I'm totally sure. And it's good to start training in the fall, when the weather is nice and cool, rather in the summer. It won't be a problem."

That was easy for Jennifer to say, she was a natural athlete. It was in her blood. But, at the same time, it would be nice to have a goal to work toward. We'd have fun, and she would make sure we stayed on schedule and would push me to my full potential.

"Okay, I'm in," I said. I was a little apprehensive but excited about pushing myself to the next level.

"Great! Then it's settled. I'll send you the link to sign up, so we can get the early bird special."

"Sounds good."

"Let's start now. I know I said we'd do four miles today, but let's go a little longer and make it five."

"You are very sneaky. I was pacing myself for four. I don't know if I have another mile in me," I said, wiping the sweat from my brow.

"You can do it. I promise," she said.

We pushed ourselves to get another mile in. It was slower than the others, my breaths were deeper, and my legs started to ache, but once we rounded the final corner and saw our homes, we both put it in high gear for the finish.

"Good run! Just eight more miles to go," Jennifer said as she gave me a high five.

I went home, signed up for the race, and marked my calendar. Five months to run 13.1 miles. Jennifer sent me the training plan and it seemed doable. We would do our long runs on Sundays, and I'd run two times during the week, mostly shorter runs. It felt nice to have a goal, something positive to work toward.

I sent Jennifer a text, letting her know I signed up.

Me: *Signed up for the race, no backing down now.*
Jennifer: *We've got this!*

Once I thought about it, I got really excited. After today's five-mile run, I knew I had a lot of work to do, but it was work that, hopefully, would result in a positive outcome. I wanted to work hard and grow stronger. I wanted to show Zoe the value of setting goals, and how great it felt to achieve them. And, who knew, maybe running half marathons would become a new tradition that Jennifer and I did together.

-5-

November

"It's my birthday!" Zoe exclaimed as she ran into my room and jumped on my bed.

I couldn't believe my little girl was really six. It seemed like the time had just flown by. This year, Zoe's birthday fell on a Saturday, which was exciting for Zoe, because her party got to be on her actual birthday. It was also ideal for me, because I only had to deal with the emotional implications of this being the first birthday her parents weren't together once.

As part of our separation agreement, Chad and I had agreed that we'd split the day. He would pick her up in the morning and spend the first half of the day with her. Then we'd both be at the birthday party with her friends from school. After the party, I would take her to dinner. My heart broke for her. I didn't want her to have to split her birthday between two sets of parents, being ping-ponged back and forth. I'd never wanted any of this for her. But I was determined to make it the best birthday, because that was what she deserved.

The night before, I couldn't sleep. I was so nervous that something would go wrong, that I wouldn't be able to handle a birthday party with Chad present, or that all morning I'd be depressed, knowing that Zoe was spending her birthday breakfast with her new family. I woke up every hour, thinking about something else that might go wrong. What if Zoe liked Courtney's gift better than mine? What if Courtney showed up at the birthday party, even though I'd explicitly told Chad not to invite her? What if I broke down sobbing at the party? There were a million other things that could go wrong. I'd stared at the clock, with Twix curled up next to me, purring loudly. I really wanted her birthday to go smoothly. I really wanted this to be her best birthday ever.

"Happy birthday, princess," I said, giving her a big kiss on the forehead as she cuddled in next to me and Twix.

"Mommy, I am so excited for today," she said. "My party is going to be so much fun. I can't wait for the trampolines."

Zoe had been talking about her birthday nonstop since I'd told her I'd booked the new trampoline park, Arc Jump. The park had opened in September, and I'd taken her there on a rainy day. We had a blast jumping around the big trampoline and playing chase, which always ended with Zoe jumping into a big pit of foam blocks. All day, Zoe could hardly contain her happiness. On the ride home, she asked if she could have her birthday party there. Luckily, they had an opening, and it wasn't too expensive. I booked it right away. When I told Zoe, she jumped up and gave me a gigantic hug.

"Me too," I said. "Come, let's see how much you've grown, birthday girl."

Zoe jumped out of bed, and I followed her into her room, where we had a chart that we used to measure how tall she was every year. She loved looking back at previous entries and seeing how much she'd grown. Last night, she'd talked about how excited she was to see how much taller she'd grown this year.

Zoe put her back against the chart. I took out a pencil and made a line, then wrote "6 years old." I felt a sharp ping of pain thinking that, next year, she might not be waking up in this house, with me, on her seventh birthday. I wasn't sure where she would be on any of her next birthdays. I held back tears, but then took a deep breath and pulled myself together. Today was about Zoe, about how great she was, not about how my life had gotten turned upside down and I was still trying to put it back right side up.

"You grew one inch! You are getting so big," I said. "You better get ready. Daddy will be here soon. Your dress is in your closet."

"Ta-da," she said as she came out of her room several minutes later.

Last week, I'd taken Zoe to Target, where she saw a sparkly purple dress with a big poufy skirt. She ran right up to it, and said, "This is the perfect birthday dress, don't you think, Mommy?" With her face all lit up, I couldn't say no. She looked so grown up in the dress. It was hard to believe my baby was turning into a young girl. Her rounded face was beginning to soften and mature. She'd lost most of her baby fat, and her legs looked longer and more muscular. I forced back tears.

"You look marvelous," I said.

She gave a little twirl, a huge smile across her face. Suddenly, we heard Chad's car drive up and Zoe ran down the stairs and out the front door.

"Daddy!" She ran into his arms.

"Happy birthday to my big girl!" he said as she scooped her up and swung her around. "How is my birthday princess?"

"I'm good. Mommy said I've grown an inch since last year."

"Wow! You are so tall. Soon you'll be taller than Daddy," he said.

"Maybe next year," she said with a giggle. "Is Courtney, Willow, and Wyatt coming to breakfast?"

Hearing Courtney's name still made me cringe. Two weeks ago,

Zoe had asked if I would come see her room at Chad's new house, so I'd arranged a time when Courtney wouldn't be home. I tried to smile and be excited while Zoe gave me a tour of their house, but, in reality, I felt nauseous the whole time I was there. As Zoe led me down the hall to her room, I tried hard not to look at the pictures on the wall. Yes, it was nice to see Zoe happy, but what I didn't need to see was a picture of another woman and my soon-to-be ex-husband cuddled up next to each other, I took a deep breath as we entered Zoe's room, she proudly showed me her bed, desk, and all of the art projects she had done with Willow.

After I left, I drove to the park and broke down, tears streaming down my face. Zoe was so happy at Chad's, and I *wanted* her to be. But it was still hard to accept that Zoe had a life I wasn't involved in and never would be.

"Yep, we're going to go home to open presents first, and then we'll have breakfast," Chad said. Ever since Chad left, our interactions had been very stale, all business. I buried all of my feelings so that Zoe wouldn't feel any tension between the two of us. I was afraid that any sort of emotion would explode, and at this juncture my feelings for Chad still were all over the place.

I was glad that Chad had at least had the decency not to bring the whole crew when picking Zoe up.

"It's too bad they can't come to my party," Zoe said.

"Maybe next year," I said as I stroked her hair. "Have fun with Daddy."

"Bye, Mommy," Zoe said, giving me a hug and a kiss goodbye.

After Chad left, I jumped in the shower. The day Zoe was born, Chad had been there, holding my hand while I pushed as hard as I could. We both cried tears of joy when she came out. She was the most perfect baby. Chad had kissed me and told me what a great job

I'd done. At that moment, I felt whole and complete. I had this perfect tiny human, and a wonderful husband. But since Chad left, all I'd felt was lost and alone. I wasn't sure who I was anymore. But I did know that I would always be Zoe's mom, and she would always be that perfect baby to me. And I knew that had to be the focus of the day.

I got dressed and headed over to Jennifer's to have brunch with Camila and Rachel. My three friends were not going to let me spend any of this day alone, and for that I was extremely grateful.

"Here you go, birthday mama," Jennifer said, giving me a hug and an already-poured Bloody Mary.

"Here's to six," I said as we clinked our glasses together.

I sat down at the table with everyone. The centerpiece of fresh flowers brightened the room. I was so glad to be with my friends and not alone right now. Last year on Zoe's birthday, she'd woken up so excited, we'd let her open one gift before school. When she'd gotten home, we'd gone out to dinner. Zoe's face had beamed as the servers sang, "Happy Birthday." Would I have done something different if I'd known it would be the last birthday we spent together as a family?

"Julian is so excited for the party this afternoon. Are Courtney and her kids coming?" Camila asked, eyeing me tentatively.

"Not if she knows what's good for her," Jennifer replied.

"I told Chad I'd prefer if Courtney didn't come. He said she wanted to show support for Zoe but understood that it would make me uncomfortable. It's not like she won't see her. They have plenty of time for birthday celebrations over at his house this morning. I told him maybe next year, but let's be real, I'm never going to be okay with this," I said, reaching for a bagel.

"All I know is that woman better not show her face on this street," Jennifer said, and she passed me the cream cheese.

"Yeah, or she's going to have to deal with us." Rachel put her hands up like fists.

"Please. Like you'd fight her," I rolled my eyes.

"I wouldn't, but Jennifer would. And I know Jennifer fights dirty." Rachel pounded her first into her hand to demonstrate Jennifer's toughness.

"That's right. I'd pull her hair," Jennifer said. We all laughed at that, knowing there was, maybe, a little truth to it. Jennifer was the middle of three sisters and had told us about some epic girl fights they'd had when they were younger. Her oldest sister always picked on the little one, so Jennifer felt like she had to protect her youngest sister. I think that's why Jennifer became such a mama bear.

"Thanks, ladies. But she's a part of Zoe's life, and I'm going to have to accept it."

"You can accept it, but you don't have to like it," Camila said.

"Thanks. I mean, I know that more love for Zoe is not bad. At least that's what I keep telling myself."

"That's a healthy outlook. Have you met Courtney's kids?" Jennifer asked.

"Not yet. But Zoe talks about Willow a lot. It seems the two of them have already created a bond."

"Well, that's nice for Zoe and Willow," Camila said as she took a bite of her bagel. She wiped her mouth and added, "I mean it's probably hard for them, too.

All of a sudden they're living with these new people, and not their dad. The whole situation must take some getting used to."

"Yeah, everything happened so quickly. I can't imagine the kids have had time to process everything," I replied. Willow was only seven and Wyatt was nine. I felt bad for them, that they had to go through this as well. Sure, kids are resilient, but it was still an adjustment.

"I don't get why they had to move in together right away. I mean, both marriages just ended. They should have spent some time apart, let people adjust," Jennifer added.

Jennifer was right. It didn't make sense that they'd moved in together right away. I guess, financially, that was smart, but it was so much for everyone to take in all at once. I think I'd have taken the news a lot better if Chad had just left to live on his own, even if there was another woman. It was one thing to be dating, and another to move in and blend families. Luckily, Zoe seemed to be doing okay.

We finished up brunch talking about our plans for Thanksgiving. My parents were coming from Nebraska, and I was excited to spend some time with them. I hadn't seen them since Chad left. They were furious with him and the way he'd treated me, but they also felt betrayed. They had welcomed him into their home with loving arms and treated him like a son. They were disappointed that he hadn't turned out to be the man he had promised to be.

"Well, thanks for brunch," I said as I gave Jennifer a hug. "It was really nice to hang out while Zoe was with Chad. I needed this."

"Anytime," Jennifer said.

As I was walking home, I noticed the UPS truck was parked in front of my house. Sean had two packages in his hands as he walked up the front steps. He turned around and saw me coming up the path.

"Hey, Sean," I said.

"Hey, Beth! Lots of packages for Zoe!" he said.

"Yeah, today's her birthday."

"Oh, wow, time does fly, doesn't it? I remember when she was just a little baby."

"I know, it seems like just yesterday we were sitting on the stoop waiting for you to come by."

"She's a really great girl. You should be proud." Sean bent down and started petting Twix, who rubbed between his legs, purring.

"Thanks," I said and gave him a smile. "Did you get a haircut?" He was looking extremely cute today.

"Oh yeah, a few days ago."

"It looks good!"

"Thanks." He rubbed his hand through his hair. "Hey, I haven't seen Chad in a while. Tell him I say hi."

I realized at that moment that I hadn't told Sean that Chad had left. It wasn't something I was broadcasting out loud, and it didn't usually come up in casual conversations with delivery drivers.

"Actually, Chad left me back in July," I said, trying not wince.

Sean looked shocked. "What? Oh, I'm sorry, Beth."

"Yeah, he actually left me for another woman. Some lady he works with."

"Oh, man, what an asshole, if you don't mind me saying."

"Oh, don't worry, I've called him much worse" I gave a dismissive wave with my hand.

Sean chuckled. "I'm sorry to hear that."

There was an awkward silence. Then Sean continued, "If I learned anything from my divorce, it's to enjoy the time you have with your kids. I feel like, when I'm with Aidan, we just have fun, and then I start forgetting about my shitty marriage."

"Good advice," I said.

I smiled and twirled my hair in my hand, suddenly feeling nervous. Sean wore the same outfit every day, but, for some reason, he looked different today. Maybe it was the way the sun hit him, or maybe it was fresh haircut.

"Well, these packages aren't going to deliver themselves," Sean finally said, when the silence had stretched out a bit to awkwardly.

I gave a little chuckle. "Have a nice day, Sean."

"Tell Ms. Zoe I said happy birthday."

"I will."

Sean ran back to his truck, gave me a wave, and honked the horn to say goodbye. I waved back at him. I liked his advice. Treasure the time with Zoe.

I brought the packages inside, and Twix followed me in and let me know she was hungry. I went to feed her and noticed a picture of Zoe and me on the fridge. It was from her first birthday party at daycare. Zoe wore a pink dress with hearts and a little party hat the teachers bought her. Chad and I brought mini muffins for the class. Her class of six kids sat around the table in their highchairs. I don't think anyone realized what was going on as we sang happy birthday, but they all seemed to enjoy the treats after.

A tear slid down my cheek. I couldn't believe my little girl had grown up so much. Five years had gone by since that picture was taken, but it seemed like it was just yesterday. Our little family unit had been so important to me. I'd always wanted a second kid, but it had been hard enough to get pregnant the first time. We'd briefly talked about having a second, but we decided that our family of three was enough.

But now, Zoe wasn't in a family of three. She was part of two families: a family of two and a family of five.

I looked at the clock and realized that Chad and Zoe would be back in half an hour, so I washed my face and got ready for the party.

When Chad's car drove up, Zoe came bouncing out of the car, holding what looked like a new Barbie. She had a huge smile on her face.

"Is it time for my party?" she asked as she greeted me at the door.

"Just about."

"I'm so excited!"

"Did you have fun with Daddy?" I asked her.

"Yeah, and look at this cool new Barbie that Willow got me." She showed me a veterinary Barbie, which came with a stethoscope, a cat, and a dog.

"Oh wow! That was really nice of her," I said.

"Yeah. I told her that, next year, she can come to my birthday. Can Daddy ride with us?" Her innocent question made my gut clench. The last thing I wanted to do was ride in a confined space with Chad.

"He's going to meet us there. He's got to pick up the cake first," I said. We had ordered a chocolate cake with white icing that had a big rainbow and said, "Happy Birthday Zoe." Zoe had picked it out the week before.

"Yummy!" she said.

"See you soon," Chad said as he headed to his car.

Nerves still clawed at my insides. I'd thought the hardest part of the day was going to be getting through the morning, but I still had to get through the party. My palms were sweaty the whole way to the trampoline park. Zoe kept on yammering on about how excited she was. She didn't stop talking the entire way. We finally arrived, and when we opened the door, we were greeted with a sign that said, "Zoe's Birthday Party, this way." The directions led us into a private room. I had told them ahead of time that we wanted purple, blue, and pink balloons.

We entered the room, and Zoe's eyes lit up. "It's so pretty," she cried, clearly delighted.

Arc Jump had taken care of all the party details. They had planned games for the kids, set up the decorations, provided goodie bags, and had even taken pictures for us. All we had to do was show up. It was so nice to have one thing off my plate and just be able to enjoy myself. I wasn't sure what to expect, but they'd really gone all out with the room. There were probably fifty balloons.

Chad came in with the cake and put it on the pink confetti-covered table. Shortly after we arrived, friends from school started to show up. Maya, one of her best friends, was the first one to get there, and she and Zoe skipped off to the trampolines. More friends started coming in, including Camila and Julian. I gave Camila a hug.

"Julian, Zoe, and Maya are already jumping," I told him.

Julian ran out the door and I turned to Camila. "I'm so glad you're here."

Most of the school parents didn't know that Chad and I had split up. I was friendly with a few of the other moms in Zoe's class, but I hadn't really told them the whole ordeal. I figured it would all come out sooner or later, but I didn't think Zoe's birthday party was the right venue. Camila nodded coldly at Chad when their eyes met, but, like always, I put on my happy face when I was around Chad. Zoe didn't need to sense any resentment or animosity.

"The place looks great," Camila said.

"Yeah, I am really impressed with how the room looks."

Zoe and her friends ran into the party room. "Mommy, will you play monster?" Zoe asked.

"Of course! I'll give you a head start." I kicked off my shoes and headed out the door. I chased Zoe and her friends around making roaring sounds. Their squeals and giggles when I'd pretend to catch them filled me with joy. We were all having so much fun, I'd almost forgotten about the uneasiness from the night before.

After about fifteen minutes of monster, I was beat, which was good, since it was time for cake.

Zoe sat in a big red throne, with Chad and me on either side of her, while everyone sang happy birthday. She blew out her candles, and part of me wondered if she wished for her mom and dad to be back together. I knew that was never going to happen, but I wasn't sure how Zoe felt about it. When the lights came on, another mom offered to take our picture. I didn't really want a picture with Chad, but I thought it would be nice for Zoe. They were about to take the cake away, but then Camila intercepted and offered to take a photo of just me and Zoe. I gave her a grateful smile.

After cake, the kids played on the trampolines for a little longer. Chad came up to me and put his arm around my shoulder. "Great party," he said.

I sidestepped so that his arm fell off me. That was the first time Chad had touched me since July, when he said he was leaving. It was confusing. It felt foreign and comforting all at the same time. I loathed this man. He'd broken my heart and ruined my life, but at the same time his touch felt familiar, and it reminded me of the moment when Zoe was born.

"Sorry," he said, looking embarrassed. "Old habits die hard," he shrugged.

That night, I took Zoe out to dinner. She asked if we could go to La Caverna, since she loved their chicken tacos, even though I thought mine were better. We got to the restaurant and saw Sebastian at the bar. I gave him a wave as we headed to a booth in the back.

"Man, I'm beat," I said.

"Me, too, Mommy. All that jumping made my legs tired," Zoe said, grabbing a few chips.

"You were a jumping machine," I said as I gave her a wink.

"I liked when you were the monster."

"Ahh," I said, putting my hands up like a monster. Zoe just giggled.

"Did you have a good birthday, sweetie?"

"Yes! It was the best birthday ever."

"I'm glad. How was this morning with Daddy and Courtney?"

"It was fun. Courtney bought me an art kit. It has paints and markers and different color papers, and it comes in this big case so you can take it around."

"That was really nice of her," I lied. It was hard to not talk smack about the woman who'd destroyed my life, slept with my husband, and who my husband had decided was worth more than me, but I couldn't let Zoe have negative feelings about her.

"Yeah. I'll make you a picture when I'm at Daddy's."

"That's very sweet. I love your pictures."

The servers came with a big slice of chocolate cake.

"Cake three times today!" Zoe exclaimed.

"You'll be bouncing off the walls tonight," I said.

I guess that was one benefit of being a child of divorce. Sure, she didn't get to celebrate with her mom and dad together, but she got two celebrations and a whole lot of love.

We got home and Zoe went to play with some of her new toys. I tucked her into bed, thinking how this day had turned out better than expected. Zoe didn't seem upset about having to split time between Chad and me and was a smiling happy girl all day. Sure, it was sad that my family life was different from the year before, but I was still able to have a good time and treasure the moment.

When Zoe was finally asleep, I opened a bottle of wine, and poured myself a drink. I sat on the couch and turned on the TV. Twix jumped up and cuddled up next to me, purring loudly. I heard a buzz on my phone. It was a text from Chad.

Chad: *I think Zoe had a good day. Thanks for organizing the party and letting Courtney and me take her out to breakfast. You're a good mom. I can't believe our baby is 6.*

I was stunned. It was the first bit of emotion that I saw from Chad since he told me he was leaving. I searched for some sort of hidden meaning. Was he implying that he didn't think I was a good mom before? Was he trying to butter me up so that I'd give him more money in the divorce? Or was he just being nice to be nice, and I was over analyzing this one text? After about thirty minutes I replied.

Me: *I know. She's getting so grown up.*

Another buzz.
I grabbed my phone with disgust, I didn't want to chat all night with Chad. To my relief it was Noah this time.

Noah: *Hey, just checking in to see how the birthday went.*
Me: *Thanks, it was good. Zoe had a good time. But I'm exhausted. Going to watch a little tv and then head to bed.*
Noah: *We still on for Tuesday?*
Me: *Yes, I can't wait.*
Noah: *Good night*
Me: *Night*

I put down my phone. It was nice of Noah to check on me, and I was happy that he was the last person I interacted with before heading to bed, not Chad.

On Tuesday, SOAR had a big Thanksgiving celebration. Noah and I both had Caleb and Zoe that day, so we brought them along with us. We thought it would be good to show them where we volunteered and figured they would have fun playing with the kids. Zoe and Caleb hadn't spent a lot of time together outside of the park, so I thought it might be weird, but they seemed to get along well.

The gym was decorated with pumpkins, gourds, and brown and orange leaves. In the corner was a big stuffed turkey. A local restaurant had donated twenty pounds of turkey, and SOAR asked the volunteers to bring a dish as a kind of a potluck. Zoe and I had made a green bean casserole, while Noah and Caleb brought baked macaroni and cheese. Two classic Thanksgiving dishes. We looked around and saw David. He gave us a wave and a big smile. Just then we spotted Christopher and Josephina. They ran over to us.

"Noah! Beth!" they exclaimed.

The four of us did our secret handshake that we had perfected two weeks ago.

"Hi, guys!" Noah said. "Josephina and Christopher, this is Caleb and Zoe. We thought you all might like to play together."

Zoe and Caleb gave them both a nervous wave.

"Do you want to play tag?" Josephina asked.

"I love tag," Caleb said.

The four of them ran off together, Josephina leading the pack, with the rest of the crew not far behind. I watched to make sure Zoe and Caleb were doing okay, since they didn't know anyone. But that is one of the great things about kids. They don't care who is around, especially if a rousing game of tag is about to start. The more players, the more exciting the game. Just then a woman came up to us and introduced herself as Maggie, Christopher and Josephina's mom.

"You must be the famous Beth and Noah," she said. "The kids talk about you nonstop. Wednesday is their favorite day since they get to see you."

Hearing Maggie say that really made my day. I was making a difference in these kids' lives and doing something productive with my time. Happiness radiated through me. When I had first signed up for SOAR, I wasn't sure what to expect. I wasn't sure what the kids would be like, and if they would take to me. Tutoring could be challenging, especially if kids were reluctant to do their homework and just wanted to play video games. But it had turned out to be a great decision.

Noah and I were connecting with Christopher and Josephina. It was also nice to share this experience with someone like Noah. He was a natural with the kids. On the car rides home, we would talk about things that worked, like dance parties and stickers, and where the kids were struggling. Last month, Josephina came to the center in tears because she had gotten a C on her science test, which she'd thought for sure she'd done better on. At first, she didn't want to talk to me about it or even go over the answers. She didn't want to do her other homework. She just sat at the table and sulked. It was one of the harder days working with her, and I couldn't figure out how to get through to her.

Noah and I talked about it after at dinner and came up with ways to get her to her talk. We decided to treat her like an adult, and it worked. The next week, we talked it out and, together, determined where she went wrong and ways that she could do better. She had another science test in two weeks, and I was eager to see how it went.

"They really are great kids," I said. "We have a lot of fun with them."

"They are." She watched the kids playing and gave a me motherly look. "I'm just so grateful for this center."

Maggie told us that Josephina and Christopher's dad had left a month after Christopher was born. He was an alcoholic, in and out of rehab, and the kids didn't have any contact with him. Maggie had to work two jobs just to make ends meet. During the day she was a teller at a local bank, and four nights a week she worked the service desk at a local gym. She didn't have much family nearby, and Josephina and Christopher used to stay with neighbors until she had heard about SOAR. She felt bad always asking people for help. Sure, they were willing to do it, but the center provided more options, and a routine for the kids, which they thrived on.

"It really changed things," Maggie said. "The kids are happy here, and they get the support they need for homework. I can't do it all, you know."

I didn't know how to respond to Maggie. I wasn't sure if she would find some solidarity in the fact that both Noah and I were single parents as well, or if she would find it insulting, since we didn't have our kids full time, had time to ourselves, and only worked one job apiece. So, I just gave her a knowing smile.

Luckily, Noah piped in. "It takes a village. I know everyone says it, but once you're on your own, you truly know the meaning. It's one of the things I learned in my divorce."

"Oh, you're divorced?" Maggie said.

"We both are," I told her.

"It's so nice of you to volunteer your time then. I know how precious it is," Maggie said.

"We really enjoy it," I said.

"I've seen a lot of improvement in Christopher's letters," Noah said. "And he really has started to pick up math."

"I'm glad you're able to work with him. School was never really my thing. But Josephina mentioned that you need to work on your dance moves," Maggie said.

We all laughed. "Well, she's right about that," I said.

The kids came back, and we all sat down together for dinner. Caleb and Josephina were talking about a new show, while Christopher and Zoe re-hashed the tag game. It was a pleasant conversation and was nice to have the three families together. You could feel the love that Maggie had for her kids. She was in a tough spot financially, and I'm sure she never had time to herself, but her face lit up as the kids gave us a play-by-play of the tag game.

After dinner, they had games for the kids including turkey bowling, pin the feather on the turkey, and a scavenger hunt, which Christopher and Josephina won. It was heartwarming to see the kids playing together. Everyone was happy and having a great time. I had an ear-to-ear smile on my face as I watched Christopher give Zoe tips on her bowling game and saw how excited Christopher and Josephina were when they finally found the last thing on the scavenger hunt, an ear of corn.

Later that night, after we read stories, I tucked Zoe into bed.

"That was really fun," Zoe said. "I wanted to win the scavenger hunt, but I'm glad Christopher and Josephina won."

Zoe was such a sweet kid, always thinking of others.

"Yeah, I think it made them feel good," I said. "I'm glad you had fun tonight. Sweet dreams."

I gave Zoe a kiss on the forehead.

"Love you, Mommy."

"Love you, Zoe."

I turned off the light, closed the door and went downstairs. Overall, the night had been a huge success. I was glad I'd gotten to meet Maggie. She was inspiring. Here she was, a single mom with two kids full time and working two jobs, but she was strong, worked hard, and was a great mother. She had overcome many obstacles and seemed like she was in a good place.

I knew I could get there, too.

-6-

DECEMBER

My company usually threw a huge holiday party on the first Saturday of December. It was often held at fancy club or an elegant hotel ballroom. All of the employees and their plus ones got dressed up in their swankiest winter outfits, drank expensive wine, and ate delicious food as we mingled. The week before, the talk at the water cooler involved reminiscing about the past year. Last year, the head of the legal team had a little too much to drink, and, to everyone's delight, he tore it up on the dance floor. Everyone was mesmerized as he flawlessly did the Dougie and Cabbage Patch moves to a '90s hip hop song. People talked about it for weeks after, and those who had left early were disappointed to have missed it. Since date nights were few and far between, Chad and I always promised ourselves that we would go all out at my holiday party. Two years ago, we'd even splurged and got a hotel room while my parents watched Zoe. It was a much-needed re-kindling to our relationship, or so I had thought.

I wasn't looking forward to attending this year's party stag. Most of the people I directly worked with knew about the divorce, but it wasn't like I had put out a blast email or anything. On our most recent long run, Jennifer convinced me that I should go, even though I was going alone. I deserved a fun night out. And it was always a good opportunity to get to know the people I managed better. I wanted to be a fun boss who seemed approachable, so the holiday party was a good place to show them that.

The day of the party, I decided to pamper myself a bit, so I went to get my hair blown out and a manicure. This year the festivities were being held at a new hotel downtown. Before I got dressed, I got on my computer to check it out. From the pictures on the website, it looked very posh and upscale. The kitchen was run by a famous chef who had a few restaurants downtown, and the food looked quite tasty. I was starting to get excited. It had been a while since I had gotten all dolled up. I decided to wear one of my favorite winter dresses. It was navy blue and hugged my body, just enough to show that I had a good figure, but not enough to show off. With the additional running, I noticed my legs were getting more toned, which was highlighted by my gold heels.

I looked at myself in the mirror, let out a deep breath, and smiled. I felt sexy and confident, two things I hadn't felt in a long time. I held my head high as I walked out the door.

When I got to the party, there was already a good crowd. I checked my coat and immediately ran into one of my coworkers, Danielle, and her husband Eric. Danielle and I had worked closely on a project together last year, but I hadn't seen much of her this year.

"Hi, Beth. You look nice," she said as she gave me a hug.

"Thanks." I grabbed a glass of wine from one of the servers and took a sip. It was flavorful and full-bodied. I could tell this was a very high-end wine. I'd gotten really into wine in college after I'd taken a wine history class. I'd loved learning about the different varietals and how each vintage changed within the wineries. I had always thought, in another life, I might even become a sommelier.

"Is your husband here?" she asked.

I started to fidget with the napkin I was holding and looked away. There it was. The first time someone asked me about Chad. On my run with Jennifer, she told me to be honest with people, but not make a big deal about it. Just say matter of fact, "We're getting divorced," and that's that. It was good advice, but hard to execute. Just hearing about Chad made me nervous. Telling people I was getting divorced made me sound like a failure. Like it was my fault I couldn't get my marriage to work. But I didn't want to go into details about Chad leaving me for Courtney. That made it almost seem worse. People would feel sorry for me, or maybe even feel like I'd led him to cheat. I was well-liked and well-respected at my job, but I was also firm and tough. I could see someone thinking that I had it coming. It was a hard area to navigate. I wasn't sure how to talk about it without going into the intimate details of my life. Jennifer assured me that people didn't want to hear about what went on behind closed doors. But I still felt the need to explain myself to my coworkers.

After a long pause I said, "Oh, actually, we're getting divorced," rather quickly.

Danielle gasped. "I'm sorry to hear that," she said tilting her head and giving me a sympathetic look.

"It's okay. Turns out he wasn't a great guy," I said, more confidently.

And that was that. Danielle didn't ask me about the details, or even seem like she wanted to talk about it anymore. Thankfully. I'd handled it well.

Danielle and I chatted a bit more about an upcoming project. She spotted someone across the room she needed to talk to and excused herself. I wandered around for a bit and noticed I needed a refill, so I went up to the bar, where I ran into another coworker, Jack.

Jack had worked at Market Insight since he'd graduated from college, and this year we were celebrating his fortieth anniversary. He and his wife had been married for thirty-five years. He was a very sweet man and knew everyone.

"Hi there, Beth, you look lovely," he said as he gave me a hug.

"Thanks, Jack. You clean up nice, too."

"What this old thing?" He gave a little chuckle.

"What are you drinking?" I asked.

"Just a beer." He held up his full bottle.

The bartender asked me what I wanted, and I ordered another glass of wine.

"So, where is that handsome husband of yours?" Jack asked.

My stomach turned a bit. I guess I wasn't *really* ready for this. Had I underestimated the number of times someone would ask me about Chad, and how many times I would have to tell them we were getting divorced? At least the wine did make it easier.

"Oh, he's not here. He's with his new girlfriend," I said.

Jack looked shocked, almost spitting out his beer. He had definitely *not* been expecting me to say that. I gave a nervous smile and took a large gulp of wine.

"Sorry, Beth. I have a neighbor who's single, want me to give him your number?"

Was Jack playing matchmaker? Was this what my life had come to? Sixty-five-year-old men trying to set me up with their neighbors?

"That's okay. I don't think I'm ready for that."

"Well, when you are, let me know."

I gave him a pat on his shoulder. "Thank you. It was nice talking to you. Enjoy the party."

I took my glass of wine and walked around. People were having a great time. A server approached me with shrimp skewers. I took a few. They were smoky and full of flavor. I made a mental note to keep my eye out for more.

Just then I spotted my good friend, Kelly. Kelly and I had gone to college together. We were in the same master's program, so we'd taken a lot of classes together. We'd started out as study buddies, but we'd instantly bonded and became fast friends. We had a lot in common, as she was also from the Midwest and liked baseball. But, in general, we just had a lot of fun together. We were both ecstatic when we got job offers at Market Insight two weeks apart.

I gave Kelly a big hug. "I'm so glad I found you. Tonight is not going well."

Kelly was already well aware of my situation with Chad. I'd told her the details shortly after Chad had told me about Courtney. It was nice to have a friend like that in the office. Kelly was often there when I needed to go for a walk and vent. She and I had a history, and she knew Chad and had been surprised about everything.

"I'm sorry. I'm here now, so you can just hang out with me and Derek." Kelly's husband, Derek, came by with two glasses of wine. He gave one to Kelly.

"Thanks, sweetie," she said, kissing him.

"Hey, Beth." Derek gave me a hug. "This is a fun party. I had been wanting to try the restaurant here, so it's nice to get a little taste."

"Yes! Have you had the shrimp skewers?" I asked. "They're delightful."

A server came by with a plate of dumplings. We each tried one. They were even better than the shrimp skewers.

"So, got your eye on anyone here?" Derek asked, taking another dumpling.

"What? First Jack, now you? No, I definitely don't," I said.

"What did Jack say?" Kelly asked. "He's married, does he have a son or something?"

"Worse. A neighbor. I am not going to date Jack's neighbor," I said.

"Ha, ha, I wouldn't let you." Kelly laughed.

"So, then why not somebody here?" Derek asked. "You can't say that, in this entire company, there isn't anyone you'd want to, you know." He gave me wink.

"She wouldn't want to what, Derek?" Kelly asked, as she put her hands on her hips.

"I don't know, make out with in the coat closet," Derek said.

The truth was, there were a few handsome guys at my company. There was Jim who worked in the graphics department. He was an excellent dresser and always smelled good, but I was pretty sure he was married. He didn't wear a ring, but he always talked about his kids and a woman named Valerie. There was also Jason. He very handsome, and I liked talking to him, but we often worked together, so if we did make out in the coat closet, it could just lead to awkward interactions down the road.

"What about Austin?" Kelly asked.

Austin was good-looking and quite foxy, but much younger. He had dark hair and piercing blue eyes. He worked out a lot and had biceps to die for. He'd started at Market Insight four years ago, and I'd met him when we both played on the softball team. Austin was the star player, which wasn't saying much. We weren't a company that was known for our softball prowess. We usually won only two or three games a season, and they would often have to call the game early because the other team was so far ahead. But it was a good bonding experience, and everyone who played seemed to have a lot of fun. I'd played in all the games before Zoe was born. Then, I tried to make it to three or four games a season, even if I could only stay for half the game. One game I caught a ball in the outfield, which may have earned me a, "Nice Catch!" from Austin. Two weeks later, we ran into each other at the coffee machine and had realized that we'd both grown up in Nebraska. After that, each fall, whenever we saw each other, we'd talk about college football, and how well the Cornhuskers were doing. That really had been the extent of our communication.

"Austin is, like, the hottest guy at Market Insight. He wouldn't go for me," I said.

"Why not?" Derek asked. "You're hot."

"Yeah, but I'm like ten years older than him, and I'm a mom. I doubt he goes out with many single thirty-eight-year-old moms."

I spotted Austin across the room. He was talking to some other guys from the softball team, but I didn't know them well. He looked good in a dark suit and light blue shirt.

"Guys like older women. And you certainly don't give off a mom vibe, especially not in this dress. Just go over there and talk to him." Kelly gave me a little shove.

"Do it! Do it!" Kelly and Derek started chanting.

I took a last sip of my wine glass and put it down on the table. I looked over at Austin and caught him looking at me, too…or at least in my direction. I gave him a smile and a wave and headed over. My heart was pounding so hard, I could feel it pulsing through my body. I realized that I'd only had a few appetizers and two glasses of wine, so I was feeling a bit woozy, but also confident.

"Hey, Austin," I said.

"Hey, Beth," he said, smiling.

"Tough loss to Wisconsin last week." Wisconsin had crushed Nebraska in last Saturday's game. We hadn't been favored to win, but it was expected to be a close game. Instead, it was a blowout, 45-12.

"Yeah, was hoping we would have won and could make it to the Holiday Bowl," he said.

I looked over at Kelly and Derek, and they gave me encouraging looks.

I started playing with my hair, trying to figure out how to flirt with this younger, very good-looking coworker. It had been a while since I'd flirted, so I was a little rusty. I wasn't getting a vibe that Austin was into me, but I also wasn't sensing that he was hoping our conversation would end.

"So, are you going back to Nebraska for Christmas?" I asked.

"For a couple of days. Then my family and I are going to Hawaii for New Year's."

"Oh, Hawaii! That should be nice. I've never been."

"We go every year; it's a bit of a tradition."

"What a nice tradition. Do you always go to the same spot?" I asked, as I brushed my hand against his arm. He didn't flinch away, which I took as a good sign.

"Different places."

Austin continued to talk about his vacations with his family, and I listened, making direct eye contact, nodding, and smiling.

"What are you drinking?" I asked.

"It's the zinfandel. It's pretty good." He looked down at his glass.

I reached out and took his drink out of his hands and took a sip. The minute I did it, I realized what a mistake it was. Why would I drink out of his glass? He hadn't offered me a sip. Was this my best attempt at flirting?

"Why don't we get you one?" he asked, heading toward the bar.

I felt my face flush. I had never been so embarrassed. What did I think I was going to accomplish with that move? I wanted to run away and hide in the bathroom, but I thought it would be better to just follow Austin the bar.

"She'll have the zinfandel," he told the bartender.

At the bar, someone came over and grabbed Austin's attention. I realized he wasn't talking to me anymore, and I was desperate to find Kelly. I started to say goodbye to Austin, but he was deep in conversation and didn't notice.

I walked around a bit and ran into a girl who worked for me, here with her husband. We chatted a bit, but I wasn't focused. I was still mortified by my terrible attempt at flirting. I saw Kelly and Derek and politely excused myself.

"How did it go?" she said.

"OMG," I said as I buried my hands in my face.

"What happened?" Derek asked.

"Ugh," I groaned. "I don't know how to flirt."

"I'm sure it wasn't that bad." Kelly tried to look encouraging.

"I took a drink from his glass. I didn't even ask him. I just took it. I don't know why I thought that would be a good idea," I said.

"Well, it's a bold move," Derek said. "But I like it. Shows you're confident. What happened after?"

"He walked me to the bar, ordered me my own drink, and then started talking to someone else." I shook my head. "What happened? Didn't I used to be good at this in college?"

"You were," Kelly confirmed. "You used to just lock eyes with a guy, go over and talk, and then you'd be playing tonsil hockey the rest of the night."

"Oh, the good old days," I said, laughing.

"Well, if it makes you feel better, he keeps looking over here," Derek said, slowly angling his head in Austin's direction.

"Yeah, he's probably thinking about how crazy I am."

"I'm sure it's not too bad," said Derek. "I think you should find a way to talk to him again."

"I don't know. I think I might just cut my losses and call it a night." My stomach started to grumble as I finished my wine. The food at the party looked tasty, but after three glasses of wine and only snacking on hors d'oeuvres, I wanted a greasy cheeseburger or a pizza.

"Okay, call me later?" Kelly asked.

I nodded and took my leave, grabbing my coat from coat check on the way out.

I walked to the nearest pizza place and ordered a cheese pizza. Tonight had been rough. I hated being alone at my work party, and I hated the pitying looks people gave me when I told them about Chad leaving. Talking to Austin had been a big mistake—I don't know why I thought he'd want to make out with me in a coat closet. I'd wanted to walk out of the party with my head held high, but, in reality, I walked out slightly drunk, very embarrassed, and sad. I finished my pizza and called an Uber. On my ride home, I sent a text to Noah.

Me: *Just made a fool out of myself at the holiday party.*
Noah: *What happened? Did you fall down?*
Me: *No. I tried to flirt with a guy. I took a drink out of his hand.*
Noah: *Not the best move.*
Me: *No. Oh well. He probably wouldn't have made out with me anyways.*
Noah: *His loss.*

I smiled. That was Noah, always trying to make me feel better. I got home and stumbled in the door. I dragged myself into bed, with my dress still on, and my contacts still in.

I woke up to Twix gently nudging me and purring to remind me I needed to feed her. I had a pounding headache and needed coffee badly. My phone showed a text from Chad.

Chad: *See you at gymnastics today!*

Zoe's gymnastics class was having an end of the year show later that morning. Zoe had been practicing her balance beam and floor routine and was eager for Chad and me to see it. I had told Chad that I wasn't ready for Courtney to be included in these types of family functions. He hadn't really put up a fight, so that was good. I was super hungover and not ready to see Chad, let alone Chad and Courtney together.

I washed my face and put on jeans and a cute blue sweater that really brought out my eyes. I still wanted to look good in front of Chad, to remind him of what he'd thrown away. Courtney might have been more "polished" than me, but I was the type of girl who looked good dressed up *and* dressed down. I pulled my hair back in a ponytail and put on a little bit of makeup, just so it didn't look like I was trying too hard.

I pulled into the gymnastics place and saw that Chad and Zoe had already arrived. I took a deep breath. These events were hard to get through. I wanted to be a united front for Zoe. I never wanted her to have to choose sides, so I put away all my anger toward Chad, for Zoe's sake. She deserved to look out into the crowd and see both of her parents together, and that was what I was going to give her. I could sit through a forty-five-minute gymnastics show next to the man who'd torn my heart into pieces if it made Zoe happy. But doing this hungover was going to be harder. What I really wanted to do was curl up on the couch and binge watch some trashy TV show on Netflix while eating pizza. But I was excited to see Zoe's routines, which she hadn't stopped talking about all week.

"Mommy, Mommy! You're here!" Zoe came running to me the minute I opened the door and gave me a big hug. She looked so cute in her purple leotard with her hair in a bun. She even had some glitter in her hair and on her cheeks.

Chad gave me a kiss on the cheek, something he had started after Zoe's birthday. I hated how he still had this kind of familiarity with me, that he thought it was okay to kiss me. I had asked him to stop, but he hadn't listened. I didn't want to make a big deal out of it in front of Zoe, so I just sucked it up.

"Well, don't you look pretty? Look at that hair; it's so sparkly."

"Thanks! Courtney did it for me this morning. Isn't it great!" Zoe said twirling around.

"So great." It was like a dagger to the heart, the idea of Courtney doing Zoe's hair. I never could have made a bun like that. If Zoe had been with me this morning, she'd be in a ponytail, or maybe a messy bun at best. But here she was with this polished hair that her "other mom" had done.

"Okay, Zoe. Go run to your class. Mommy and I will get seats," Chad said, giving her a kiss.

"Okay, Daddy," Zoe said, running off to join her friends.

Chad led us to some seats front and center. I plopped on the folding chair and let out a little sigh.

"I know that look. Rough night?" Chad said.

"It was my office holiday party last night." I hated that he knew my looks. Granted, we were married for ten years, but still. He had no right pointing out my looks. He'd lost that right when he decided to leave me for Courtney.

"Oh, fun. Where was it this year?"

"They booked a room at that new hotel downtown. It was nice."

Chad put his hand on my neck and started to massage it. He used to do this when I was stressed or tired. After ten years of marriage, and three years of dating before that, he knew exactly what I needed and what felt good. I wanted to push his hand away, but I was tired and hungover, and I hadn't had someone touch me in months.

He then leaned in and gave me a kiss on my head. I wanted to put my head on his shoulder.

And then I snapped out of it.

This wasn't Chad, my husband. This was Chad, the guy who had cheated on me for three years. The Chad who'd left me for another woman.

I pushed his hand away.

"What? You know you liked it," he said, leaning closer.

"Are you serious?" I hissed. "One, we are at gymnastics show for *children,* and two, you left me for Courtney. Remember? Our divorce hearing is literally next month."

"I know, Beth. I just miss you." He looked at me with what he clearly thought were loving eyes. The look he used to give me across the dinner table. That look used to make me melt, but now it just made me angry. But I didn't want to make a scene at Zoe's gymnastics place.

"Well, too bad," I said in a harsh tone.

"Can't we be friends?"

"No, we can't be friends. That's not how this works." I couldn't believe him. After he'd stomped all over my heart and treated me like complete garbage, he wanted to be friends? As if I'd just forgive him. "You don't want to be married to me, then you don't get to be friends with me either. We can be civil, for Zoe's sake, and go to these things together, but that's it."

He tried to put his hand on my leg, but I pushed him away.

"Chad, I mean it. Please stop." I gave him a dirty look. I was not in the mood for this.

My head started to throb. I was hungover, and my soon-to-be ex-husband was trying to act like cheating and lying to me was no big deal, like five months later I'd just toss up my hands and say, "It's no biggie, let's be friends."

"Okay, okay," he said, putting his hands up, surrendering.

I tried to focus my attention on Zoe. The first event was a group floor routine with Zoe and four other kids. They had a choreographed dance, followed by each kid doing a forward roll, a backward roll, and a cartwheel. Zoe looked like she was having a lot of fun, but then she was really concentrating on the solo acts. She'd improved her forward rolls and was starting to perfect her cartwheel. I was so proud of her for trying. She wasn't at all nervous. The entire time she had a huge smile on her face.

After the floor routine, each of the kids got to pick one event to do on their own. Zoe had chosen balance beam. Before she started, she gave me and Chad a big wave. It made me so happy to see *her* happy and excited to do something, and I was glad we could both be there to support her. By the end of the show, I had put the conversation with Chad out of my mind.

After the show, Zoe ran up to us.

"You were terrific. Nice job on the cartwheel," I said, giving her a high five.

"You really were great," Chad agreed. "I think that deserves some ice cream."

"Yeah!" Zoe jumped up with delight.

"Maybe even sprinkles," Chad said, giving her a smile. "Courtney said she'd meet us there. I sent her some pictures of your beam routine."

"Have fun," I said, giving Zoe a hug. "I'm really proud of you. You did great."

"Thanks, Mommy."

I walked to my car. I couldn't wait to get home and sit on the couch. When I pulled into the driveway, Jennifer was out walking her dog.

"How are you?" she said with a smile.

"I've had better twenty-four hours," I said, giving her a look of exhaustion.

"Want to come over later?"

I wasn't in the mood to talk or relive my night. I just wanted to relax on the couch.

"Thanks, but I've got some work to do."

"No problem, see ya!" she said as she waved goodbye.

I went into the house, ordered some pizza, and plopped on the couch. Twix cuddled up next to me. I turned on a show and kind of zoned out. About two hours later, I got a text from Chad.

Chad: *Zoe did great, didn't she?*
Me: *Yes, she did. Our little gymnast.*
Chad: *I do really miss you.*

I wasn't going to respond to that. He didn't deserve a response. Him missing me was not my problem—I had plenty of other problems to deal with, problems that *his* infidelity had caused. I was working on getting over him, getting on with my life. If he missed me, that was his doing.

I tossed the phone on the coffee table and turned my attention back to Netflix.

The week before Christmas, Zoe and I went over to bake cookies with Camila and Julian. We decided it would be fun to make and decorate cookies for all the neighbors. Zoe started with putting the flour and butter in the mixer, but she turned it on too high, and flour went everywhere. Zoe and Julian laughed hysterically.

"Oh no! I'm covered in flour," Zoe said, trying to brush it off.

"You're all white!" I said.

I brushed flour off Zoe's clothes, and out of her hair, and grabbed a broom to sweep up the flour.

"I can do it!" Julian said. He took the broom from me and started sweeping the flour into a pile, while Zoe manned the dustpan. Julian swept the flour into the dustpan and Zoe took it to the trash.

"What good helpers!" Camila said.

We cleaned up the mess and started making the dough. Julian reminded Zoe to be careful with the mixer this time. They had a blast making the dough but were disappointed that we had to let it sit in the refrigerator for thirty minutes. While we waited for it to chill, Camila and I sat at the kitchen counter drinking coffee while Zoe and Julian picked out cookie cutters at the table.

"So, are you excited for your trip?" Camila asked.

"Yes and no. I'm going to miss not going to Minnesota," I said.

Chad and I had considered ourselves lucky. Since I'm Jewish, and he isn't, for the past twelve years we'd never had to fight over whose family we spent Christmas with. It was a done deal that we would visit his family in Minnesota at Christmas. As part of our custody arrangement, Chad got Christmas with Zoe and I got her for Thanksgiving. I loved the time we spent up there and looked forward to it ever year. Chad's mom went all out. She decorated the house with Santa everything, including bath towels and night lights. We spent the days listening to Christmas music, talking, and playing games like Scrabble and Monopoly. At night, my mother-in-law, sister-in-law, and I would drink wine and talk in the family room. The kids played and Chad, his brother, and dad cooked up a feast of steak, crab legs, and side dishes galore. On Christmas Day, Zoe, my niece, and nephew would run into the living room to see a mountain of presents under the tree, each one of them bursting with joy as they tore through the wrapping paper.

I'd miss them this year, and every year after that. The thought of Courtney sitting at the table instead of me made me feel like I was being replaced. Like I was just picked up, and Courtney dropped into the Christmas scene in Minnesota, as if I was never even a part of it.

Since Chad would be gone for a few days with Zoe, I thought I'd use the time to catch up on stuff around the house. But the thought of being home alone felt depressing. Christmas was supposed to be a time filled with joy, not a time to feel sorry for myself. I didn't want to think about the family I had lost, and the good times I was supposed to be having in Minnesota. I thought about visiting my parents in Nebraska, but it felt weird to see them without Zoe. If

I went there, it would be a constant reminder of my failed marriage, and my life being torn apart. I really needed to decompress and take some time to myself that wasn't spent doing chores or working.

A month ago, I'd been surfing the internet, and stumbled upon a luxury hotel nestled in the Blue Ridge Mountains. The pictures looked peaceful and serene, like the type of place I could really unwind. A change a scenery was exactly what I needed. I saw they had some availability and booked two nights.

"I'm ready for some R&R," I told Camila.

"If anyone deserves some R&R, it's you," Camila said. "So, what do you have planned?"

"I'm hoping to recharge the batteries. I've booked a few appointments at the spa and checked out two books from the library."

The past five months had really taken a toll on me, emotionally and physically. I'd found a groove to balance work, childcare, friends, volunteering, housework, and errands, but it was all very exhausting. I figured this trip would be a good time to focus on me and clear my mind a little. I'd never traveled by myself outside of work. I was a little nervous to go by myself—what if I got lonely?—but I was looking forward to the adventure. The idea of two full days where I wasn't running around or doing chores, where I got to do whatever I wanted, and it didn't matter what anyone else wanted, sounded very appealing.

"Sounds nice. I'm kind of jealous," Camila said.

I felt a sharp pain in my stomach. I know she didn't mean it that way, but this trip wasn't anything to be jealous of. This trip was a necessity, because my life got turned upside down. I would much rather be spending the holidays with my daughter and extended family. Even though I was Jewish, I still very much enjoyed celebrating

Christmas with Chad's side of the family. And I was heartbroken that wasn't the case this year and would never be the case again. This trip was about trying to turn a negative situation into something good. I wanted to take the opportunity and go out and do something new.

"Well, just get divorced and you can join me," I said, only half kidding.

Camila gave me a sympathetic smile. Just then the timer went off, and Zoe and Julian jumped up.

"Cookies!" they cried in unison.

Camila got out the dough and rolled it out.

"I'm going to make candy canes," Zoe said.

"I'm going to make trees," Julian said.

We stamped out the dough and put them on the cookie sheet. Camila put the first batch in the oven while we created some more candy canes, stars, Santas, and snowmen. When the first batch was cool enough to decorate, we made stations for icing and sprinkles. Zoe and Julian decorated while Camila and I put the cookies in boxes that looked like gingerbread houses.

"Zoe, stop licking your fingers," I said.

"But the icing is so good," she replied.

"You're going to get a belly ache. Go wash your hands."

The cookies turned out great. We had made enough for all the neighbors and even made a batch for Sean.

"I can give it to him," I offered.

"Oh, I bet you can," Camila said, giving me a sly smile.

Since I'd told Sean about Chad leaving, we seemed to be getting closer. I couldn't tell if he was flirting with me, or just being his friendly self. Two weeks ago, we were talking about Thanksgiving. I told him about how my mom and dad made all this food, but Zoe decided she would only eat chicken nuggets and tater tots right from the freezer. He laughed and told me his son went through a similar phase. Before he left, he mentioned that he liked the shirt I was wearing. My face got hot when he smiled at me. We had locked eyes for a brief second before he headed to his truck, my heart beating fast.

"What? I'm just expecting a package this week."

I'd bought Zoe a Barbie camper for Hanukkah. She'd been talking about wanting one all year. The tracker said it should come on Monday by way of UPS.

"It's Christmas; we're *all* expecting packages," Camila said, giving me a little wink.

I rolled my eyes and changed the subject.

"Okay, kids, let's get you cleaned up and then help Ms. Camila clean this kitchen. There's icing everywhere."

I arrived for my flight two hours early. After checking in and going through security, I found a wine bar close to my gate. I sat down and ordered a glass of wine and some salmon cakes. I was reading my first book when the waitress brought me my food and wine. I took a drink of wine and already started to feel the stress rolling off my shoulders.

I pulled into the hotel around dinnertime. I got out of my rental car and looked around, taking in the vastness of the Blue Ridge Mountains. The air was clean, and there was a purity and freshness that felt cleansing. The hotel was absolutely stunning, with high ceilings and marble floors. Every room had a view of the mountains. I checked in and headed upstairs. All around me were happy families in their Christmas attire. I thought, for a second, this was probably not a great idea. I should have found some singles' cruise or something. But I was already here and had to make the most of it.

When I got into my room, I put my suitcase in the corner and laid on the bed. It was soft and fluffy and felt as if I was lying on a cloud. I unpacked and took a long hot shower, that was lovely. The water felt invigorating streaming down my back. I put on a plush robe and ordered room service.

The next morning, I got up and did a nice long run. Jennifer said that I needed to do eight and a half miles if we wanted to keep up with our training. The previous Sunday, we'd gotten up to eight miles. The strength I'd gained through the training impressed me. My legs didn't ache as much, and we'd even picked up our pace a little during the long runs. We'd been averaging ten-minute miles until last week, when we'd shaved five seconds off each mile. I wasn't looking forward to running eight miles by myself, not having Jennifer to distract me or encourage me, but I got lost in the mountain views, and the time ended up flying by.

I ended my run at a small coffee shop so I could have a little breakfast before my spa appointment. I headed back to my room and quickly changed out of my running clothes. A day at the spa would be wonderful. I hadn't had a massage in over a year, and I was due. I could feel the tension in my back.

The spa was tranquil and calming. Between appointments, I spent time in the steam room and sauna. I started to feel relaxed, and the stress was fading away. I felt like I was on air, like the hardships from the past few months were starting to diminish. After my appointments, I sat by the pool—it was too cold to swim, but it was refreshing to sit and look at the mountains while I read. Across the way, a mother and daughter smiled and laughed, clearly enjoying their time together. A warmness filled my heart. It was as if I was looking into the future and seeing the bond that Zoe and I would always share. I breathed deeply and took everything in. I felt free. This trip had been seriously needed. If only for today, it was well worth it.

After the spa, I took a shower and headed down to the restaurant for dinner. The dining room bustled with families having a good time, but the adjacent bar seemed empty. I sat down and ordered a glass of red wine.

"Merry Christmas," I said to the bartender.

"Merry Christmas," she replied.

I turned my attention to the TV. Football was on and the playoffs were just about to start.

"Who's winning?" I asked.

"Buffalo is up by a touchdown," she said. She set down my wine, and I ordered a steak.

"So, what brings you to Asheville?" she asked.

"I'm on vacation."

"Oh, you here with your family?"

"No. Just me, myself, and I. I'm going through a divorce, and my daughter is with her dad, so I figured I'd take some time to myself. Beats sitting at home alone."

"Good for you. So, what are your plans while you are here?" she asked.

"I'm not sure. I went to the spa today. Was planning on doing some hiking tomorrow."

"You should check out Mt. Mitchell. It's a bit of a drive, but beautiful."

"Thanks for the recommendation."

The bartender brought me my steak; it was perfectly mid-rare, just the way I liked it. Day one had turned out to be a huge success.

The next morning was Christmas Day, and I woke up feeling down. I knew, at this very moment, Zoe would be ripping through her Christmas presents, while the smell of bacon filled the air of Chad's boyhood home. I wondered if Zoe was getting along with her cousins. I missed seeing their faces light up as they unwrapped each gift. I missed the feeling of family together, laughing and smiling.

I stared at the ceiling, taking deep breaths. The point of this trip was to be adventurous, not to feel sorry for myself. I got up and looked out the window. The sky was blue, and the sun was shining. It was a great day for a hike, and Mt. Mitchell was calling my name. I filled up my backpack with snacks and water and set off. It was about an hour drive, but it was very scenic along the way. The mountains were extremely soothing, and I marveled at their beauty and vastness. I got to the parking lot and found the trailhead. I looked up. It was going to be a long and strenuous climb to the top.

The trail was empty since it was Christmas Day. I appreciated the stillness as I walked, taking in the nature. The trees were bare, and there were leaves on the ground. I felt like those trees. The past five months I'd felt empty, as if I had lost everything. My family had been torn apart, and I didn't know who I was anymore. I climbed higher and stopped at a lookout. The mountains around were so massive, it was almost humbling. In all this greatness, I realized I was just one small part of a larger world.

I continued up the trail as it got tougher and steeper. As I pushed myself further, I thought about how strong I had become, both physically and emotionally. How I held my tongue while Zoe gushed about her time at Chad's and how much fun she had with Willow and Wyatt. How, as a single mom, I never got a break when

Zoe wouldn't go to sleep and I needed to work, or was full of energy and I just wanted to relax, but I did it. I thought about how happy volunteering had made me, knowing that I was making a difference in Christopher and Josephina's lives. I thought about how daunting it had felt at first taking care of all the home maintenance, but I'd figured out how to fit it in, even the never-ending pile of leaves this last fall.

When I got to the top, the views were breathtaking, and I could see for miles and miles. The few other people at the top, some clearly seasoned climbers, were not as worn out as I was, but I was proud of myself. I had done it. I reached the top and let out a big yell! I felt empowered and strong. I was ready for whatever else was coming my way. I asked someone to take my picture and did a super woman pose with my hand on the hips, and then one with me flexing. At that moment I felt like I was on top of the world, and I could accomplish anything.

-7-

JANUARY

The night before my divorce hearing, it started to snow. Outside my bedroom window, small flakes dropped onto the ground. The green grass slowly became a blanket of white. The weatherman said it was just going to be about an inch, but I didn't know what that meant in terms of traffic. The hearing was supposed to start at nine, and I didn't want to be late. I paced around my room, trying to choose the perfect outfit. I wasn't sure what I was supposed to wear. I wanted to look sophisticated and elegant. I knew my marriage was over, but I didn't want to feel like this was the end. I wanted to it to feel like a new beginning. I pulled out a few options: a black suit with a green striped shirt, and a navy suit with a pink camisole. I settled on a charcoal suit with a light blue camisole and black pumps.

I tossed and turned all night and woke up well before my alarm clock went off. The snow had stopped, but there was still a bit on the ground. The sky was gray, and it looked like more snow was heading our way. I was itching to get a move on, so I jumped in the shower, hoping it would calm my jitters and loosen the knots in my stomach. I wanted today to be over, and quickly.

My lawyer had explained that today was just a formality, since we had already agreed on everything two weeks earlier when we'd finished mediation. Overall, the process had gone smoothly. Chad had originally asked for alimony and child support, since I made a lot more money than he did. I'd been furious. Why should I have to pay him alimony, seeing as he was the one who had left? He was the one who had decided our marriage was over, not me. I worked hard for my money, and it didn't feel fair that I should have to give him any of that. It wasn't my fault he didn't have the drive to advance in his career. I wanted to stay on my street, in my house, and I was willing to be responsible for the mortgage and other expenses on a single income.

Luckily, my lawyer fought back, and we compromised with just child support. It still didn't seem fair to me, but my lawyer convinced me that it was good for Zoe, and there was no way I could fight it. We divided up all our assets, including me buying him out of the house, and him paying me for his car. We'd gone through all our bank statements carefully to decide how everything should be split. It felt invasive. When Chad decided to leave me for Courtney, he should have had to forfeit any of our assets. In terms of custody, we agreed to joint legal custody and a 70/30 split. We went through all the holidays and figured out even and odd years.

It was all so surreal. After three one-hour sessions, we were completely de-coupled. It seemed like it should have taken more, that our life together had been more entwined. But we signed the papers and that was that.

Even though today was just a formality, it still weighed heavily on me. This was the final nail in the coffin. This was the official ending to my marriage with Chad. I was on a roller coaster of emotions. I was disappointed that this was where my romantic life was. That I was alone. It still pained me to think that Chad didn't want to be with me anymore. But I was also still extremely angry with him.

For what he'd done to me and our family. I still couldn't get past the deceit and betrayal.

There were still little triggers in my everyday life. Last week, I'd gotten a bill for our annual wine club. Before Zoe was born, Chad and I had taken a trip out to Napa. We'd had an amazing time touring the wineries, eating delicious food, and relaxing at the spa. We'd really enjoyed one of the wineries, Matchbook Vineyard, and subscribed to their wine delivery. Every year we got a case of their wine. Seeing the bill took me back to those days when we were carefree and in love. And here we were now, getting a divorce.

But then, I was also excited. After climbing Mt. Mitchell, I'd gained a new perspective of my situation. I was strong. I was empowered. And I was ready for what my future might hold. I got out of the shower and dressed. I pulled my hair back in a slick ponytail and went to check on Zoe. Of course, of all the days, today Zoe was dragging her feet a little. She couldn't decide between the unicorn shirt and the mermaid shirt. I was envious that this small decision was going to be the toughest part of her day.

"Let's go, Zoe. Mommy can't be late today. Just pick a shirt and brush your teeth," I said trying to hurry her along.

"Okay, okay," she said, as she quickly put on the mermaid shirt and headed into the bathroom.

Somehow, we made it out the door ahead of schedule. I dropped Zoe off at school and arrived at the courthouse around 8:45, even though we weren't supposed to start until nine. It was my second time in the courthouse—I had been called for jury duty a year ago. But today was going to be a different experience. I would be sitting in front of the judge, not beside him. I walked down the hall, hearing the echo of my pumps on the marble floor.

Chad sat on a bench just outside of the room, drinking coffee and looking through the morning newspaper. I smiled to myself. Of course, he was early, just like me. That was one of the things Chad and I had always agreed upon—we were always early or on time. I wondered if Courtney was also punctual. I paused for a moment and watched him sitting there. A wave of nostalgia came over me. I started thinking about when we first met, and the first year we were together. How happy we were. I thought about all the good times we'd had, the vacations to the beach, going to Nationals games. Was it all worth it, knowing that I'd end up completely heartbroken?

I sat down across from him and gave him a slight nod.

"Hi," he said, before lowering his head and fidgeting with his coffee cup.

"Hi," I said. I tucked a loose strand of hair behind my ear.

You could feel the awkwardness in the air. Here we were, two people who'd once been in love, who had once wanted to share a life together, and now we were ending that dream. I'd wondered if Courtney would be coming, too, for support. I'd thought about asking Noah to come, but decided it would be weird, so he'd agreed to meet me after for breakfast.

"How was Zoe this morning?" he asked.

"She was good, couldn't decide between wearing mermaids or unicorns. You know, six-year-old problems," I said.

Chad smiled and went back to reading his newspaper. I scrolled through my phone. There was a text message from Camila wishing me good luck. Another one from Jennifer with hearts.

At 9:00 a.m., they called us into the courtroom. I sat with my lawyer on one side, Chad and his on the other. It felt strange to sit across from him and in such a formal setting. The knots in my stomach grew. My lawyer put her hand on my back and told me to breathe.

"This is just a formality. I'm going to ask you a few questions, so the judge knows that this is what you both want."

The judge came in and both Chad and I took an oath to swear that we would tell the truth.

My lawyer asked me questions, confirming the agreement we'd both signed at mediation and the understanding that I would pay child support. I told her that I was fine with that situation.

The judge looked me square in the eye and asked if I saw any way of reconciling our marriage. I looked over at Chad. He was staring at his hands. I knew it was over and didn't want to get back together with a liar and a cheater, but I was still coming to terms with the fact that there was no future with Chad. It was hard to get the words out, but I managed to tell him that, no, there was no way of reconciling our marriage. He wrote something down and then asked Chad the same question. Without missing a beat, he said, "No, it's over." I swallowed hard to hold back the tears. He didn't even hesitate. This was what he had wanted for a long time.

The judge looked at both of us and granted us the divorce. He banged his gavel, and just like that, I was legally divorced. I had also decided to go back to my maiden name, Beth Bradley, so the judge also granted me that. It was an odd feeling to get permission to go back to a name I had used for twenty-eight years, but I guess that was the process.

My lawyer walked me out of the courtroom.

"So, it's done. You'll get the official paperwork in two to three weeks so you can go down to the Social Security office and change your name and driver's license."

When I got married, it had been such a pain to change everything. You never realized how much your name was tied to, until you decided to change it. It wasn't as simple as just going online and updating your last name on your accounts. They needed proof that your name had changed. I even had to mail in a marriage certificate to get my airlines miles changed, as if someone would want to steal my 40,000 Delta points. Thinking of going through the arduous process again, I laughed at myself, because after we got married, I told Chad we better not get divorced, since I didn't want to do this all again. Famous last words, I guess.

"Thanks for everything," I told my lawyer and gave her a hug.

I went out to the parking garage and saw Courtney and Chad together. I hurried to my car, hoping they wouldn't see me. Before I could turn the car on, tears started streaming down my face. This was it; I was a divorced woman. I was in a place in my life that I never thought I could be.

I wiped away the tears, took two deep breaths, and texted Noah.

Me: *I guess I'm a single lady now.*
Noah: *That was quick. The Sizzling Griddle in 15 minutes?*
Me: *See you soon.*

The Sizzling Griddle was a 1950s-style dinner, complete with red plastic booths and amazing milkshakes. When I arrived, Noah was already sitting at a booth. He waved at me, and I walked over.

"I went ahead and ordered you a coffee," he said.

"Thanks," I said.

The waitress came over and put down two steaming cups of coffee.

"I'll give you a few minutes," she said.

"Thanks," Noah and I said in unison.

I opened the menu and checked the breakfast options. I didn't really have much of an appetite, but the coffee was hitting the spot.

"So how do you feel?" he asked.

"Emotionally, I'm all over the place. When we signed the separation agreement two weeks ago, I was really upset. How my life was now essentially dictated by this legal document, including when I could and couldn't see my daughter, and how I had to pay Chad child support, even though he was the one who cheated and decided to end the marriage. So, I thought, since today was just a formality, I wouldn't really feel anything. But something about a judge putting down their gavel and saying, I grant you a divorce, just made it seem more real. Like the last thirteen years with Chad had been a waste."

"It's not a waste, but I get it. Like, after my divorce, I just wished I could go back to twenty-four-year-old Noah and say, 'Don't do it! Don't do it! She's the worst. She'll rip your heart out.' But I can't. And if I could have, who knows where my life would be? Who's to say I would have been any happier? What I *can* say, is that, because of my marriage, although it was crappy, I have a great son, and I met you."

I smiled at that sentiment. It was true. Without Chad, I wouldn't have moved to Highland Avenue, I wouldn't have had Zoe, and I wouldn't have had a lot of the other good things that had come into my life.

"For what it's worth, I'm proud of you," he said.

"Proud of me?" I asked, surprised.

Noah looked me straight in the eye. "In the past six months, you've come a long way. Back in July, you felt like there was no way to move forward, and now look at you." He put his hand on mine, and I felt a moment of relief. Being with Noah made me forget all about the knots that were still in my stomach.

"You are a strong woman, and a great mom. And I know this is just the beginning, but you're going to come out on top. I know you are."

"Thanks," I smiled.

"Are you sure you don't want breakfast? My treat." Noah opened the menu.

"Well if you are paying, maybe I will get something," I said, winking.

After breakfast, I went home and changed out of my suit. On my dresser lay my engagement and wedding rings. I hadn't put the rings on since Chad told me he was leaving, but I'd kept them on my dresser, thinking maybe this was all a dream, maybe my life was going to go back to what it had been. But I knew that wasn't going to happen, and it was time to say goodbye to our relationship.

I put the rings in a small box and headed to the basement.

In a box labeled "Chad and Beth," I had already put a few things away for Zoe that I thought she might like someday. Just because we weren't married didn't mean Zoe wouldn't want to know about her mom and dad when they were younger. In the box were our wedding pictures, the ticket from our first baseball game together, and other mementos. I added the rings to the box and wrote a letter.

Dear Zoe,

There once was a time when Mommy and Daddy loved each other very much. And that love brought us you, the greatest daughter anyone could ever ask for.

Love,
Mommy

I put the letter in the box and sealed it up. I crossed out Chad and Beth and put "For Zoe" on the box. I hoped that, when she was older, she would be able to see and feel the love we'd had, and know that she was a result of that love, and, because of her, I wouldn't trade in the hurt I was feeling for anything in the world.

Two weeks later, there was a big snowstorm. I woke up to a foot and a half of snow on the ground. I poured myself a cup of coffee and surveyed the big pile of white in front of me. It was still early, so nobody had been outside, and I took in the calmness. I loved the look of fresh, untouched snow. Fresh snow always made me think of my brother. Growing up, he always made me walk in his footsteps so we could preserve the snow. He wanted to make sure we could maximize our sledding time.

I was jealous that Zoe was at Chad's, and she'd probably be building snowmen and making snow angels with her new family. I pictured her all dressed up in her purple snow overalls and pink snow boots, sledding with Willow and Wyatt, having a snowball fight with Courtney and Chad, and then coming in from the cold for hot chocolate, her cheeks red and her nose runny. I hoped that we'd get another snow day this year, and it would happen on a weekend when Zoe was with me so we could have some fun playing together.

Out on the driveway, the snow looked wet and heavy, and the task of shoveling seemed daunting. It was something Chad had always taken care of. Being from Minnesota, he loved the snow, and he was usually out with the shovel before 8:00 a.m. He'd pop out of bed, pour coffee into a large silver thermos, and get to work while Zoe watched out the window. But now, like everything else, it was my responsibility.

I finished my second cup of coffee, laced up my boots, grabbed a shovel, and headed outside. The sky was a bright blue, and the sun was shining, but it was still freezing. Luckily, last year, I had invested in a nice pair of gloves, and they kept my fingers warm and toasty.

There was so much snow. I knew from my days in Nebraska that it was best to get some momentum going, so I started with the sidewalk. I was the first one out on the street and enjoyed the quietness. With the sound of my boots crunching on the snow and the shovel scraping against the concrete, I got into a rhythm, and my heart started beating faster as I moved along. I was starting to break a sweat, and my arms and legs felt the burn from lifting the heavy snow. After thirty minutes, I had finally finished the sidewalk. My cheeks burned.

Down the road, Michael came out with his shovel. I waved and smiled as I headed to the end of my driveway.

"Hey, Beth. Quite the snow we got!"

"I know. I think they said it's about sixteen inches."

"Need any help shoveling? The twins are going to help here, and we could come by after we finish," Michael said.

I was a tad jealous that Michael got help from Nicholas and Tyler. Even if Zoe was here, she probably wouldn't last that long with the shoveling. She liked to help, though. Last year, when we got a light dusting, she helped me brush the snow off my car. But this was lot of snow, and after I had piled up what was on the sidewalk, the banks were almost half her size. Michael, Jennifer, and the twins were born athletes—I was sure they'd have their driveway and walk done in no time. But I was making progress and feeling good.

"No thanks, I'm kind of on a roll," I said, looking at my clean sidewalk.

"Okay, let me know if you change your mind."

"Thanks."

I started on the driveway, pushing the snow from one end into the grass. The workout was great—my arms felt tired. About an hour later, I was halfway done with the driveway, and Camila and Sebastian came out with Julian and Arlo. Julian was helping Sebastian with a little red shovel. He wasn't moving much snow, but that didn't stop him.

"I'm so strong, Daddy," I heard him say.

Arlo was wrapped up like a snow bunny in a blue fleece coat and was having fun exploring the snow. I decided to take a break from shoveling and walked across the street to say hi.

"Hey, girl. Your driveway is looking good," Camila said.

"Thanks." I held out my arms and pretended to flex. "But I'm not as strong as you," I said to Julian. He chuckled and started flexing his arms.

"I heard on the news that this was the biggest snowstorm in five years," Camila said.

Zoe was just two months old during that snowstorm, and we had gotten twenty inches. Chad spent all day shoveling while Zoe and I stayed inside. I watched Chad out the window while I nursed Zoe to sleep sitting next to the crackling fireplace.

"I believe it, and so do my arms," I said.

Julian ran over to Arlo and started making snowballs with him.

"Can Zoe play?" Julian asked.

"No, she's with her dad today. Maybe on Monday, if the snow is still on the ground, you could make snow angels."

"That'd be fun," Julian said.

Arlo started to fuss—he was no longer loving the snow. It was too cold and wet.

Camila scooped him up and made faces to entertain him.

"Well, I've got to get back. That driveway isn't going to shovel itself," I said.

"Come by for hot chocolate later. You know, my secret recipe!" Camila made this delicious bourbon hot chocolate, complete with marshmallows and whipped cream. It would most certainly be a well-deserved treat when I was done.

"I think I'm going to need a hot shower after this, but I'll stop by after," I called as I headed back across the street.

I continued removing the heavy snow, back and forth across the driveway. It made me feel stronger and more powerful. I was like a machine, moving this snow off my driveway, and nothing was going to get in my way. Just like in life. I could handle just about anything. These past six months had been the hardest of my life, but here I was, still standing. And not just standing but *thriving*. I could have asked someone to shovel my driveway, but I hadn't. I was training for a half marathon and was a director at work. I had supportive friends who were there for me, and most importantly, I had an amazing daughter. Even though I didn't have a husband, and the family I thought I'd wanted was no longer an option, I felt more optimistic about my future.

When I finished the driveway, I pumped my fists in the air. I'd done it.

I looked next door at Gregory's driveway, which was still covered in snow. Chad had always shoveled his driveway and walk after ours. So, I got to work.

Gregory came out on his front porch.

I smiled and waved at him.

"You don't need to do that, Beth. I'll find someone else to do it," he said.

"Really, it's no trouble at all. I've got a good momentum going, and I could use the exercise."

"Thanks," he said. "You really are a great neighbor."

Michael saw me at Gregory's house and came by with the twins.

"We can help you with this," he said.

"Thanks, Michael. With the four of us, we should be able to knock this out pretty quickly."

After finishing Gregory's driveway, I was beat, and my arms and legs felt like jelly. I went inside for a hot shower, which felt amazing. I sat in the tub with the water beating down on my body. I felt invigorated and fresh. I had shoveled two driveways. I felt strong, like I could accomplish anything. I didn't want this feeling to end. Feeling good about myself was so much better than being the sad, depressing, Beth. I didn't want to be the person whose husband had left her. I wanted to be the person who could do anything. I wanted to take this opportunity and figure out how to become a better version of myself. I needed to take everything I liked about myself and enhance it. I wanted to become a new me, someone my daughter could look up to. Someone who got through tough times with grace and resilience.

I got out of the shower and put on yoga pants and a sweatshirt. Still feeling empowered, I went over to Camila's for the hot chocolate she'd promised me.

"Here you go. You deserve it. You were a shoveling machine today." She slid over a blue mug with white polka dots.

I took a whiff of the hot chocolate. It gave off an intoxicating aroma.

"Mmm, smells delicious."

The mini marshmallows danced in the brown liquid. Adult hot chocolates really hit the spot on a day like today.

"So, how does it feel to be officially back to Beth Bradley? Has it sunk in yet?" she asked.

The paperwork for my name change had finally come through. I had appointments lined up next week with Social Security and the DMV to get the never-ending process started.

"I never thought I'd be back to Beth Bradley, but it feels good. Kind of like starting over."

"Yeah, it's a new you, a new year—anything is possible."

I told Camila about my thoughts in the shower, about how I wanted to become a better person.

"I think that's a great attitude. Most people in your situation would still be reeling with hatred."

"Oh, don't get me wrong, there're still some negative feelings for Chad and Courtney," I said. "I mean, *strong* negative feelings. But what good does it do me to hate them? It's not like it affects their lives in any way."

"That's true. I don't think they sit around talking about whether or not you hate them."

"I'm pretty sure they haven't thought about me or my feelings...ever. If they did, they wouldn't have had an affair, or at least would have told me about it sooner." I swallowed the last of my hot chocolate.

"True," Camila said just as Arlo woke up from his nap.

"I better get going. Thanks for the hot chocolate."

As I was leaving, Julian ran up to me and said, "Tell Zoe I can't wait to have a snowball fight with her."

"Will do!"

I crossed the street and found a tin on my front stoop. There was a note from Gregory.

Thanks for shoveling the driveway. I'm truly blessed to have such great neighbors.

—Gregory

Inside the tin were some oatmeal chocolate chip cookies. Zoe would be excited for these when she came back on Monday. Gregory made the best cookies.

I was exhausted from the shoveling, and the spiked hot chocolates were starting to go to my head. I laid down to take a little nap and woke to a text from Noah.

Noah: *Do you want to build a snowman?*
Me: *OMG I'm so tired. I shoveled two driveways and am already deep in spiked hot chocolate. The couch is calling my name.*
Noah: *Want company? I'll bring wine.*
Noah knew me so well. There was no way I was going to say no to wine.
Me: *You've made me an offer I can't refuse.*
Noah: *I'll be over in 10 minutes.*

Noah arrived, bottle of red in hand.

"You certainly know the way to my heart," I said as I opened the door.

"Good job with the shoveling. I'm impressed. That was a lot of snow."

"I also did the neighbor's." I took two glasses out of the cupboard as Noah opened the wine.

"You're like superwoman."

"Don't forget it," I said and gave him a little nudge with my elbow. "Popcorn?"

BETH BRADLEY 2.0

"Sure!"

I popped some popcorn and put it in a big bowl to share, and we headed on the couch. I always enjoyed chilling with Noah. I could relax around him and just be myself.

"What do you want to watch?"

"I don't know. Let's see what Netflix recommends."

We settled on one of the Marvel movies. Halfway through, I must have fallen asleep, because I woke up with my head on Noah's shoulder, and the credits were rolling.

"Oh, look who's up," Noah said.

"Next time, I get to pick the movie."

"Deal," he said.

Noah helped me put the wine glasses and popcorn in the sink and headed for the door.

"I'll see you later," Noah said as he left.

I watched Noah climb into his car. He was a great friend, and I was glad to have him in my life. It was nice to have another friend I could just bum around with, watching TV, and drinking wine.

I put the dishes in the sink and went upstairs, where I fell asleep as soon as my head hit the pillow.

–8–

FEBRUARY

After the snowstorms we had in January, February turned out to be unseasonably warm. It was a sunny Saturday afternoon, in the low 60s. The wind was calm, and it was one of those days where you just had to be outside. Zoe and I decided to take a bike ride to Backyard Bistro to grab lunch. It was one of our favorite places to eat and was in the same complex as Sebastian and Camila's restaurant. Zoe loved that every kids' meal came with an ice cream. We had been there enough that most of the employees knew us.

Zoe and I parked our bikes and headed inside. The hostess recognized us right away.

"Hi, guys," she said with a chipper smile. "Taking advantage of this amazing day, I see." She glanced over at both of us carrying our helmets.

"Yes, Mommy and I rode our bikes here," Zoe said, holding up her pink and purple helmet.

"I see," she said. "You must have worked up an appetite."

She grabbed some menus and led us to one of our usual tables, right by the window. Zoe and I liked to watch the people coming and going from the shopping center. Everyone seemed to be in good spirits. It was amazing how a sunny day seemed to lift everyone up.

We'd all been hunkered down during January, and now people were eager to get out and feel the warmth of the sun on their skin.

The waitress came by and put down some bread and garlic sauce on the table. The bread here was such a comfort food. It came out warm, and every bite brought me back to happy, simpler times.

"What a beautiful day," I said to Zoe, taking a piece of bread and dipping into the sauce.

"Yeah," Zoe said, "but I wish it would snow again."

"Oh yeah, so you can help Mommy shovel the driveway this time?" I asked.

"No, so Julian and I can have another snowball fight," she said.

I had been lucky enough to get another snow day with Zoe. There wasn't as much as the time before, but a few inches did manage to accumulate. Zoe and I spent the afternoon making snow angels, before we had a full-on snowball fight with Julian and Sebastian. The kids laughed all afternoon—it was such a delight. I was glad we'd been able to do it, because it didn't seem like it would snow again this winter.

Zoe and I talked while we waited for the waiter. She told me about school, and how they were learning all about the presidents.

"Maybe after lunch we can head to the library and find a book on George Washington," I suggested. The library was just a quick five-minute bike ride from Backyard Bistro and would be a nice place to go so we could continue our afternoon bike ride.

"Sounds fun," Zoe said.

The waiter arrived with an iced tea for me and a milk for Zoe.

"So, what will it be?" she asked.

"I'll have the corn and avocado salad," I said.

"Chicken nuggets and French fries," Zoe said with excitement.

It was one of our usual lunch orders.

"Coming right up," the waitress said with a smile.

Zoe colored on her menu and did the maze, while I stared out the window and took in the day. A group of high school girls enter the bistro, their giggles infectious. I stared at Zoe. I couldn't imagine a time when she'd be old enough to *walk* here, probably with Julian. She was still my little girl, and she loved going on adventures with me. We were two peas in a pod, but I knew there would be a time where I'd become lame Mom.

We finished up lunch, Zoe relishing her ice cream.

"Yummy!" she said, as she licked the last bit.

"Shall we?" I said stepping out of the booth.

We left the restaurant and were heading to our bikes, when I heard Zoe exclaim, "Daddy's here!"

"What are you talking about?"

I looked up, and Chad and Courtney were coming across the parking lot, hand in hand. They looked so carefree and happy. Chad had a big smile across his face, and it looked like he had just made Courtney laugh. My heart sank. Was this really happening? Did they have to come to the shopping center right by my house? Wasn't there a place closer to them for lunch?

I put my helmet down and started messing with my hair. I hadn't seen Courtney since our conversation in August, and I was pretty sure I was rocking some major helmet hair. Luckily, I always kept a ponytail holder with me, so I quickly pulled my hair back.

Courtney and Chad came closer. Of course, Courtney looked completely put together and polished. Her lips were shiny with lipstick, there wasn't a hair on her head out of place, and she walked with a sense of confidence. I didn't want to feel intimidated by her, so I stood taller, threw my shoulders back, and put on my biggest fake smile as they approached.

"Hey there, Zoe," Chad said, looking surprised to see us.

Zoe ran up to him and gave him a big hug and giggled. Then, in front my own eyes, she gave Courtney a hug. I wanted to throw up. I wanted to cry. I wanted to scream. This was not something I'd ever wanted to witness. My own daughter, hugging my ex-husband's girlfriend.

"Hi, Chad. Hi, Courtney. What brings you this way?" I said. My cheeks cramped from smiling so much. I toned it down a little, afraid I might look like I was trying too hard.

"Courtney wanted to try the Backyard Bistro. She told me she had never been, even though I always raved about their flat bread pizzas."

"Well, enjoy!" I said.

Chad and Courtney looked happy, like they didn't care how hurt I'd felt the past couple of months. They didn't care about the damage they'd done with all their lying and cheating. They didn't care about anyone but themselves. I needed to get out of here.

I reached for my helmet, hoping they felt the same urgency for our encounter to end. Unfortunately, Courtney wanted to chit chat.

"Yes, Chad told me how much he loved the pizzas. I've never been," Courtney said as she nuzzled up next to Chad. Chad put his arm around Courtney's shoulder, and she moved her arm around his waist. It felt like she was rubbing it my face, that he chose her. "Chad said I had to try the fig and prosciutto one."

Of course, he told her about that one. That was *our* pizza. We ordered it together all the time. We would often split the fig and prosciutto pizza, a Caesar salad, and a bottle of wine, while Zoe munched on chicken nuggets. It was our tradition, a quick outing when neither of us wanted to cook. And now he was going to share it with her. I wondered if she knew, and that's why she brought it up. To rub it in my face. Not only did she take my husband, but she was going to enjoy our favorite pizza, too.

"It's delicious. I'm sure you'll enjoy it." I pressed my lips together tightly, fuming inside. I hated this woman and all that she represented. I hated that she had a relationship with Zoe, that she had the audacity to canoodle with my ex-husband in front of my face.

"I told him it's probably not as good as the one at The Upper Crust. We went there two weeks ago, but Chad insisted this one was the best."

What was with her? I get it! You and my ex-husband love eating fig and prosciutto pizzas. You and my ex-husband go out to dinner together. You and my ex-husband have each other. And I have no one. I still didn't understand why she wanted to talk. I needed to end this quickly, but Courtney definitely wasn't taking the hint.

Chad gave her a little nudge. "I do love my pizzas, and this one is the best."

Courtney let out a little laugh, like there was some inside joke I wasn't getting. I didn't want to be any part of any inside joke the two of them shared.

Just then Zoe exclaimed, "This one time, Daddy ate a whole pizza." She made a big circle with his arms. "Wyatt didn't think Daddy could, but he did, and we all just laughed."

My heart sank even more. Zoe was apparently in on this inside joke as well.

Was I the only one feeling that this was a super awkward situation?

"Well, I hope you like it. We were just on our way to the library, right, Zoe?"

"Right, Mommy. We're going to find a book about George

Washington," Zoe said. "Did you know that he was the first president? And he was a general in the army."

Of course, Zoe wanted to show off all she now knew about George Washington, but she was also ignoring my hint that we needed to go.

"Oh really, Zoe? What else do you know?" Courtney asked.

"Well." Zoe tilted her hand and put her finger to her chin.

"That's why we need to go the library," I interjected.

"Yes!" Zoe agreed. "So I can find out more facts."

"So, we better get going. Enjoy your pizza." I put on my helmet and grabbed Zoe's.

Zoe gave Chad another hug. Courtney leaned in for a hug, too. This woman was ruthless. My husband, my pizza, *and* my daughter. What else did she want from me?

"Bye, Daddy. Bye, Courtney. See you soon," Zoe said as she waved. She put on her helmet and, we peddled away.

"To the library!" I said as we rounded the corner.

"That was fun seeing Daddy and Courtney," Zoe said. "Too bad we had just finished eating. We could have had lunch with them."

"Too bad!" I said, keeping my now-perfected happy face on. Lunch with my ex-husband and his girlfriend was not on my list of to-dos. In fact, there were a million things I'd rather do, than go through that experience. Running into them was bad enough. Sharing an impromptu meal was out of the question.

"It would be fun to have lunch with everyone. You, Daddy, Courtney, Willow, and Wyatt. Maybe we can do that sometime," Zoe said.

I loved Zoe for her innocence. She had no idea of the situation we were in. She just wanted everyone to get along. I'd decided I would remain civil to Chad, knowing that we had a future with Zoe together, and I wanted her to feel love and support from both of us. But it was hard to accept a scenario where Courtney would be included. If it was just Chad and me, then we could just be divorced parents. But, if Courtney came along, she would be a constant reminder that he'd left me for her. And then, with Willow and Wyatt in the mix, suddenly, I became the odd man out of what used to be my family. Just thinking about that made my hear sink. I knew these people were part of Zoe's life, but I still just couldn't get used to it.

"Maybe. We'll see," I said.

"Last weekend, when I was with Daddy, we went to Wyatt's soccer game, and his dad was there. He sat with us. And Wyatt scored a goal. It was so exciting."

It must have been nice for Wyatt to have everyone there supporting him. I wondered how Wyatt's dad did it. How he sat and watched a game with his ex-wife and her new boyfriend, the person who had ruined his marriage.

I started to feel guilty. If Courtney's ex could do it, then why couldn't I? Was he more mature than me? Was I being petty and not putting my child's happiness first?

I tried to shake off the feeling. I do everything for Zoe. But maybe, in this instance, I was wrong?

"That's really cool. Did they end up winning?" I tried to keep my voice neutral.

"No, his team still lost, but we all went for ice cream after."

"Even Wyatt and Willow's dad?" I inquired.

"Yep. He told me I could get sprinkles on mine."

Everyone acting in a civil manner, making it fun for Wyatt, but also making Willow and Zoe feel included. I didn't think I could do that. Not now, knowing that the two of them had been lying to me for three years. I just wasn't there yet. It was hard enough being around Chad. I didn't have the energy to face the whole crew. Maybe in the future I'd find a way. Courtney, Willow, and Wyatt were all a part of Zoe's life, and I'm sure Zoe would love the support, but these things were going to take time. It was hard enough getting over the end of my marriage.

We got to the library and Zoe picked out two books on George Washington. She didn't want to wait to get home to read them. We sat on a bench, and I pulled out one of the books. Zoe crawled on my lap as we learned about how George Washington led the Continental Army against King George.

As we rode back from the library, I thought more about Courtney's ex-husband, and I felt like I was failing at this co-parenting thing. I had done all I could to keep a good relationship with Chad, but I was ignoring the other people in Zoe's life. I'd never even met Wyatt or Willow, which seemed odd now, seeing as Zoe talked about Willow all the time. But here Courtney's ex was, going to soccer games and out to ice cream with all of them. I wanted to know how he did it. Maybe he'd realized that his marriage was over sooner than I had, which was why it didn't sting so much. Or maybe he'd also had an affair.

Later that night, I got a text from Chad.

Chad: *Sorry that was awkward today.*
Me: *Yeah.*
Chad: *Funny running into you.*

I wasn't sure where he was going with this. Did he have a point? I kept thinking about Courtney's ex, so I figured I'd see if Chad could give me any more insight into him.

Me: *I heard Zoe met Courtney's ex-husband.*
Chad: *Yeah, he's nice. A good guy.*
Me: *Did they have an amicable split?*

Chad took a while to respond. I kept seeing the three dots appear and then disappear.

Chad: *Why do you ask?*

I guess it really wasn't any of my business, but I was just so interested. Here I was, seven months later, and seeing Courtney still made me cringe. How could he sit with them through an entire soccer game?

Me: *Just curious.*
Chad: *It was tough at first, but they've been separated longer than we have.*

The three dots kept on appearing and then disappearing. Finally, I got another text.

Chad: *She ended things with him six months before I did. I just had a harder time ending things with you.*

I was taken aback by this information. Courtney had left her husband a whole six months before Chad left me? I had mixed reactions to this news. I didn't know if I had more respect for Courtney for ending her marriage earlier, or more anger knowing she'd just spent her days waiting for Chad to drop me.

And what about Chad? Had he been leading me on, or leading

Courtney on? Did they decide to leave their marriages together? If so, what kind of man has his girlfriend end her marriage with a promise of getting together, but doesn't follow through on his end? It just solidified the fact that Chad wasn't the person I thought he was. I wondered what Courtney must have thought, waiting for Chad to end things with me. What an awful position to be in. Had she been afraid he wouldn't do it? Did she pressure him more? Did she give him an ultimatum? And, if so, what was it?

Six months ago, this news would have put me in a downward spiral, with lots of tears and lots of wine. But I wasn't reaching for the bottle, and there weren't any tears. I was just angry, angry at both of them. They were horrible people who only cared about themselves. They deserved each other.

I focused my attention back on Courtney's ex-husband. In a year, it seemed like his wounds had healed enough to spend time with Chad. Maybe I could get there, too. I already felt stronger and more confident. Maybe I would become comfortable, little by little, with not only the thought of Zoe's insta-family but with sharing moments that were important to Zoe with them.

"So, Chad and Courtney's ex are best friends?" Jennifer said, after I told her about what Chad texted me.

"No, I didn't say that. It's just that Courtney's ex is able to tolerate him, for the sake of his kids. I think it's nice."

"This is going to be an interesting run," Jennifer said.

"Yes, but are you sure we have to do nine and a half?" I groaned.

"Yes, Beth. C'mon, we better start now."

We headed down Highland Avenue toward the bike trail. The

plan was to do four and a half miles, turn around, and the do a big loop when we got to Highland Avenue. That would be nine and a half. The week before, we'd done the same run, but it was a lot windier. Around mile seven it had started to rain. Nothing too bad, but enough to get a squishy feeling in my socks. My legs ached when we got to Highland Avenue, and I tried to convince Jennifer to skip the half mile loop. I told her I was tired and cold, but she wasn't hearing any of it and pushed us through the full nine and half. Afterwards, I just about collapsed on my driveway, but Jennifer revived me with a hot cup of coffee. I was hoping that, since it was nice today, the run would go a little smoother.

"So, are you thinking of spending more time with Courtney?" Jennifer asked.

"I wasn't *planning* on it. But maybe Zoe would like it," I said.

"Has she asked you? Like for her next gymnastics show, did she ask if Courtney could come watch?"

Zoe's next recital was coming up at the beginning of March. Chad and I hadn't talked about whether or not Courtney could come, and Zoe hadn't brought it up, either. I kind of figured I'd just keep kicking that can down the road, and then maybe it'd be too late, and Courtney would have plans.

"She hasn't. But I just feel like I'm the one limiting Zoe from having Courtney in her life."

"I wouldn't think of it that way. It's not like she asked and you flat out said no. Besides, I don't think anyone blames you for not wanting to spend time with the woman who wrecked your marriage."

"I guess I just feel like I'm holding onto something, and maybe I need to let go."

The healing process was a complicated one. I wanted to move forward with my life, but these wounds were deep, and I needed to do what was best for me and what was best for Zoe. It was a tricky situation, and I wasn't sure how to navigate it. But maybe putting this wall up with Courtney was prohibiting me from healing some of my wounds.

"Are you ready to let go?" she asked, giving me a quizzical look.

"No, I still hate her, and I hate what she and Chad did. I'm just not over it."

"Then give it time. If you rush into this, it could be bad."

I thought about what Jennifer said. I couldn't heal all my wounds at once. I had to keep doing what I'd been doing since July—taking it one step at a time. If something in my gut was telling me I wasn't ready, then I should listen to it, and not be so hard on myself.

"I guess so. I wouldn't want to explode at the next gymnastics show."

"No, you don't want to be *that* mom. I mean, I've been there."

Last year, Jennifer had been at Tyler's basketball game, and a kid tripped Tyler as he was going for a lay-up. The ref didn't call a foul, but as Tyler got up with blood streaming from his nose, Jennifer lost it. She went right up to the ref, two inches from his face, and started screaming. She called him reckless, blind, and a few other colorful words. She had to leave the game and ended up writing an apology to the ref and the league.

"Sometimes I wish I had your mama bear reactions. You don't let anyone mess with the people you love," I said.

"It's a blessing and a curse. But you do have mama bear reactions. You're just a little tamer."

I laughed. We reached the four-mile mark and turned around. The run was turning out to be a pretty strong one. Jennifer told me we were running three seconds faster than last week. My heart beat fast, pumping blood throughout my body as the wind blew my hair. This was probably the best run we'd had yet. It felt good to move and to move fast, like all of my problems were fading away.

It was still warm on Tuesday. It was one of my work from home days, so I sat out on the front porch while I did some work. I was typing away, editing a report that was due to an important client at the end of the week, when I heard the rumble of the UPS truck pulling up.

"Hey, Beth. How's it going?" Sean said, giving me his signature grin. I didn't know how he did it, but he was always happy and in an upbeat, chipper mood. I didn't think I'd ever seen him not smiling.

"Hey, Sean." I put my laptop away and gave him my full attention.

"Enjoying the sunshine, I see."

I loved when he smiled, showing off the dimple on his left cheek.

"Yeah, I figured I'd get some vitamin D while I finish up this report. How have you been?"

"Can't complain. Things are always slow this time of year, after the big Christmas push."

"I guess it's a nice change of pace." This past December, Sean had told me how hectic his days were. Everyone loved to do online shopping over the holidays, and he was working ten-hour days, six days a week. He was exhausted, but the money was good.

"I bet. You deserve a break," I said.

Sean went into the back of his truck and pulled out a large box for me. "Got a big package for you today," he said.

I laughed. I was pretty sure that was how most porno movies started. Sean must have realized what he said, too, once he saw my face.

"Oh man, I don't mean that. Get your head out of the gutter, Beth."

"What?" I said, holding up my hands and smirking. "I ordered a new table and chairs for the patio out back."

I was really enjoying changing up the rooms, getting the Chad out, and making everything mine. The house was really coming together. Last month, I redid the guest room. I got a new rug, bedspread, and curtains. I also picked out some new art to give it a homier feel. This month, I was working on the backyard. I had found a new table and chairs that I loved and was going to string some lights across the deck. I wanted to be ready for spring, so I could host some backyard get-togethers.

"Very nice. Do you need any help putting it together?" he asked.

"Thanks, but I'm sure I can handle it."

"Really, it's no problem."

"Seriously? You don't need to do that."

"I don't mind at all."

"That would be really great, thanks. Zoe is with Chad tomorrow. Do you want to come over then?"

"Yeah, I'll swing by after my shift. Would 7:30 work?"

"That'd be perfect." I gave him my number in case something came up. "You're the best."

"Not a problem! See you tomorrow."

Sean jumped in his truck and gave me a little honk and a wave goodbye.

The next day, Sean arrived at 7:30 on the dot. It was nice to know he was another punctual person, like me. It was weird not seeing him in his normal uniform—I realized that, even though I had known Sean for over six years, I had only seen him in the signature UPS brown, which he pulled off nicely. Tonight, he had on dark jeans and a red Nationals hooded sweatshirt.

"Come on in. I hope you found the place okay," I joked. I realized I was nervous. Thankfully, he laughed at my sad attempt at humor.

"Do you want something to drink? I have beer."

"Beer would be great. Thanks."

In the kitchen, I pulled out two IPAs. I put them in Nationals koozies, one blue and one red. "Red or blue? Zoe is usually particular, so I'm in the habit of asking," I explained.

"Ha ha, Aidan was the same way. Blue's fine." He grabbed the beer and took a sip. "I like the koozie."

"Thanks! We can work out on the patio. I've gotten as far as taking everything out of the box."

"Sounds good." He took his sweatshirt off and wore a standard white T-shirt underneath, which showed off his muscular arms. He really pulled the look off well.

We started putting the table together. Sean read the directions, and together we got the legs on. As we assembled the table, we mostly just talked baseball.

"So, what do you think about the Nationals this year? Think the team looks any good?" I asked. Spring training games had just started, and I was excited for the regular season to begin.

"We never have good relief pitching. We blew more saves than any other team last year. It's infuriating," he complained.

"I know, and what does the team do? Spend more money on hitting."

The Nationals had signed a former silver slugger last season for a huge five-year contract. He was a welcome addition to the team, but everyone on the sports radio circuit thought that the money could have been spent elsewhere.

"We don't need hitting. What good are runs, if your set-up man and closer can't get anyone out?"

"I couldn't agree more."

Sean tightened up the last leg on the table.

"Ta-da." Sean set the table upright.

I tested it to make sure it wasn't wobbly.

"It looks great! Now on to the chairs. But first, another beer. Do you want one?"

"Sure!" Sean said, and I headed into the kitchen and grabbed us another round.

Returning to the backyard, Sean hesitated and then said, "Hey, Beth. I know this might be uncalled for, but I'm really sorry about Chad. That guy was a damn fool to leave you."

I blushed, my face getting hot. "Thanks, Sean."

"I'm serious. You're a rockstar."

I didn't know what to say. It was one thing when your best friends tried to pump you up with lines about being awesome, but it was different coming from someone else. Someone who was just there to help put together your table and chairs and wasn't expecting anything in return.

"Well, I wouldn't say that," I said.

"No, it's true. You work hard, you're a good mom, you do it all. I just don't know how someone would walk away from you and Zoe. Like I said, that guy is a damn fool."

My heart started beating a little faster, and my palms grew sweaty.

"That's very sweet of you to say. But I'm better off without him." I gave a dismissive wave.

"That's for sure. That guy doesn't deserve you."

As much as I wanted to keep hearing Sean say nice things about me, I needed to change the subject before my face got any redder. "I never asked you, what happened with your marriage?"

"Just one of those 'we grew apart' things. We were always fighting and found ourselves looking forward to time when we were apart versus time we were together. She said I worked too much, taking too many extra shifts, but the truth was, I worked because I knew I wouldn't have to go home to her. I wanted to make it work because of Aidan, but we had a big fight about me not doing my share around the house, and it was just my breaking point. I miss not being able to see him every day and getting him off to school, but it's better than being in a bad marriage."

I wish Chad had had the maturity to do that. To end things with me, knowing he wasn't happy, rather than cheat on me for three years and *then* leave me.

"How did you know it just wasn't a rut?" As soon as the words left my mouth, I wished I could take them back. I felt like I was getting too personal, and I didn't want Sean to think I was digging into his private life.

"We tried therapy, and other things, but I guess we just weren't meant to be." He gave a little shrug.

"I'm sorry, I don't mean to get too personal."

"Don't worry about it. I'm the one who started it and brought up Chad."

Sean and I continued talking while we finished putting together the rest of the chairs. It was the longest we had hung out, and we had a lot in common, outside of our love of the Nationals. We talked about the struggles of single parenthood and staying positive for your kids. He told me about his family, and how he felt like he'd let his mom down when he got divorced. He told me about playing basketball in college, and how it was the best time, hearing the roar of the crowd, and how he missed it, being part of something bigger like that. It was a great conversation, and I felt like we really connected.

Sean looked at his watch. "Oh, man. Look at the time. I better run."

"Really? What time is it?"

"Almost eleven."

"Oh, wow. That is late, way past my bedtime. Thanks for helping with the table and chairs, and the company."

"Sure thing. I had a good time," Sean said.

There was an awkward silence. I didn't know if I should hug him, shake his hand, or give him a high five. I settled on a hug.

Sean left, and I looked down at my phone to see three texts from Rachel:

What's Sean doing at your house? [7:30]
Is Sean still there? [9:30]
Are you and Sean doing it?" [10:30]

Rachel must have been dying for my response.

Me: *He just helped put together my table and chairs.*
Rachel: *Is that what we're calling it?*

I put down the phone and laid in bed with a huge smile on my face. It was still there when I woke up the next morning.

The following weekend we were all over at Camila's for an after-noon BBQ. The kids played in the yard while the adults sat on the patio drinking a crisp white wine.

"So, have you talked to Sean since he came by to 'put your table together,'" Rachel inquired.

"Yea, he was over for a long time." Camila noted.

"He sent me a text saying he had a good time, but that was about it," I said.

"Is there anything going on with you two?" Jennifer asked.

"We're just friends," I said.

I had thought a little bit about Sean the last week, in a more-than-friends capacity, but I wasn't sure if it was something I wanted to peruse. I felt very fragile and wasn't even sure what Sean thought about me. It would take a lot for me to make a move. What if I em-barrassed myself like I had at the Christmas party with Austin? I would never be able to order a package online again. I'd have to go back to shopping in an actual store.

"Have you thought about dating at all?" Rachel asked.

"Not really. I'm not sure if I'm ready," I shrugged.

I wasn't sure if I was ready to put myself out there. I didn't want to admit it to my friends, but I was afraid. What if nobody liked me? What if I wasn't good enough? Chad left me for Courtney, so who was to say it wouldn't happen again? I was a terrified of getting hurt again. I just couldn't take any more heartbreak.

On the other hand, I would be lying if I didn't say I was just a tiny bit curious what it would be like. I was also craving some sort of intimacy. It had been a while since I'd even kissed another person.

"Just dip your toe in the water. Get dressed up, have someone buy you a drink. See what happens," Jennifer suggested.

"What if I like someone and he rejects me? Or what if I go on a date with some creepy guy? Who even knows what the over-thirty-five dating pool looks like?" I asked.

"It's not like we're saying you have to find another husband. Just go out and see what it's like. Then you'll know," Camila said.

"Come on. Let's do an online dating profile. My coworker swears by Here Comes Love," Rachel said.

"Love? I'm not ready for something *that* serious. I don't know if I'll even be able to love again," I protested.

"Whatever, drama queen. Give me your phone. We're doing this." Rachel stuck out her hand.

I reluctantly passed her my phone, and she downloaded the app.

"Okay, first the profile. Let's see… 'Avid runner and baseball enthusiast seeks hot hunk.'" Rachel began typing into the phone.

"Let's keep it simple," I said.

I was nervous about online dating. It hadn't been a thing when I was single. I used to just meet people out at bars or on intermural sports teams. That's how Chad and I met—we both played soccer. He was on a different team, but we always ended up talking after the games at the bar. The last night of the season, he finally asked me out, and the rest was history.

"Should I mention that I'm a mom?" I asked.

"Maybe, just a slight mention, like, 'Enjoys dance parties with my daughter,'" Jennifer said.

"Okay, how about this: 'Newly single and dipping my toe in the dating pool. I like to spend time running, watching baseball, and having dance parties with my daughter. Interested in meeting up for a drink.'"

"Perfect," said Jennifer. "Now it's time for pictures!"

We settled on three photos. One of me crossing the finish line from one of the 10ks that Jennifer and I had done last year, one of me taken at happy hour with friends (cropped), and, finally, a picture I'd taken at the top of Mt. Mitchell.

Rachel handed me back my phone.

"Keep us posted on any prospects," she said.

"I think you all are going to enjoy this more than me," I added.

Later that night, I got into bed and started swiping. I was surprised by the number of people who bragged about how many countries they had visited. I didn't realize that was so important and was embarrassed that I had only been to ten, compared to Xander's twenty-seven. A shocking number of men took selfies in public restrooms. Who was ever in a public restroom and thought, "This is a great place to take a picture!" Was that what people liked? I was way behind the times. And then there were the guys who took selfies in dirty mirrors. How hard was it to spray some Windex before snapping a picture? If someone couldn't be bothered to clean his mirror, I didn't think we'd be a good fit.

Still, there were some potential matches on the site. A good number of single dads who were also attractive. They hadn't succumbed to the dad bod yet. I started getting excited about the possibility of a first date. Maybe this wouldn't be so bad after all. I kept swiping and then ended up with my first match. His name was Tom, and he was thirty-five, had no kids, was originally from Australia, and worked in finance. He seemed like a promising first date.

"This is exciting! Your first date!" Camila said.

Camila had agreed to help me get ready for my date with Tom. We were up in my room, and she was helping me pick out an outfit.

All day, I'd been so nervous that I could barely eat. I kept having this feeling in the pit of my stomach. Was I really ready to date? I had been through so much, and it felt like I was setting myself up for more failure. Being cheated on had really done a number on myself self-esteem. I was convinced that any guy I liked wouldn't like me back. I thought for sure that Tom would take one look at me and run in the other direction. When I ran, and when I was with my friends, I felt amazing, like I could take on the world. But this was different. This was putting myself out there, and it was terrifying.

"Where is he taking you?"

"We're meeting for drinks at Luxe Lounge."

"Oh, I've been wanting to try that place. I've heard good things."

"Me, too."

Luxe Lounge was a classy new wine bar that had recently opened a few miles away. The first two months it was impossible to get a reservation, and the bar was always packed, no matter what time of day it was. They had a well-crafted wine list, and the food was supposedly delicious. I was really glad that Tom had picked it.

I pulled out two different choices for shirts. One was purple, made my eyes pop, and went well with my dark jeans, which showed off my slim figure. The other was a light green cowl-neck.

"Which one?" I asked as I held each one up to my body.

"Definitely the purple one. And are you wearing your hot jeans you got last week?"

"Of course. They show off my best feature…my butt."

"Since you and Jennifer have been running more, your butt is looking even better. Not that I've been looking."

"I know you can't take your eyes off my backside," I said with a giggle. "Okay, now hair—sexy pony, or down?"

"Down! You look hot when your hair is down. Are you nervous?" she asked.

"A little. I guess."

Besides the fact that I was convinced this night would end with me getting rejected, I also had first date jitters. I hadn't gone on a first date since Chad, and that was back when I was in my twenties. And when I *had* gone on a date before that, I had usually known the guy already. This was essentially a blind date—outside of a few messages, I didn't really know much about Tom. I wasn't sure how to act or what to say. There were so many questions racing through my mind. When I saw him, should I shake his hand or give him a hug? Should I offer to pay, or split the bill? What if he stood me up? What if he didn't look like his picture?

I tried to think of all the possible scenarios of how this date could go and what might happen. But the more I thought about it, the more uneasy I felt.

"I'm trying not to think too much about it, set my expectations low," I lied.

"Uh-huh?" She tilted her head. Camila saw right through me.

"Okay, I'm scared out of my mind. This is not a place I thought I'd be." I sank onto the bed and put my hands in my head. Camila came over and sat beside me.

"Look. It's just a date."

"Easy for you to say," I said. "You're not the one who has to go on it."

"I know, but look—what's the worst that can happen?"

"Oh, I've been down that road. There are some pretty bad things." Earlier in the day, I'd thought about the possibility of me trying to kiss him, and him just backing away. Or him leaving halfway through the date to go to the bathroom and not coming back.

"Okay, well there is a very small chance any of those things will happen. And, to be honest, there is a very small chance you two will fall in love, or even want a second date with this guy. Most likely what will happen is you will have a conversation with a nice man over a glass of wine, and that's it."

"You're right."

"Of course, I'm right. Just go and have fun, or don't have fun."

What Camila said made sense. This was just a conversation with a guy. I had to put all of my fears aside. I was going to have to start dating eventually, so why not now? And even if he did leave halfway, I'd just pay the bill and go home. I probably would crawl into bed and not date again for another six months, but at least then I could tell people I'd tried.

I put on my shirt and finished my makeup. I glanced at myself in the mirror. I looked pretty good. I was going to do this—have a glass of wine with a guy.

I spun around to show Camila. "So, how do I look?"

"You look great!"

"Thanks. This is scary, but I'm strong. I can handle a glass of wine with a stranger."

"That's the attitude!"

I gave her hug, then put on my shoes, grabbed my keys, and we headed out the door.

"Have fun!" Camila shouted as she walked across the street back to her house.

I arrived for my date at 7:00 p.m. sharp. Tom was already at the bar. He looked just like his picture, so that was already one in the plus column. Luxe Lounge was packed and had a dark, cozy vibe. I was glad that Tom had chosen to sit at the bar, rather than at a table. Just drinks was way less pressure than drinks and dinner.

"Tom?" I asked, as I approached him.

"Beth!" He got up and gave me a hug.

I guess that was the answer to one of my questions. This date would start with a hug.

"How are you?" He still had his Australian accent, which was very sexy.

"I'm good. This place looks great. I've been wanting to try it since it opened. I'm a big fan of wine."

"Yeah, you mentioned that on your profile. A friend of mine recommended it," Tom said.

I sat down on the stool next to him. He seemed nice and pleasant. I took a deep breath. It's just a simple conversation over a glass of wine. I've got this.

The bartender came by and I ordered myself a zinfandel. Tom got a merlot.

"When I was in college, I would never have believed I'd be sitting at a wine bar, on a date, drinking this nice of wine," he said.

"I actually took a wine class in college," I said. "That's when I started to get into it."

"Really?" Tom said.

"Yeah, I signed up because I needed a few more credits, and it sounded like fun. I really enjoyed learning about all the grape varietals and the differences in the vineyards."

"Oh no, did I order the right wine? You're probably thinking I'm a fool."

I gave a little chuckle. This was going pretty well. Tom was cute and nice, and it was refreshing to talk to someone new. The knot in my stomach seemed to go away.

"Don't worry, I won't hold it against you," I said. Tom smiled.

The bartender brought us our drinks.

"Cheers," Tom said, as we clinked glasses. "I wasn't sophisticated enough for a wine class. I was in a fraternity, and we used to throw crazy parties with jungle juice. Man, I can't believe I used to get so drunk off that cheap stuff."

"Oh, yeah, the palate does change with age," I said.

I took a drink of my wine. The zinfandel was delightful, I could really taste the cherry and black pepper. It was probably one of the best ones I'd had in a while.

"Oh man, this one time, we threw a big toga party, and me and my buddy, Pete, drank so much, we decided to run around the party naked. Everyone was laughing. It was a hoot."

This was an odd story to tell so early in the date, but I guess talking about college was sort of an ice breaker.

"Were you in a sorority?" he asked.

"No, they didn't have many at my school."

I'd gone to a small liberal arts school, so Greek life hadn't been that big of a deal.

"Oh man, you missed out. My fraternity brothers and I are tight. It was really a bonding experience," Tom said.

I figured I needed to steer the conversation out of college and onto something else. We obviously didn't have the same Greek life experience, which seemed so important to Tom.

"That's really a nice thing to have. So, how do you like the finance world?"

Tom had mentioned over short message conversations that he was a financial consultant.

"I really like it. I travel a lot, but I get to go to some fun places. Just two weeks ago, I was in Switzerland. Went skiing in the Alps."

"Oh, that sounds awesome."

"You ever been?"

"No, but it's on my places to go."

"Switzerland is great, but Barcelona is by far my favorite. Right by the beach, and a great nightlife."

"How often do you travel?"

I was glad that the conversation had moved away from the college talk. I hadn't realized Tom was such a traveler. He wasn't one of those guys who'd put how many countries he had been to on his profile. I kind of liked that it wasn't something he felt the need to brag about. I didn't travel internationally much, but I did like hearing about other people's adventures. Chad and I always thought seeing America was adventurous enough while Zoe was young, and then, when she was older, we'd thought we might go abroad together. I guess that was just another plan that had disappeared. I tried not to think about it and focused on my date.

"Usually, two weeks out of the month I'm away," Tom said.

"That seems like a lot of time away. Do you ever just want to stay home?"

"Nah, I love it. I work hard, and then it's party time," he said, as he took a gulp of his wine, not really savoring the flavor. "I've been to bars all over the world. It's kind of fun. My coworkers and I get along, and we're always taking our clients out to the best places with the best drinks."

I started to realize why Tom was still single at thirty-five. He wanted to live the life of a party boy and never grow up.

Our date continued, and Tom talked more about work and told stories about traveling and drinking. I tried to keep the conversation going, politely asking questions. He didn't really ask any questions about me. This was not an ideal first date, but at least the wine was good. I wondered if most online dates went this way.

"Another round?" the bartender asked.

Tom looked at me. I wondered if he was having a good time, or if he could sense that *I* was having a *terrible* time. I glanced at my watch and realized it was only eight o'clock.

"Have anywhere to be?" he asked.

He'd put me on the spot, and I didn't really have a good reason to leave, although I wanted to go home and watch Netflix. I didn't want to hear any more stories about Tom drinking. But I didn't want to hurt his feelings, either, leaving the date after just an hour. Maybe he'd get better. Maybe we could move on to a different topic of conversation. Maybe he would start asking questions about me.

Before I could say anything, Tom said, "Another round," to the bartender, who came back with two more glasses of wine.

"So, you're divorced?" Tom asked.

I was stunned; it was finally a question about me. Not a great one, but still about me.

"Yeah, it was finalized in January. So, this is actually my first date."

"Really? I feel so honored," Tom said.

I smiled. Okay, the second glass was going to be better. I was convinced.

"And just the one kid?"

"Yeah, Zoe. She's great."

"I have two nieces. They're six and four. A handful, I don't know how my sister does it. I like hanging out with them for an hour, but, after that, I'm done."

"A lot of energy?" I asked. I knew how Zoe could be, bouncing off the walls at times.

"Something like that," Tom said. "I guess I'm not really a kid person."

I was so confused. If Tom wasn't a kid person, why had he even swiped right for me? He knew I had a kid. What was the point of this date?

"So, after these drinks, do you want to go back to my place?"

I almost spit out my wine. Was he serious? What made him think that I wanted to sleep with him after this terrible date?

I put my glass down. "I don't think so. Actually, I have to do a long run tomorrow morning. I should go."

I was about to take out my wallet and pay, but then Tom said, "Don't worry, I'm sure I can get that girl to go home with me." He nodded at a blond girl sitting at the bar, looking at her phone.

I left in disgust and headed to the parking garage. On the drive home, I replayed the date. Parts of it had been fine. Tom had seemed like a normal guy, and I did enjoy talking to him…a little. But, mostly, he was pretty awful, talking about getting drunk and then, out of nowhere, asking me to go home with him. Did he think that, because of his sexy Australian accent, girls would just flock to him? Ugh, men were seriously the worst. Was this what was out there?

When I got home, I saw Camila and Sebastian sitting on their porch, enjoying the nice night.

"How did it go?"

"Were you waiting up for me?" I asked.

"Maybe," she grinned. "So?"

"Tom and I are *not* a match. I had two very nice glasses of wine while listening to a man talk about all the places he'd traveled to and got drunk. Though I did get offered sex. When I said no, he told me he'd hit up some other girl."

"Ugh, sounds awful, but yay about the sex, at least you know it's out there. Want a glass of wine?" she asked.

"Thanks, I think I'm going to call it a day."

I walked to the front door, and Twix ran inside, where I fed her and collapsed on the couch. The date had been a definite dud, but, on the plus side, at least I hadn't gotten rejected. I guess it couldn't hurt to see where another date took me. I got out my phone, opened Here Comes Love, and started swiping.

-9-

MARCH

It was a busy day at work. I had back-to-back meetings until 2:00 p.m. with just a short break for lunch. I knew I had to leave early to pick up Zoe, so I hustled around trying to get everything done before 4:00. I'd have some work to do when she went to bed. There was a meeting with an important client next week, and my team was working hard to get everything ready in time.

After my 2:00 meeting, which ran long, I got back to my desk and found a text from Chad.

Chad: *Hey, do you have a minute to talk?*

My heart sank. Chad never texted me in the middle of the day. Was Zoe okay? Had the school called? I looked at my missed calls and didn't see anything from the school, and no emails. After my mini freak-out, I wondered what he wanted. There were still thirty unread emails in my work inbox that needed my attention, but I figured I wouldn't be able to concentrate anyway, knowing that Chad "needed to talk."

Sure. I'm free now, I texted back.

The phone rang right away, and I picked up.

"Hey, what's up. Everything okay?" I asked.

"Yeah, I just wanted to touch base about something."

He kind of paused, the same pause he'd made when he told me he was leaving me for another woman. I wasn't sure what was so important that he had to call, and not email, and I started to worry.

"Okay."

He took a deep breath, and then out it came. "I just wanted to tell you, in case you had heard it from somebody else, or on social media, but Courtney and I are getting married."

Shocked again. I felt my stomach turn to knots. We had been divorced for less than three months, we hadn't even been separated an entire year, and now he was marrying his mistress? It was a new blow. I didn't understand why he needed to get remarried so badly. What was the rush?

I just stayed silent. I didn't know what to say. I started to feel sick to my stomach.

"The wedding is in August. Zoe and Willow are going to be flower girls," he continued.

It felt like someone had kicked me in the stomach. August! Like, August of *this* year? That was six months away. A year and change after he'd left me. I knew that they had been together for three years before that, but it all felt so soon, so sudden. My heart beat faster, and my face flamed. I shoved my fingers onto my temples and rubbed.

"Beth?" Chad said.

I realized I had stopped listening. Was he giving more details about the wedding, or was he waiting for me to say something? What did he want, for me to give him my blessing? Not that it would have mattered, he was getting married anyway. Married. I just couldn't believe it. I wanted to vomit.

"Okay," I said. There was a big lump in my throat, and I was holding back tears. I wanted to get off this phone call quickly so I could burst into tears without Chad on the line.

"Okay. I just felt like I should tell you."

"All right, I have to go."

I hung up the phone before he could get another word in. I shut the door, sank down in my chair, and let the tears start to flow. Marriage was permanent. Marriage wasn't a mid-life crisis. Marriage was something that he expected would last. Moving in with his paramour was bad enough, but marriage was official. Marriage was saying that their story was a true love story, that, although people had been hurt, it was worth it, because they were in love, and they were destined to be together. Chad and Courtney didn't need to get married, and they didn't need to rush. It was like they wanted to sink their claws into each other and really lock it down. Like they needed to prove something. I guess when your relationship starts with each of you having affairs, there is a level of trust that is broken. Maybe marriage was a way for them to seal that trust.

I stared at my reflection in the window. My makeup was smeared all over my face. I hadn't cried like this since July, when Chad told me he was leaving. The past few months I'd felt like I was making some progress in my healing. I was starting to feel better about this situation, but now I just felt like crap. All of the old feelings of not being enough, like I wasn't worth it, were coming back.

I checked my inbox and there were now forty unread emails that were definitely not going to get read until later today. I texted Kelly instead.

Me: *CHAD IS GETTING MARRIED*
Kelly: *WHAT???*

Me: *Is it too early for a drink?*
Kelly: *I think a half glass is okay.*

Kelly met me down in the lobby and pulled me into a hug.

"I'm sorry, Beth. You don't deserve this."

I felt like those words had been on repeat from everyone I knew for the past nine months. I was getting sick of people feeling sorry for me, but, more importantly, I was getting tired of Chad hurting me. Of making me cry, of making me feel bad about myself.

We headed to a bar down the street. It was a popular spot for office happy hours, and the bartenders there knew us pretty well. On Fridays, Kelly and I would sometimes go for a quick drink before heading home. We sat at the bar, and Kyle, the bartender, poured me a half glass of their house cabernet.

"Nothing for me," Kelly said.

I gave her a puzzled look. She was usually one to join me for a glass of wine, if needed.

Kelly stared back, and started to smile, looking almost giddy.

"Um…" She bit her lower lip. "It's early, and I haven't told anyone, but I'm pregnant."

"What!" I nearly jumped out of my seat and threw my arms around her. "That's so exciting! How far? Oh, my, I'm speechless."

"Nine weeks. Derek and I are really excited, but it's still too early to tell people."

"I am so happy for you two."

And I was. I really was happy for Derek and Kelly. They'd been having a hard time getting pregnant, and I knew that they really wanted this. Kelly swooned at any baby she saw and joked how her ovaries would flutter anytime anybody even said the word "baby."

"You two will be great parents."

"Thanks, Beth."

"Well, here's to you," I said as I took a sip of wine.

It was nice for Kelly to have something good happen. I was glad to know that her life was going in the direction she wanted, even though my life felt like it was in shambles.

"So, Chad and Courtney, tying the knot?" she asked, changing the subject with a cringe.

Tears immediately formed at the corner of my eyes. "I just don't get it. Why do they have to get married?"

Kelly put her arm on my shoulder and said, "Because they are selfish and insecure."

"Maybe." I shrugged.

"Maybe? Definitely."

"Maybe their love is true, and they want to share it with the world. Maybe they were destined to be together."

"No love that is true started with an affair on both ends. You know that, right?"

I stared down at my glass. I wanted to believe Kelly. But in the back of my mind, I kept thinking, maybe Chad and Courtney were meant to be together. Maybe Courtney was everything that Chad wanted, and I was nothing.

"I'm sure that's not true in all cases."

"It's true in this case."

I wiped the corners of my eyes.

"I just feel so defeated. Them getting married, it's really a hard pill to swallow. We were married for ten years, and now he's marrying someone else, and so quickly. Like our entire relationship meant nothing."

I put my hands on my head and took a deep breath.

Here I was, drowning my sorrows again. Letting Chad and

Courtney's actions affect the way I felt. How much more damage could Chad do to me? Kelly was right. I wanted to go back to the way I'd felt on top of Mt. Mitchell. How I'd felt like I was strong and could accomplish anything.

But all I felt now was sad and pathetic. Chad didn't want to be with me. He wanted to spend the rest of his life with Courtney. All of the dreams we'd shared for the future were now officially over—I had to find new dreams, a new me, but Chad and Courtney were starting a life together. They weren't going to break up. They were going to legally bind themselves together.

"I'm sorry, Beth. I know this is hard, and shocking. But remember when you were climbing that mountain and how good you felt? You've come so far, and you should be proud of that. You're an amazing person, and you deserve better."

I tried to force a little smile.

"Thanks. And thanks for letting me vent."

"That's what I'm here for," she said.

I went to pay Kyle. "This one is on me," he said. "I can't believe that jerk is getting remarried so soon."

"Thanks, Kyle," I said.

Before heading home, I went to the bathroom and looked at myself in the mirror—tears were rolling down my face...again. This year had been the worst, and every time I felt like I was moving forward, another setback knocked me down. I took a deep breath and splashed water on my face and headed toward my car.

I had texted the girls about Chad as soon as I got home. Twenty minutes later there was a knock on my door, and it was Rachel and Avery.

"We are going out," Rachel declared. "Avery will watch Zoe."

"I just got home," I protested.

"Camila is working at La Caverna tonight, and Jennifer said she'd meet us once Michael gets home."

"Can't I get in the door? I haven't even fed Zoe." I asked.

"Zoe, do you want Avery to cook you her famous mac and cheese?" Rachel yelled in the door.

Zoe ran down the stairs in excitement. "Yes! It's my favorite."

Zoe grabbed Avery's hand and led her into the kitchen.

"Okay, it's settled. Grab your purse," Rachel said.

I gave Zoe a kiss goodbye and told her I'd be home later.

We got to La Caverna, and Camila already had two glasses of Sangria poured.

"You all don't have to do this, I'm fine." I explained.

"We know," Camila said.

"But we just didn't want you to be alone," Rachel added.

"Thanks." I said. "I think I'm still in shock."

"Understandable. I can't believe he's getting married. When I told Travis, he nearly spit out his wine," Rachel added.

"Kelly and I went for a glass of wine, and I could barely hold it together, and now I'm just so angry that his actions keep affecting me like this. I want to feel strong, not sad."

"You should feel strong," Camila declared.

"You are Beth-Fucking-Bradley," Rachel added. "You can do anything."

Just then Jennifer came bouncing into the door and plopped onto the stool next to me.

"What'd I miss?" she blurted.

"We were just going on about how awesome Beth is," Rachel gushed.

"Oh, I like this game," Jennifer said with a smile.

I smiled back at her.

"What, it's true, Beth." Jennifer continued. "You are still kicking ass." She explained.

"Definitely," Camila added. "It's only been two months since your divorce has been final, and you're starting this new life for yourself. It's very admirable."

Just then an idea dawned on me. "I should have a party."

"A party? Like a Fuck Chad party? I'd definitely be down with that," Camila said, bringing us a plate of manchego cheese.

"No, Chad doesn't deserve to be talked about anymore. I'm done wasting my time on him and what he did to me."

"Okay, then, what kind of party?" Rachel questioned.

"I don't know, like a celebration of the new me. This new chapter in my life. How I'm going to move forward."

"That's brilliant! I can cater," Camila said.

"No, no, no," I said waving my hands. "You already do too much for me. I couldn't ask you to do that."

"I want to."

"I want you to have fun at my party! I want you to celebrate with me, and I want to celebrate my friends as well. And all you have done for me. I truly am grateful for all of you. All of my friends, really. I know that I've been a bit of the center of attention lately."

"You're going through some pretty life changing stuff." Jennifer said.

"I know. And I seriously don't know what I'd do if I couldn't just walk to any of your houses and just unload."

"So, this party. I love the idea. If I can't cater, at least let me bring dessert" Camila said.

"Deal."

I started thinking more about this party, and what I wanted it to represent. I wanted to focus on my accomplishments these last nine months, and the things I had learned about myself. I wanted it to be about the strong person I had come. The warrior that was inside me this entire time.

"I think I'm going to make it like a 2.0 party. Beth Bradley 2.0, the new and improved version of me," I said.

"To Beth Bradley 2.0," Jennifer said, as we all clinked our glasses together.

I was getting really excited about this idea. I needed a project, something to look forward to, and it would be amazing to do something for my friends at the same time.

Online dating had proven to be extremely difficult. I had realized that "matches" fit into a variety of categories. The first category were the immediate ghosters. You would match on the app, and I would send a quick hello, nothing too crazy. But they would never respond. I imagined these guys played the numbers game and just swiped right on everyone, waiting to see who actually responded.

The second category included the pen pals. You would have long conversations through the application. Every day, they would ask you questions about your life and your day, but they never made a move or asked to meet in person. I currently had three of these types of conversations going. And, like clockwork, they would all message me every morning, asking if I had a big day planned, or comment on the weather and ask if I would be getting outside. These conversations had lasted at least two weeks without an in-person meet up. It wasn't even because our schedules didn't align…they just never asked. I wasn't sure if they were waiting for *me* to ask, but I figured, if *they* did, I might as well say yes, so I kept the conversation going just in case.

The last category was the psych guys. They would message you, and you'd finally lock down a time for a date, and then, right before the date, they'd say, "Psych!" and unmatch with you. Those guys were the worst. Two weeks ago, I was talking with a guy, and we had planned to go out on a Wednesday evening. I was actually looking forward to it. Our online banter was playful, and he was definitely attractive, at least according to his pictures. We hadn't decided where and what time we were going to meet up. On Wednesday morning, I messaged him, saying I was looking forward to hanging out and was wondering about the details. An hour later he un-matched me. I was really confused but tried not to take it personally.

Overall, the process was exhausting. So much swiping, so much texting back and forth, and nothing to show for it.

I finally nailed down a date with a guy named Justin. He was thirty-eight and also recently single. It seemed like we had a lot in common, as he was also a runner. I had mentioned my upcoming half marathon, and he shared a story about one of his best runs. After my date with Tom, I realized you couldn't judge anyone from a brief online profile and conversation. I was going in with very low expectations, but something about Justin seemed like it was going to be better. At least I knew Justin liked kids, since he had two. He lived a half hour north of me, so we decided to meet in the middle, at a Mexican restaurant, for drinks. I put on my "date night" jeans and a green tank top. I glanced at myself in the mirror and smiled. Man, I looked good. I snapped a picture and then texted Camila, Jennifer, and Rachel.

Me: *Ready for date number 2*
Camila: *Good luck!*

Jennifer: *Hope it goes well.*

Rachel: *If he's hot and asks for sex, just say yes, then at least you'll get laid.*

Justin was already waiting for me at the bar, which was a good sign.

"Justin?" I asked.

He turned around and smiled. He was much cuter than his picture. He had dark brown hair, bright green eyes, and an inviting smile.

"Beth?" He got up and gave me a hug.

Justin was extremely attractive—I probably wouldn't say yes to sex, but maybe I'd make out with him a little. I was in desperate need of physical connection. I was really starting to miss it. I knew I wasn't ready to have sex with someone else, but I really wanted to feel a warm embrace from someone who wasn't just a friend. I missed the feeling of someone's lips on mine, their softness, and the tingling feeling I got. If this date went well, maybe Justin could be a viable candidate for a little lip locking.

I sat down next to him.

"So, how are you?" I asked.

"Glad it's Friday," he said.

"Me too. How was your week?"

Justin shifted in his seat. "Ugh, like all the other weeks. Working in an IT department is exhausting."

"I bet. Lots of issues?"

"You don't realize how stupid people can be with computers. This one old lady asks me the same question once a month. I have to walk her through fixing the issue all the time. I don't know how to get it through her thick skull. She can't handle the technology, but I'm not her personal IT guy. I've got other things to do."

I was stunned. Justin's tone was so sharp and mean. But I tried to cut him some slack. Everyone had hard weeks, and I knew what it was like to have people pulling you in every direction. I also knew how hard the IT people worked at Market Insight. Just last week, I'd needed someone to help me because my email wasn't working. It was the worst possible time. I had a big report that was due later that day. The IT guy had to download a lot of new software to get it working again, and I lost three hours of my day, but I'd been patient, knowing that I had no idea how to fix it, but magically he could.

"Sounds frustrating," I said, trying to sound sympathetic. "How long have you been doing IT?"

"About ten years."

"That's a long time. Do you like it?"

"Not really. I studied computer science in college and was hoping to do something else, like develop a new app, but I couldn't get anything off the ground. I needed money, so I took this job, but it's just not satisfying."

I kind of felt bad for Justin because your job was so much of your day. I couldn't imagine being that unhappy for ten years. Though, maybe he was just having one of those weeks. I thought about changing the subject. Talking about work seemed to be putting him in a foul mood.

The bartender came by and we ordered drinks. I thought that would be a good time to change the subject. Since Justin and I were both runners, I figured getting on some common ground couldn't hurt. In our brief online messages, he'd mentioned that he preferred trail runs to running on the pavement, since it was better for the knees.

"So, have you found any new trails to run on?" I asked.

"Not really," Justin said.

"What's your favorite one? It might be nice to mix it up," I said.

Justin looked down and checked his phone. His eyebrows lowered and pulled closer together before he slammed his phone face down on the bar.

"I'm sorry, just got a text from the dreaded ex," he said.

The bartender brought out drinks, and I took a swig of my margarita.

"What was it you asked me?" he said.

"Oh, I was just wondering what your favorite trail to run was. My friend and I run around the neighborhood a lot, and we're looking for new places to go."

Justin took a sip of his drink. "Oh, I usually run Blue Diamond River on the weekends. It's a eight-mile loop that's pretty challenging. But definitely worth it. There's a great view of the Potomac River about four miles in. Last week, I finished in just under an hour. It was my personal best, and I felt amazing afterward."

"Sounds cool. I'll have to check it out."

"Don't feel bad if you don't run the whole way and have to walk a bit the first time. It's pretty steep."

"Well, I'm pretty strong," I said flexing my muscles and giving him a playful smile.

Justin smiled back at me. He had a nice smile. But then his phone buzzed. He picked it up again, and his face turned completely sour.

"Ugh, bitch," he said under his breath.

Excuse me? I couldn't believe he'd just called his ex-wife a bitch only thirty minutes into our date. I wondered what she was like, what she was doing that was so terrible that he couldn't focus on our date.

Chad and I got into a lot of arguments over text message. Just last week, he'd sent Zoe to school with a huge bag of gummy bears and chips in her lunch. He also packed an apple and a sandwich, but she didn't eat any of *that*. I tried to play it cool and explain that you can't give a six-year-old an extra-large bag of gummy bears; that just giving her one or two would have been better. He mentioned the apple and sandwich, but when I told him she didn't eat it, he said I had no right to tell him how to pack her lunch. I was furious that he just couldn't see the compromise—it was his way or the highway. He cared more about getting his way than helping Zoe make good nutritional choices and setting boundaries. All he saw was me being controlling. But, still, if I was on a date, I would have saved that conversation for another time.

"I'm sorry. It's just my ex-wife is being ridiculous," he said, rubbing his hands through his hair.

"It's no problem. I know how that goes."

"I asked if I could have the kids tomorrow so I could take them to the Nationals game, but she keeps insisting we keep to the schedule. She says this is her weekend, and I can see them next weekend. All I want to do is hang out with my kids, but she's being unreasonable."

"Well, could you take them to the game next weekend? They're still going to be at home," I asked.

"Yeah, but I wanted to go tomorrow. My son is a huge fan of Max Flick, and he's pitching tomorrow," he said.

I understood about the downfalls of shared custody. There were so many times I wanted to do something with Zoe, but it was her time to be with Chad. If there was something really important, like Julian's birthday party, Chad would adjust the schedule. But, a lot of times, I had to just find a workaround. I sympathized with Justin, but, at the same time, the season had just started two days ago, and Max Flick would certainly be pitching at home at least twenty times this year, if not more. I was sure he could find another time to go with his son. It felt like Justin just wanted what he wanted, when he wanted it.

"One of the downfalls of divorce." I shrugged my shoulders.

"I don't see why we have to be so rigid," Justin said.

"I guess it's just to be consistent. It helps the kids and makes things fair," I said.

I wasn't necessarily taking Justin's ex's side. I just knew that the rules were there for a reason. I hoped to change the conversation again. Work and family were both apparently triggers for Justin. I wanted to get back to running, or maybe we could even talk about baseball, since he'd had brought up the game.

I twisted my glass in my hands. This was not going well. Was this going to be how it was? I wait three weeks to finally find a time to go on a date, and the guy turns out to be a total jerk?

"She's just being a bitch. It's not like she had something planned with them."

That was the second time he had called his ex-wife a bitch. I wasn't one of his buddies that he could complain to. We were on a date. I would never call Chad terrible names on a date, especially not a first date.

The bartender asked if we wanted another round. I took a look at my watch. I didn't want to be on this date anymore. This guy was just in a bad mood, and I wasn't having a good time at all. It was only 7:30, so I couldn't say it was getting late. I needed an excuse.

"I should go. I told a friend I'd meet her for drinks later."

"Whatever," Justin said. Then to the bartender he said, "We're good, and we'll take separate checks."

I handed the bartender my credit card and gulped down the

rest of my margarita. Justin was still on his phone, looking pissed off. I thought about saying goodbye, but instead I just left.

I felt so defeated. Another bad date. I was zero for two. Dating in your late thirties was so hard. It was hard enough getting to the meet-in-person stage, but when I did get there, it was a bust. All I was looking for was a decent conversation, but Tom was stuck in college and Justin had a chip on his shoulder.

The night was still early, and I didn't want to waste a night out, so I walked around a little bit and stumbled into a sports bar to watch the Nationals game.

I sat at the bar and ordered a beer. The Nationals were playing the Phillies, and they were up 3-2. It was only the fifth inning, so there was still half a game to watch. I figured I'd settle in for the remainder of the game before heading home. I asked the bartender for a menu. I was deciding between the burger or the tacos when someone came up behind me.

"Excuse me, is this seat taken?" a familiar man's voice said. I turned around and was surprised to see Sean.

"Sean! What are you doing here?" I asked, excited to see him. "Please sit down." I patted the stool next to me.

"I live right around the corner. I figured I'd stop in for a beer and baseball," he said, sitting on stool next to me. "The more important question is, what are *you* doing here?"

"Just left a bad date. We were over at Picante's. But the guy was a dud. I didn't want to go home, so I guess I'm also here for a beer and some baseball."

The bartender came by.

"Hey, Sean. The usual?" he said.

"Sure thing, Randy," Sean said.

Shortly after, a waitress came by with his beer.

"Hi, Sean," she said.

"Hey, Kaitlin. How's it going?"

"You know, same old," she said.

"So, do you know everyone here?" I asked.

I wasn't surprised to see that Sean was friends with the entire staff. Sean was friends with everyone.

Sean chuckled. "Well, you could say I come here a lot."

"A lot! That's an understatement," Randy said.

"Okay, maybe once or twice a week. This place has the best hamburgers."

"Good to know. I was trying to decide between that and the tacos."

"Definitely get the burger, it's the best in town. So, why was this a bad date?" he asked.

"Ugh, the guy was bent out of shape about everything. I came up with an excuse to leave, and he asked to split the check."

"Rough."

"Well, to being single," I said as we clinked our beers.

"To being single," Sean said, with his signature infectious smile.

Sean and I sat at the bar, watching baseball and drinking beers.

"So, is Zoe with Chad this weekend?" Sean asked.

Under the bar, my knee gently brushed up against Sean's knee, and I felt a little tingle inside of me.

"Yeah. Is Aiden at his mom's?" I asked.

"Yep. I try to stay super busy when he's gone, just to pass the time."

"I know what you mean," I said.

The bartender asked us if we wanted another round. Sean and I both got another beer as the waitress dropped off our burgers.

"So, what are your plans this weekend?" he asked.

"The usual. Cleaning the house, mowing the lawn, grocery shopping. Brunch with friends. Nothing too exciting."

"A lot on your plate," he said, taking a bite of his burger.

"Plus, I've got to get in a long run," I added.

"How long?" Sean asked.

"Ten miles. I'm training for a half marathon."

"A half marathon! Wow. I didn't know you ran those," Sean said excitedly.

"It's my first one," I said. "Jennifer convinced me to do it. It's at the end April."

"You truly are incredible," he said. "Doing it all, raising a daughter, working hard, doing yard work, and still finding time to run ten miles. I'm impressed."

I smiled. A feeling of warmth radiated within me. Sean was such an encouraging person, and I felt giddy whenever he complimented me. It felt genuine, like he really thought I was this amazing person. He wasn't just saying it to make me feel better. He believed it, and he believed in me.

Sean and I continued talking and watching the game. The Nationals ended up winning 4-2.

"Good game," I finally said. "I better get going home. I'm really glad I ran into you."

"Me, too. I'm sorry your date sucked, but hopefully the night was salvaged."

"It was more than salvaged. Good company, and the Nats won. What more could a girl want?" I asked with a smile.

"I'll walk you to your car," Sean said.

"You don't have to."

"No, I insist."

When we got to my car, Sean hugged me. It felt good being in his arms.

"Drive safely," he said with a wink.

The next day I met the girls for brunch at Backyard Bistro. We were sipping on mimosas as I told them about my terrible date.

"Ugh, he sounds horrible," Jennifer said.

"What did you end up doing with the rest of your night?" Camila asked.

"I went to a sports bar and watched the Nationals game. But guess who I ran into?" I teased.

"Who?" they all replied in unison.

"Sean."

Rachel almost spit out her mimosa. "It's fate!" she replied.

I think she was more excited than I was.

"We had a good time watching the game together," I replied. "He's a lot of fun." I could feel my face getting red.

"I think you have a crush," Camila said, winking.

"Maybe. Hanging out with him was a lot better than my date. But he's just a nice guy." I finished my mimosa and motioned to the waiter for another one. "Ugh, I don't want to continue online dating. It's so much work. Finding a decent person to talk to over a glass of wine is like finding a needle in a haystack."

"Well, you know what they say…you've got to kiss a lot of frogs," Jennifer said.

"I don't want to kiss frogs, and I don't even want a prince. I just want to have a normal conversation with someone and maybe make out with them. It took a lot to put myself out there, and it's not feeling worth it." I sighed deeply.

"It's just been two dates. Maybe the third one will be better," Camila said.

"Or maybe he'll just be crazy. And that's if I even find someone to have a third date with. You wouldn't believe the type of people on this app. Two days ago, I got my first an unsolicited dick pic."

"What!" Jennifer said.

"I want to see," said Rachel.

"Yeah, I was just texting this guy, Sam. And then, before I knew it, he sent me a selfie of himself in the mirror, completely naked."

"Oh my! Did he look hot? How was his penis? OMG, do you still have it?" Rachel squealed, barely able to keep it together.

"At first, I was so surprised! I was in total shock. But then I gave it a longer look. The guy did have a nice body and well-defined ab muscles, but still. Who does that? I ended up blocking him," I gave Rachel a pointed look. "So, no, I don't still have the dick pic."

"Don't give up. Sure, there are going to be some weirdos out there, but at least you have good stories at brunch. The best I can talk about is how Michael and I thought about having sex last night, but then we both fell asleep," Jennifer said.

"Yes, Beth. We need more stories. They're keeping our brunches exciting," Camila said.

Easy for them to say. They didn't have to go through with the dates. They just got to live vicariously through me, laughing at my horrible experiences. They weren't the one summoning up enough courage to put themselves out there, just to find out the guy was a jerk. They weren't the one who had to figure out how to navigate dating as a single mom. They weren't the one whose heart was completely broken and didn't even want to be in this position.

My phone buzzed, and I saw I had a text from Noah.

Noah: *Hey, are you home? I have something for Zoe.*
Me: *Just finishing up brunch, will be home in twenty minutes.*
   Stop by then.

We wrapped up brunch, and I headed home. A few minutes later, Noah showed up with an art easel.

"I saw someone was giving this away. I know you mentioned that Zoe had wanted an easel, so I cleaned it up for you. It should be in good shape. I also brought Zoe some chalk."

The art easel had been freshly painted, and he'd even put Zoe's name at the top. There were two sides, one with a chalkboard, and one with a clip for paper. Noah had obviously put a lot of effort into restoring this. Zoe would be ecstatic.

"Thanks, Noah. That's really sweet. She'll love it." I said, giving him a hug.

"So, what did you do last night? Hot date?" Noah said.

I think it was in jest. I hadn't told him that I was dating again.

"Don't even ask," I said as I rolled my eyes.

"Oh really? I didn't know you were dating."

"The girls made me sign up for one of those apps. It's resulted in some bad dates and a picture of a naked guy. I'm not sure if I'll continue."

"Give it some time."

"Why, because it's been so successful for you?"

"You definitely don't want to take dating advice from me. I have no idea what I'm doing." Noah laughed.

I knew he'd done a little online dating at first but didn't like it because he'd had about the same luck as me. He'd also let his friends set him up a few times. He'd dated this girl for a few months, but then she decided to get back together with her boyfriend. Noah took it as a sign and decided to hold off on dating for a while longer.

Noah left, and I went ahead with my normal weekend chores. By the end of the day, I was beat, but I was still curious about what was out there on Here Comes Love. I opened the app and kept scrolling for another match, or at the very least another interesting story for our next brunch.

-10-

April

finally found a time to meet up with my latest match, Daniel, a forty-two-year-old software engineer. As I got ready for my date, I felt even less excited than I had with Justin and Tom. I was convinced that I'd never find someone who lasted more than one drink, someone who wasn't a disaster and that I could have a pleasant conversation with, or someone who could help me feel that I was worth it again. I had been on the app for six weeks now, and everyone had been a dud. Why should Daniel be any different? But I still had a little hope. There was a little piece of me, deep down, that still wanted to see if maybe this would work. I wasn't completely defeated yet.

We decided to meet for drinks at Uncorked, one of my favorite wine bars. I arrived five minutes early, and Daniel wasn't there yet, so I sat at the bar and ordered a glass of wine. The bartender brought me my drink as Daniel arrived.

"Beth?" he said.

"Yep." I got up and gave him a hug.

The first thing I noticed was how good Daniel smelled. His cologne was almost heavenly. He was also extremely tall—he had to be well over six-two, and I went up on my tippy-toes to hug him.

"I'm so sorry I'm late," he said. "I'm usually on time, but my daughter realized that she forgot her stuffed pig at my house, and I had to take it to her or else bedtime would have been a disaster."

"Oh, I totally understand," I said as he sat down on the stool next to me. "If my daughter left her monkey at my house, it would be all hell."

Daniel gave me a sweet smile, and his eyes crinkled.

"What are you drinking?" he asked.

"I went with the house merlot," I said, taking a sip.

"Any good?" he asked.

"Yeah, one of my favorites," I said.

Daniel motioned to the bartender for another one for him. The bartender brought his glass right away.

"Cheers," he said as we clinked glasses. "Oh, wow, this *is* good. You were right."

"Well, I got into wine in college," I said.

All of a sudden, I had déjà vu. This was exactly how my date with Tom had started out. I hoped that wasn't a bad sign.

"Really? Tell me about that?" he said.

Daniel looked right at me as I told him about the wine taking class I took in college. He asked a lot of questions, as he continued to make eye contact. It was a nice and pleasant conversation, exactly what I'd wanted. But I was still not getting my hopes up. We hadn't finished our first glass of wine. There was still time for Daniel to fail.

"So, are you going to teach your daughter about wine?" he asked.

"Well, not now." I laughed. "She's only six. But I did hear about a place you can go pick grapes and then make your own grape juice, so I might do that with her."

"Sounds fun," Daniel said.

We continued talking about our kids. Daniel had two, a boy and girl. The girl was four and the boy was seven, so close in age to Zoe. He told me about how hard his divorce had been for his kids. He and his ex-wife had split up two years ago. No matter which house she was in, his daughter had missed the other parent terribly, and would cry, while his son had been convinced that they'd split up because he didn't clean his room when he was asked.

"I'm sorry. That must have been really hard," I said.

"It was, but we got through it," Daniel said. "Now we're a well oil-machined. The kids are used to going back and forth. We call each other every night so we can say goodnight, and my daughter even made me a bracelet, so I don't forget her."

Daniel held up his sleeve and showed me a purple and pink beaded bracelet. "I told her I would never take it off."

My heart swooned at the sentiment. Daniel was clearly an extremely caring person, and he loved his kids. He was not like Tom or Justin. This was what I'd wanted all along: a pleasant conversation over a glass of wine with a good-looking guy.

The bartender came by and asked if we wanted another round. I looked at my watch and realized that Daniel and I had been talking for an hour and half. It had gone by so quickly, but I didn't want it to end.

"I'm game if you are?" he said, smiling.

"Sounds good." I stared into his green eyes. My heart started beating just a little faster.

The bartender brought us our drinks.

"So, how long have you been in the area?" I asked.

"I came after college, when my now ex-wife got a job with the government. It was easy enough for me to find work here."

"Where did you go to college?"

"I'm a proud Wisconsin Badger," he said.

"Oh no!" I said.

"What?" he said. "Is that bad?"

"I'm from Nebraska. Go Huskers!"

Daniel put his hand on my shoulder and looked me straight in the eye. "I'm sorry about that game last December."

"It was the worst! We were up by fourteen points, and we blew our chances for a good bowl game," I whined.

"Well, the Badgers are just better."

I gave him a nudge. "We'll get you this year."

Daniel tipped his head and smiled thoughtfully. "Wow, smart, beautiful, *and* a football fan. I think I just hit the jackpot."

My face flushed. Staring at Daniel, a feeling came over me. I wanted to kiss him…really badly. But I didn't know how to make a move. This date was going really well, and it seemed Daniel agreed.

I turned so that our knees were touching. He put his hand on my knee. The warmth spread through my body.

The bartender came by and asked if we wanted another. I looked at my watch again and saw it was already ten o'clock. I needed to get back, since Avery was watching Zoe.

"I would love to, but I need to go free the babysitter," I said.

"Not a problem. We'll take the check," he told the bartender.

Daniel paid the bill, and we walked out of the bar. I was worried that I'd ruined the moment. That Daniel would think I wasn't interested. When we were staring at each other, was there a sign I was supposed to make to indicate I wanted him to kiss me? Why hadn't he kissed me in there? Was it bad that I said I had to go? He seemed to understand, but, still, I was afraid I'd blown it. I finally had a date that I liked and, somehow, I messed it up.

We stood outside the bar for just a bit.

"I had a nice time," I said. I gave him a smile and then bit my upper lip.

"Me too," he said, his gaze drifting briefly to my mouth.

I just stood there, waiting for him to make a move. It felt like forever—why wasn't he going to kiss me?

I snapped out of it and dug into my purse to grab my keys. "Well, I'm parked over there," I said, motioning to my left, trying not to show my disappointment.

But, before I could move, Daniel pulled me toward him and kissed me. I felt like I was going to melt in his arms. My heart pounded in my chest so hard, I was sure he could hear it. His scent was intoxicating. I didn't want the kiss to end.

When we did pull apart, I got off my tippy-toes and looked at him.

He brushed a hair back behind my ear, and smiled, his eyes crinkling again. "Can I walk you to your car?" he asked.

He put out his arm, and I took it. We walked down the street toward my car in silence. I was grinning from ear to ear. This would be a good story for the girls, and finally one that had ended well.

When we got to my car, Daniel kissed me again and opened my door for me. I got in, and he gave me another kiss on my lips.

"Have a good night," he said.

"You, too," I said back.

He closed the door and walked away. I just sat there for a minute, waiting for my heart to stop beating so hard.

The following weekend was my half marathon. The night before, I'd swooned over Daniel as I carbo-loaded with the girls on homemade pasta with veal and pork meat sauce at Camila's house.

"I'm really glad you got a little make-out session in," Rachel said. "You definitely deserved it."

"Man, it was so great," I said. "Daniel is an amazing kisser."

"You look happy. I'm glad," said Camila. "Like, there's a brightness in your eyes that hasn't been there for a while."

"I *feel* happy," I said. All week Daniel and I had been texting back and forth. We were still trying to find a time to meet up again. Just the buzz of my phone, and seeing a text from him, made my heart skip. But I was afraid that I was rushing into things. I was still fragile and didn't want to get hurt. I was trying to just take it one step at a time. "But I can't think about Daniel now. I've got to focus on my race."

"We are going to own those thirteen miles," Jennifer said, as she shoved some more pasta in her face.

We wrapped up dinner, and I headed home. I didn't think I'd be able to sleep, since I was nervous for the race, but, as soon as my head hit the pillow, I was out like a light.

The morning of the half marathon, my alarm buzzed at 6:00 a.m. I already had two texts one from Jennifer saying she'd by in twenty minutes, and another from Noah wishing me good luck. I put on my running shorts and tank top and washed my face. I took a look in the mirror and said, "Let's do this." I wasn't trying to get a good time or anything; I just wanted to finish the race. Thirteen miles was a long way to run, but it was possible. I was proud of myself for coming all this way. Back in October, the thought of running a half marathon had seemed daunting—I hadn't thought I could do it. But Jennifer and I had worked hard to get to this point.

When we got to the starting line, I was surprised to see how many people were there. Everyone around us seemed to have their own little routine. Some people were stretching, others were jogging in place. Two girls walk past me with pink tutus and ribbons in their hair. They were smiling and laughing, like running 13 miles was just another Saturday to them.

The first five miles were pretty solid. Being with the other runners was inspiring. All of these people together, just running. It was a sense of community with people who I'd never met, bonded by the fact that we were going to run these thirteen miles together. The people along the sidelines of the race, cheering us on, gave me power. I had no idea who these people were, yet their support lifted me. Jennifer and I were in sync. The breath-in, breath-out tempo mimicked our stride. I felt strong. We were on pace for nine-minute miles, but I knew we still had a lot of the race left. I didn't want to tire myself out. This was, by far, the fastest we had ever run.

We hit mile six, also known as Heartbreak Hill. It had a steep incline, and a lot of other runners had already started walking, but I knew that Jennifer and I could do it. "We can do this. We are strong," we kept telling ourselves as we powered through. We made it up the hill, but it slowed down our pace a bit. Even so, we were still doing our best.

By mile eight, I felt euphoric and empowered. We were halfway done. I'd already gotten this far. Bring on the next half.

By mile ten, I hit a wall, and I felt like I was running through Jell-O. I knew my legs were moving because I wasn't standing still, but I couldn't feel them. I was tired, and the euphoria was wearing off. We still had three more miles to go, and it was a gradual incline for the next two. My toes hurt, and I could feel the blisters rubbing against my socks. I wanted to stop. We had started out too strong, and now I was tired. We had considerably slowed down our pace, and other runners were passing us.

"Ugh, I'm so tired," I complained to Jennifer.

"We're so close. Taste the finish," Jennifer said, ever my cheerleader.

Jennifer was in better shape than me. I *wanted* to power through, but it was hard. I knew I could finish. I just needed motivation. I couldn't stop. This race could not turn into a failure like my marriage.

But my *marriage* hadn't been a failure. Chad had been the failure. He was the one who'd lied, who'd deceived me, the one who'd thrown it all away. And nine months later, I still wasn't completely over it, but I was stronger for it.

Thinking of all that Chad had done, and how far I'd come, I kicked it into high gear. I'd finish this race strong. I was going to prove to myself that I could do this.

"Screw Chad," I said, under my breath.

Jennifer shot me a confused look but went with it. "Yeah," she said. "Screw him and his lying, and his cheating."

"Yeah," I shot back. "Screw him and Courtney for rubbing their relationship in my face."

I pushed onward and ran the last three miles as fast as I could. All my anger and hate for Chad and Courtney propelled me forward. All of my feelings about the past nine months came in the form of power and speed. I felt strong. I felt powerful. I felt invigorated. The sweat was streaming down my forehead as I charged forward. I could hear the crowd cheering us along and I kicked into high gear.

We crossed the finish line with our fists pumping in the air after two hours and ten minutes of solid running.

At the finish line, we collected our medals and a much-needed glass of water.

"We did it!" I exclaimed, giving Jennifer a high five.

After the race, we treated ourselves to a big brunch with Rachel and Camila.

"Good job, girls!" Rachel said. "I'm glad you all ran thirteen miles to give us an excuse to have brunch and drink mimosas."

"Like we need an excuse," Camila replied, as we all clinked our glasses together.

After brunch, I got home and took a shower, followed by a very long nap. I woke up to a text from Noah.

Noah: *How did the race go?*

I responded with a picture of me and my medal and told him I'd finished strong at two hours and ten minutes.

Noah: *Great job, Beth. I'm really proud of you! You should feel accomplished.*
Me: *Thanks. Want to have coffee tomorrow?*
Noah: *Yes! I want to hear all about your race.*
Me: *Great! See you tomorrow.*

After our first date, Daniel and I texted each other and had learned we were both watching the TV series *Vampire Academy*. Every few nights, we'd make sure both of us were caught up, and then chatted about all the characters and unexpected twists. It was fun to have someone to talk to about the show. Since we both had shared custody, we couldn't necessarily watch it together, so this was the next best thing.

Finding time to meet up proved to be difficult, but we figured it out. On our second date, Daniel and I went for a hike. It took us an extra-long time, because we kept stopping to make out. Daniel was an excellent kisser, and we couldn't seem to keep our hands off each other. We had good chemistry. Being with him felt natural and carefree.

But, after our date, I obsessed about every little detail. What if he found something wrong with me? Lying in my bed, I replayed every minute, wondering if I'd said the wrong thing, or done something that might have turned him off. When he told me about a problem he was having at work, did I come off as sympathetic enough? Had I changed the subject to my issues too quickly? I was the one who had decided we'd go on a hike—had he wanted to do something else instead? He seemed to enjoy it, but maybe he thought it was lame? If Chad could up and leave me after thirteen years together, why wouldn't Daniel want to leave me after two dates, even if they had seemed to go well?

I didn't like feeling like this. It had been two days, and Daniel hadn't texted since our hike, which wasn't *that* odd. He'd said he had a big work project coming up, and his kids were back at his house. But, still, I couldn't shake the feeling that I'd done something wrong, that he didn't think I was good enough, just like Chad hadn't thought I was good enough.

I checked my phone for the millionth time. No message from Daniel. Should I text him first? Would that seem desperate? I wanted to seem cool and relaxed around him, but that was hard to do. My heart raced, and I felt like I was having a full-blown panic attack. And for what? A guy I had been on two dates with and watched vampire shows with?

I was about to jump in the shower when my phone buzzed.

Daniel: *So, when do I get to see you again?*

A huge sigh of relief came over me.

Me: *Zoe's with her dad this weekend. Does that work?*
Daniel: *How about Saturday?*
Me: *Perfect*

I got in the shower with a smile on my face. I'd been worried about nothing. I was going to have to find a way to remain calm and not overanalyze every detail of every encounter we had. A lot harder to do in practice than on paper. I was still new to dating and getting over heartbreak, but the only way to fix that was to work through my issues, one day at a time.

Saturday afternoon, Noah and I went to SOAR to help set up their new playground. They had gotten some funds for a new teeter-totter, slide, and jungle gym. The center needed help putting things together, so they planned a picnic to get the kids and volunteers together to help out. Noah and I were both free, so we decided to help. I'd really looked forward to this. I had grown to love my time at SOAR and was excited to help out with other events, not just tutoring. It was rewarding spending time with the kids, and it gave me that warm, fuzzy feeling inside. Noah and I had become staples at the center, getting to know a lot of the other kids, not just Josephina and Christopher, as well as some of the other volunteers. It felt like I was part of something, something that I wouldn't have experienced if Chad hadn't walked out on me.

Noah picked me up and we headed over. It was a gorgeous spring day. The sun was shining, and there wasn't a cloud in the sky. It was a perfect day for doing some work outside and enjoying the company of friends.

When we got there, David was working with another volunteer, putting together the teeter-totter. Noah and I walked over to say hi.

"Need any help?" I asked.

"Actually, yes," he said. "We just started, but you two can take over. I was going to see about helping the kids set up the mural."

Since the center was putting in new equipment, they'd decided to spiff up the rest of the playground. One of the volunteers was an art teacher who had the idea to make use of the cement wall and create a mural that the kids could all work on. They also planned to plant some flowers around the playground. Everyone was working hard and having a good time.

"Well, let's get started," Noah declared.

I grabbed the directions. It seemed simple enough.

"I think we need to start with screwing the base in," I said, handing him a screwdriver.

Noah and I made one hell of a team. We had a good rhythm and were making great progress on the teeter-totter.

"So, any more dates?" Noah asked.

"I've got a third date with a guy named Daniel," I said.

"Third date, huh?" Noah said. "I take it this guy is tolerable."

"He's actually really nice and also loves *Vampire Academy*," I said.

"Oh my, Beth. You finally found another adult who watches that show. He's a keeper," Noah said with a laugh.

Noah always made fun of my TV choices. Lately, my mind had been all over the place, and I liked to settle in with some mindless TV. Sure, *Vampire Academy* was geared toward high school kids, but it had everything I needed, including ridiculous drama. What more could you expect from a vampire show?

"Oh yes. We could have a vampire-themed wedding," I said in jest.

"Wow, it's that serious?" Noah teased.

"No, I was just saying…since you said he's a keeper. Never mind." I shook my head.

"But you like him?" he asked.

"I do. We have a good time together. But I'm afraid that he's going to disappear on me. I feel like I can't be my full self around him, because what if he doesn't like the real me?"

I handed Noah a wrench to tighten some of the bolts.

"So what if he doesn't like the real you?" Noah asked.

"I think I'll be crushed."

"Crushed?" Noah asked, giving me a quizzical look.

"Yeah, Chad left me, and we had promised to love each other in good times and bad. What's to say Daniel won't walk away?"

"Nothing, I guess."

"Thanks a lot," I replied, slightly annoyed at his implication.

"I just mean, you can't live your life wondering what if. You've got to take risks."

"Dating is a *big* risk."

"It is. And it's going to have its ups and downs, but you can't let what Chad did dictate how you live your life. Then he wins."

"Maybe."

"Maybe? You know I'm right."

I sighed deeply. "I know you are. I'm just scared."

"It's okay to be scared. But it's good you're out there. So, have you slept with him?"

"Noah!"

"What?"

"Not appropriate."

I definitely had *thought* about sleeping with Daniel. I wasn't sure I was ready, but I figured, after three dates, he might be expecting something. He'd made a few comments about me having a nice figure, and I was sure he'd imagined me naked. But having sex with someone who wasn't Chad was a big step. Getting intimate always seemed to complicate things, especially emotionally. I did like Daniel, but I was terrified of getting hurt. I wanted to put myself out there, but how out there did I need to be?

Then again, if I didn't sleep with him, would he dump me? I just didn't know what to do.

"Sorry. Just asking."

"Well, no, I haven't. But we're going out tonight, so maybe."

"Well, just have fun. Don't overthink it."

"Ha ha, easier said than done."

Noah and I finished up the teeter-totter.

"Looks great," I said, giving him a high five.

We went to join the others at the mural and then grabbed some lunch. While we ate, Charlotte, a girl I had been working on fractions with last week, came up to us.

"Is he your boyfriend?" Charlotte asked, pointing to Noah.

"No," I said with a smile. "We're just friends."

"Well, he should be your boyfriend, because you two are always together."

Noah and I laughed. We finished up our lunch and went to go check on the progress with the mural.

After Noah dropped me off at home, I fed Twix and jumped in the shower to get ready for my date. I kept thinking about whether or not I was going to sleep with Daniel. I liked him, I felt like we had really good chemistry, and I enjoyed being in his company. He was a great dad and understood the ups and downs of being a single parent and going through a divorce. He seemed to be really interested in me, and I thought he liked me.

A million questions raced through my mind. What if I wasn't good at sex anymore? What if it was so terrible that he decided I wasn't worth it? How would I feel after having sex with him? Would I be reminded that this wasn't my husband? That I was being intimate with someone else? Would I cry after? Would I be happy after? Also, what were the rules for having sex? We hadn't had the conversation about seeing other people. I wasn't ready for that, but did I need to talk it out before we slept together. If I was going to sleep with him, I didn't really want him sleeping with other people.

I realized the shower had turned to cold. I had forty-five minutes before Daniel would arrive. I was still so confused. I didn't know what to do.

The doorbell rang. When I opened the door, Daniel gave me a long kiss hello.

"I've been thinking about that all day," he said.

I started to blush.

"Me, too," I admitted.

"Ready to go?"

"Yep, let me just grab my shoes."

Daniel walked me to his car. We'd decided to go bowling. I was a decent bowler, so I was happy when Daniel suggested it.

We got to the alley, and I put on my shoes.

"I can't believe you have your own bowling shoes. You must be pretty serious."

"Nah, just not a fan of wearing the same shoes as fifty other people," I said.

Chad and I had really enjoyed bowling. Our first Christmas together, he'd gotten me the bowling shoes. I hadn't been bowling since he left. Tying up the laces, I thought about the first time I had gotten a "turkey," and how excited Chad had been at my three consecutive strikes. It was a nice memory, and at that moment, I realized this was the first time I'd had a memory about Chad that was just that. A memory. I didn't get sad. I didn't get angry. I just thought about the time and smiled. Maybe I didn't have to let the past thirteen years be defined by Chad's eventual betrayal and infidelity. There were things that I could remember and not feel like I had to have a reaction. I could remember the good times, especially when they revolved around my accomplishments.

I picked up the ball and rolled a strike.

"Okay, maybe I'm a little good," I said, giving Daniel a sly smile.

"I'm in trouble," he said as he kissed me. Probably to try to distract me. He wore the same cologne from our first date. I took a deep breath in. He smelled amazing.

In the end, I ended up beating Daniel with a score of 154, but he put up a good fight, bowling a 146. It had come down to the last frame, but Daniel didn't end up picking up his spare. I got up and did a victory dance. Daniel grabbed me and kissed me.

"Want to get out of here?" he said.

"Yes, very much so," I said, as I gave him a kiss and grabbed my shoes.

Daniel held my hand the entire car ride to my house. It was only a fifteen-minute drive, but it felt like a lifetime. I was still debating whether or not I wanted to sleep with him. His hand in mine felt comforting. My heart was saying yes, but I felt like my mind was trying to protect me from something. I thought about what Noah had said, that holding back because of what Chad did, meant that Chad won. I didn't want his actions to define my life, and I had to take risks. But I wanted to be ready for the consequences of those risks. I felt like I needed to protect my heart.

When we got to my house, I put my bag and shoes down, went into the kitchen, and poured us each a glass of wine. We headed to the couch. Daniel told me a story about camping in the backyard with his kids. His son had told him he really wanted to go camping in the woods, but his daughter was a little apprehensive, so Daniel had decided to do a test run. I thought it was a cute idea. Whenever Daniel told stories about his kids, his face lit up, and he got excited. He loved them with all his heart. He didn't want to just be the fun dad; he also wanted to shape his kids into good people. He wanted to be the dad who took an interest in doing things with them and also taught them about life.

"And then it started to pour, so we ran inside the house and just set up blankets in the living room. The kids were happy to be dry, and we had a really good time." Daniel smiled, his eyes crinkling.

That was it, that was the moment I needed. I put my wine glass down, straddled him, and kissed him deeply.

"Are you sure you want to do this?" he said.

"Yes." I kissed him harder, my hands running through his thick black hair.

He looked into my eyes. My heart was pounding.

"You are so beautiful," he said.

He kissed me again. I took his hand and led him to my bedroom. He kissed my lips, and then my neck. His kisses sent shivers down my spine. He took my shirt off.

"Wow," he said.

I just smiled at him and slipped his shirt off. He had a great body. I put my arms around his neck and kissed him. His skin felt cool next to mine.

He lifted me up and put me on the bed, kissing me all over. I closed my eyes and breathed in his smell. His hands gently glided over my body. His touch electrified my skin.

He kissed my neck again. "You're amazing."

An hour later, I laid in his arms, our legs tangled together.

"That was incredible," he said with a smile.

My heart was beating fast. I hadn't known what sex with another man would be like, but with Daniel, it had been great. He was kind and gentle, and then, when the moment was right, he took command. It was just what I'd needed.

I kissed him gently on the cheek.

He brushed the hair away from my face and looked at me. "You are so sexy, Beth. Really. I've enjoyed our last three dates and am looking forward to spending more time with you."

I smiled, ecstatic. I'd taken a risk, and it had paid off. Who knew what the future with Daniel would entail? Sure, he could call me tomorrow and tell me he didn't want to see me again. But I wasn't going to worry about that. I couldn't control the future, that I knew. I would just enjoy this moment. I was going to enjoy the feeling of being in Daniel's arms. A guy, who, at this point in time, thought I was worth it.

-11-

MAY

"Ladies, we need a theme. Last year's movie theme was a huge success," Jennifer said.

It was the first of May, and just like every other year, we were all at Rachel's house planning our annual block party. Over the years, the block party had turned into quite the ordeal. We shut down the street and had all sorts of activities, including a bounce house, face painting, and water balloon toss. Last year, we'd done a movie theme with a big popcorn machine and a movie projected on Rachel's garage door. Looking back, it was weird to think that my entire life was going to change just two days later, when Chad told me he was leaving me. I tried to recall if he'd acted any differently in those days, but all I remembered was the three of us snuggled up on the blankets watching *Finding Nemo* in Rachel's yard. I'd been happy and thinking about how much I loved my neighbors...and my family.

"We could do a luau. Sebastian's been wanting an excuse to roast a pig on a stick," said Camila.

"That sounds delicious," Jennifer said, licking her lips. "I'm definitely in."

"Me too," I said. "It'll give me an excuse to buy a coconut bra."

"Then it's settled. Okay, now decorations. I can go to the store the day before," Jennifer said, jotting everything down in her note-book labeled "BLOCK PARTY." All of the notes from previous years planning sessions were in it. It was fun to see how far we'd come.

"We have to have a limbo contest!" Rachel said

"Oh, and a tiki torch ring toss," Camila added, making a toss motion with her hands. "The kids will love it."

"Okay, I'm writing this all down. Good stuff," Jennifer said. Her pen couldn't move fast enough.

The decorations and games were all planned out, and we were ready for our second pitcher of Sebastian's famous sangria. Luckily, Camila had come prepared.

"Okay, now, in addition to the roasted pig, what else in terms of food?" asked Jennifer.

I loved the way she always took charge at these planning parties. She made sure we had everything covered before our third round of sangria. We had learned our lesson. With each sangria, we had to have one glass of water. The first year that we'd had our block party planning party, none of us made it to work the next day, which was why we'd also decided to move it to a Friday night.

"We could also do kabobs on the grill and a pineapple dessert," Rachel suggested.

"Finally, the gift basket. We can add luau-themed items like SPAM and macadamia nuts," Jennifer said, as Camila moved on to the third pitcher of sangria.

Each year, we put together a gift basket and held a raffle, rais-ing money for a charity. We each donated items for the gift basket, including toys for the kids and wine for the adults. We even had some local businesses donate gift cards. Camila and Sebastian al-ways put in a $200 gift card for their restaurant.

"Any ideas for a charity?"

"How about SOAR, where Noah and I volunteer? The center can always use some help, so maybe we could give the money to them?" I asked.

"Good idea. Will you organize this again?"

Putting together the gift basket and selling raffle tickets was always my contribution to the block party. I wasn't good at cooking or decorating, but I could organize and sell. I liked the idea of the raffle, and in the past, we had raised a lot of money. I was glad that we could give to SOAR.

"Sure, I'd be happy to," I agreed.

"So, now, the question we've all been wondering: are you going to invite Daniel?" Rachel asked.

I hadn't thought about asking Daniel. Things between the two of us were going well, but I wasn't ready to introduce him to my friends, and definitely not to Zoe. Daniel and I still needed to get to know each other and figure each other out. Dating when you're divorced means there's a lot of baggage. It wasn't always *bad* baggage, but it was there. Both people had been hurt by previous partners. Both people balanced kids, house things, and work, and it was hard to find time for each other that lined up. I wanted to move slowly with Daniel—I didn't need to invite him fully into my life, and I didn't want to be introduced to his quite yet. I enjoyed it just being the two of us.

"I don't think so. Seems like a big step."

"You'll need a new partner for corn hole, and this year Travis and I are determined to win," Rachel said.

Each year the block party also had a corn hole tournament, which was essentially just a glorified bean bag toss. For the past two years, Chad and I had made it to the finals, winning last year in an epic showdown. I wanted to be able to defend my title, but I would need a good teammate. Maybe I would just skip this year.

"True," I said. "But what if Daniel is terrible at corn hole? If he cost me the championship, I would have to break up with him, and the scx is just too good for that."

"Oh, please, do tell," Rachel said.

"A lady doesn't kiss and tell," I said.

"Please." Jennifer rolled her eyes.

"Let's just say, that the man knows how to satisfy me." I smiled slyly.

"We should invite Sean to the block party," Rachel suggested.

"Sean?" I asked.

"Yeah, aren't you *friends* now?" Jennifer inquired.

"This way Sean and Daniel can fight over you," Rachel said, winking.

I threw a throw pillow at her.

"One, Daniel isn't coming, and two, Sean and I *are* just friends."

"Oh, that's right, he's a friend who helps build your table and chairs," Rachel said, putting "build" in air quotes.

I threw another throw pillow at her.

"I'm being attacked by my own pillows!" Rachel shouted.

She threw her pillows back, and we all started to giggle.

"What's going on down there?" Travis asked from above.

"Nothing, honey. We've just finished our third glass of sangria," Rachel yelled up.

"Oh, that explains a lot," Travis said.

Daniel picked me up for our date at six. He knocked on the door and greeted me with pink carnations with white lilies. My favorite.

"What are these for?" I asked.

"I saw them, and they looked pretty, just like you."

I put them up to my nose and took in their fragrance.

"Thanks. I love lilies," I said.

"I remembered," Daniel said. "I also remembered you said you always enjoyed fresh flowers, and after your ex-husband left, you made sure to always have some. Now you won't have to get any tomorrow."

"That's very sweet."

I'd said all that to Daniel on our first date. When we were talking about changes we'd made after getting divorced, I told him about the fresh flowers I usually picked some at the farmers market on Sundays. I was impressed with what a great listener Daniel was.

I gave him a deep kiss.

"Let me go put these in water, and I'll be ready to go. Come on in."

Daniel came in, and I went to grab a vase. I put them on the windowsill and smiled. I wasn't sure where my relationship with Daniel was going, but, at that moment, it felt like the start of something good. It was our sixth date, and Daniel had turned out to be a pleasant surprise. He was more than someone to have conversation with over wine. I found myself thinking about him at little moments, like on the train, or in the store if I saw something he'd like. My friends had also noticed a hop in my step lately. At drinks with the girls a few days ago, they'd mentioned that I was beaming, and I couldn't stop smiling. I was happy. This was good. I was glad that I'd kept up with the online dating and was glad that I had found Daniel.

"Shall we?" he said, as he took my arm to lead me to his car.

He opened the door for me and helped me inside. I was really getting used to his chivalry. He certainly treated me like a princess.

Earlier, Camila had reminded me that I *was* a princess, and I deserved it.

Daniel and I went to a new sushi place for dinner. I loved going out for sushi, since it wasn't something I'd normally eat with Zoe. She was more of a chicken nugget and pizza kind of kid. The restaurant was very intimate, and they brought us to a table in the back.

"So, how was your day?"

"Pretty good. Just a normal Saturday. Errands, running, mowing the lawn."

"Have you signed up for any more races?" he asked.

"Jennifer and I were talking about another half marathon in the fall. I told her I'd be down."

"Not going to go for the full marathon?"

"Thirteen point one is good enough for me."

"Fair enough."

I smiled at him, staring into his eyes. He looked very handsome in his blue polo. Daniel always wore a polo shirt on our dates. I was convinced that he must have over twenty in his closet. On our first date, he'd worn on a green one, which brought out his eyes. On our bowling date, he wore a striped one. He even wore one hiking. Even though he always wore polos, they seemed to match the mood of our date. I was impressed with this skill. I wanted to bring it up, but every time I thought about saying something, I figured he would take it the wrong way. Like he might think I didn't like the way he dressed, or that he didn't have style. I liked to think he would see the humor in it, too. But I was afraid that he'd get mad and leave.

I realized there was a lot I still held back from Daniel, afraid to be my true self around him. But I was trying to open up a little more.

"What did you do last night?" I asked.

"Out with some friends from work."

"Fun."

I wondered if he might still be going on dates from the Here Comes Love app. We hadn't talked about whether we were in an actual relationship or just something casual. We hadn't discussed if either of us were seeing other people. I wasn't even sure how that protocol went, especially with online dating. We both still had our profiles up, but I had no idea what that meant. I wanted to delete mine, but I wasn't sure what kind of message that was sending. Would he interpret that as me being too serious too quickly?

On the other hand, the message it was *currently* sending was that I was still virtually out there.

I wasn't sure I even wanted to be fully committed to Daniel yet. I wasn't emotionally ready for that. But I also didn't like the idea of him dating other people. What if I sent him a racy text message while he was out on date or making out with another girl? That would be embarrassing. I wanted to bring it up with him. But I just didn't know how. Whenever I asked him about his weekend or evenings, I always looked for signs that he was still dating.

But then I realized I didn't know what those signs would be.

"Harper has her first swim lesson this week. She's so excited," Daniel said, breaking me out of my thoughts.

"Oh fun!" I said. "Zoe loved swim lessons. I need to sign her up for more, especially now that the pool is open again."

Daniel took a sip of his wine and took my hand across the table. "This is nice," he said, as he rubbed his thumb against my knuckles. Daniel stared into my eyes and smiled. He looked at me like I was the only person in the room, the only person in the universe. His hand felt calming in mine.

"I'm really glad we matched," he said.

"Me, too," I said.

The waiter came by and brought us our order. The food looked delicious. The tuna had a nice color to it. I couldn't wait to try some.

I reached across and took a bite.

"Mmm," I said, as I closed my eyes and took in the flavor.

"Best sushi?" he asked.

"Without a doubt."

We continued eating and talking about our weeks. Daniel excitedly told me about a project he was finishing up at work, and I shared about a problem I was having with a coworker. It was nice that we were learning about each other. After my last bite of sushi and our wine glasses were empty, Daniel signaled for the waiter to bring him a check.

"Thanks for dinner," I said as he paid the bill. "It was really nice."

"I'm just happy to get to spend time with you," Daniel said. "Want to go to my place or yours?"

"Either works."

We ended up going to his house. We got in the door and immediately started making out like teenagers. Daniel was a great kisser, and we always felt in sync. He lifted me up and carried me to his bedroom, my legs wrapped around him, still kissing.

Then, he threw me on the bed, and started kissing every inch of my body, while slowly removing my clothes. I breathed in as he made his way past my belly button. There was just something about Daniel—he knew exactly how I wanted it, without me having to say anything. Being with him gave me goose bumps and made my legs tremble.

A half hour later, we both fell back onto the bed, breathing heavily.

"Phew, that was amazing. I love having sex with you," he said as he laid on the bed with his arm around me.

Something inside of me felt weird as the word "love" hung in the air. I know he hadn't flat out said he loved *me*, but no guy since Chad had ever started a sentence that began with "I love" and ended with "you." I wasn't sure how I felt about it. I liked Daniel, but I definitely wasn't in love with him.

"I know, I don't remember the last time I had sex this good. It's really fun." There was no way I was using the word love, even if it was just in reference to having sex.

"Good, I'm glad," he said.

We stayed in his bed a little longer. I stared up at the ceiling, watching the fan spin. Something about this night felt different. The flowers, the intimate dinner, him using the L word. I felt like things were moving fast with Daniel. I really liked hanging out with him, and the sex was extremely satisfying. But there was a feeling inside of me, that said I needed to protect my heart. Moving too quickly felt like I was more likely to get hurt, and that was the last thing I wanted.

"I'm going to get a glass of water, want anything?" he asked, kissing me on my forehead.

"Water would be great. Thanks."

Daniel came back with a glass of water, two empty wine glasses, and a bottle of wine. "Another drink, too?"

"Of course," I said.

We laid in bed, naked, drinking wine and talking. There was something about being naked and exposed that made people more real when they talked. I looked over at his shelves and noticed a picture of three kids standing in front of a dock. I picked up the picture to examine it.

"Is that you?" I asked.

"Yep, me and my sister and brother. I think I was eight in that picture."

"You all are cute."

"Thanks," he said.

I hadn't heard much about his brother and sister, just that they existed.

"Do you keep in touch?" I asked.

"My brother and I are close. He lives in Oregon, so we don't see much of each other. I haven't talked to my sister in ten years."

"Oh, I'm sorry," I said.

"It's okay. We had a big falling out. It's sad that my kids don't have a relationship with their aunt or their cousins though."

I wanted to ask about the falling out, but I wasn't sure how much he wanted to divulge. I wasn't sure if this was girlfriend/boyfriend talk or not.

I gave Daniel a kiss on the lips. He put down his wine glass and took mine. Then he pushed me back and kissed me.

After another round in the hay, Daniel fell asleep with me lying in his arms. I stared at the ceiling, curled up next to him. It had been a perfect night. The food, the company, the amazing sex, the connection.

But as I laid there, a million thoughts raced through my mind. Was this when we were supposed to have the boyfriend/girlfriend talk? Part of me wanted to take this to the next level, but I was scared. What if I became emotionally invested and he decided I wasn't worth it? I would be crushed. I was also scared to even bring it up. What if I wasn't reading the signs correctly? What if Daniel was just a nice guy and I was blowing everything out of proportion? What if I wanted to think that he liked me this much because

I wanted someone to look at me like I was the only person in the room, when in reality, to Daniel, I was just one of the girls he was seeing? What if that was his game? What if he *was* dating other people, and I asked him about it? How would I react to his answer? Would I be okay with that? Would I make him choose me? What if he didn't choose me?

I got up on the pretense of going to the bathroom and turned to look at him. He looked so peaceful sleeping. Could I be okay with putting myself out there, with Daniel? Part of me said yes, be brave, be bold, don't hold back, you can do this. The other part replayed Chad telling me that he didn't love me anymore. I couldn't take that kind of heartbreak again. That part started taking hold of me. It felt like I was there again. But, instead of Chad, it was Daniel telling me that he'd decided I wasn't worth it anymore. That I wasn't good enough.

I felt like I couldn't breathe. Everything was happening too quickly. I wasn't ready for this kind of intimacy with another person. I wasn't ready for the doubt to take hold of me.

I ran into the bathroom and splashed water on my face. I had to get out of here. I wasn't sure what I was going to say to Daniel, but I knew I had to get home. I was in a full-fledged panic attack, and I didn't want Daniel to see me like this. I didn't know what I was doing anymore. I just knew I wanted to get home.

I threw on my clothes and wrote him a note. I decided to say the sushi wasn't agreeing with me and I'd decided to go home. I called an Uber.

When I got in, I just sat in the back and cried.

The next weekend I took Zoe to an afternoon Nationals game. They were playing the Mets, and it was a fun mother-daughter adventure. We rode the metro down to the park. Zoe wore her favorite Nationals dress and had her hair in a ponytail with Nationals ribbons. I had on my lucky tank top. We always sat in right field. It was one of my favorite sections to sit in because it was in the shade, you got a good view of the ballpark, and my favorite BBQ stand was right behind us.

"I hope we catch a home run ball," Zoe said.

"That would be exciting, wouldn't it!"

The Nationals started the game with a two-run homer in the first. Zoe was beyond excited. She jumped up and down, and we did our home run dance. The men behind us chuckled. When the Mets tied it up in the second, with an overthrow at first base, Zoe let out a loud grunt.

"Come on, guys," she screamed. "Let's focus. You can do this." In her mind, all the team needed was some encouragement, and she thought that she was the right person for the job. She got up and started chanting. "Let's go, Nats!"

It filled my heart with joy to see how excited she got at baseball games. We didn't have a big-league team in Nebraska, but, growing up, I used to go with my dad to the Omaha Storm Chasers games. They were a triple-A affiliate for the Kansas City Royals, and it was exciting to see the up-and-comers. My dad and I probably went to fifteen games a year. I was glad that Zoe wanted to continue our tradition.

At the start of third inning, Zoe wanted to get a snack. I reached into my bag to get my credit card and checked my phone. I hadn't heard from Daniel in a few days. I had texted him on Thursday to see if he wanted to get lunch next week, but, two days later, there was still no reply. Things with us had changed after I'd left the house in the middle of the night. He called me the next day, making sure I was okay. I told him I was sorry that I'd just up and left, but I'd had a bad stomachache. We went out on Wednesday night, but things felt...off. Daniel seemed distant. He didn't hold my hand like he normally did, and later, when we had sex, it didn't seem like we were connecting. He made a bad joke about making sure I wasn't going to leave again, and maybe he needed to tie me down, which didn't sit well.

I'd left the next morning, early, without breakfast. He kissed me on my check as I left. When I got to my car, I had a feeling in my stomach that it was over between me and Daniel. I was afraid to tell him how I really felt, to be vulnerable with him, which had probably left him confused.

"Let's go," I said to Zoe.

She grabbed my hand and we skipped through the ballpark to the BBQ stand. I ordered a pulled pork sandwich, while Zoe got a hot dog and chips. I told her that, in the sixth inning, we could get popcorn.

Back at our seats, we continued to watch the game. There was a little excitement, and I kept checking my phone every inning. Still nothing from Daniel. I just knew something wasn't right. He'd never failed to text me back. I wasn't sure if I should send a follow-up text. Maybe he hadn't seen it. But, at the same time, it wasn't like he was asking me to hang out. I looked over at Zoe and saw how much fun she was having. I wasn't going to let Daniel ruin this moment. I was going to have fun with my daughter. If he didn't want to text me back, that was his problem. This was Zoe and Mommy time. It was precious.

The bottom of the ninth inning, the game was still tied 2-2. Our star player, Isaac Fox, stepped up to the plate.

"I bet he's going to hit a home run," Zoe said.

"I hope so," I said, giving her a smile.

The first ball was thrown, and Isaac swung and missed. Strike one. The second ball whizzed right by him. Strike two.

"Let's go," Zoe shouted. The entire stadium was on their feet, clapping. You could feel the excitement around us.

The third ball was thrown and *crack!* You could hear the ball hit the bat. It soared our way. Everyone in our section tried to catch the ball, but I hovered to protect Zoe. The crowd cheered, and Zoe and I gave each other a high five.

"We won!" I screamed.

"Yay, Nationals!" Zoe screamed.

The entire crowd erupted in excitement.

A man sitting a few rows back had caught the ball.

"That's so cool he got the ball. I wish I had it," Zoe said.

"Maybe next time."

Just then, the guy came up to us. "Here. You should have this." He handed Zoe the home run ball. "You're probably a bigger fan than I am," he said with a wink.

"That's very nice of you. Zoe what do you say?"

"Thank you! Thank you! Thank you!" Zoe exclaimed.

"Just keep rooting for the Nationals," the man said as he left.

On the ride home from the metro, Zoe held onto her ball tight.

"I'm going to show all my friends at school," she said, with an ear to ear smile the entire ride home.

As we got to the door, I put my key in and heard my phone buzz. I pulled out my phone and saw a text from Daniel.

Hey, I'm really sorry, but I don't think we should see each other anymore. It just feels like we are in different places right now.

Shock slammed through me. I dropped the phone back into my purse, opened the door, and started to cry. I didn't want Zoe to see me upset, so I ran into the bathroom.

I'd been right. I *wasn't* worth it to Daniel. He *wasn't* going to be there for me while I worked out my insecurities. I wasn't sure how to navigate dating, and, after the betrayal from Chad, it wasn't going to be easy. I wished that Daniel had been willing to figure it out with me. Of course, it would have been easier if I'd been willing to talk about it. But, after just one "off" night, he'd distanced himself and gave up. I didn't need that.

Big tears fell down my face. I felt so defeated. I was mad at myself for breaking down at Daniel's house and ruining everything. I was mad at Daniel for just giving up, for not even giving me the time to explain myself. I was hurt that, a week ago, I'd felt like I was on the top of the world, that maybe Daniel and I could be the start of something new. That I was truly happy.

There was a sadness and an emptiness inside of me. I had put myself out there, and now here I was, back where I'd started. I was more upset than I had been in a while. I was angry with myself for letting Daniel make me feel this way, but I just couldn't shake it. I was mad that I couldn't be myself with him.

I felt like Chad had won. That this was his fault. I wouldn't even be here if it wasn't for him. I got knocked down. I got up. And I got knocked down again. How much more pain did I have to go through? Was this even worth it? All of the swiping, bad dates, and then, when it did finally amount to something, heartache. Absolute heartache.

I took a deep breath and wiped up my tears. I sent Camila a text.

ME: WTF, Daniel just broke up with me...over text!
Camila: Want to come over?

I came out of the bathroom. Zoe was playing with her Barbies. I put on my brightest smile.

"Want to go to Julian's house?"

"Yes! I can show him my baseball."

When we arrived across the street, Zoe showed Julian her base-ball right away, and they went off to the backyard.

"I can't believe he broke up with you via text. Who does that?" Camila said, pulling me into one of her signature hugs. Her embrace made me feel so much better. Just the physical connection with a good friend could get me through anything.

"I know, he could have at least called."

"Did you have any idea this was coming?"

"Well, it's been weird since my great vanishing act," I admitted. "But he didn't give it time. I know I needed to talk to him about it, but I was just scared."

"Well, on the plus side, at least the sex was good." Camila added.

"That's true," I chucked. "And Daniel made me feel sexy and it was nice to connect with someone new," I added.

"So, not a total waste of time," Camila said.

"No, not at all," I shrugged.

"I guess it's back on the app?"

"I don't know. I constantly worried that Daniel was going to leave me, and it was kind of stressful. Dating is supposed to be fun. Maybe I wasn't as ready as I thought I was. I might give it a few more months, keep focusing on Beth Bradley 2.0."

"At least you tried. I'm proud of you."

"Thanks. I'm glad I did it, even though it was scary. I faced my fears, and I'm still standing."

"And if you can get over Chad, I'm sure I'll bounce back from Daniel in no time."

"Daniel who?" I asked with a smile.

"That's the spirit."

After volunteering with Noah on Wednesday, we grabbed pizzas at Backyard Bistro and went back to his place to have some wine and play cards.

"How are things with your boyfriend?" he asked.

"He's not my boyfriend. Actually, he ended it over the weekend."

"I'm sorry to hear that. "

"It's fine. I mean, it kind of sucks, but I'm over it."

Noah took a sip of his wine. "He's an idiot. Doesn't know a good thing when he has it. Any guy would be lucky to go out with you."

I blushed. Noah smiled at me.

"Gin!" I laid down my last card. "Want to play again?"

"Sure!" He shuffled the deck and I poured us another glass of wine.

I glanced up at Noah as he dealt. It might have been the wine, but his eyes looked especially blue today. I swung my legs under the table and gently brushed his leg. I felt a sudden flutter in my stomach, and my palms grew sweaty. He gently brushed my leg with his foot as he swung it under the table. Had it been an accident?

"So, back to the drawing board?" he asked, glancing up at me expectantly.

"What do you mean?"

"With dating?"

"Nah, I think I'm going to give a few more months. Turns out, I might need some more time healing. What about you?"

"There are just no quality women out there."

I gave him a sly smile.

"Your standards are too high," I said.

"I just want someone I can be myself with, someone I can hang out with, have a glass of wine with and have it feel natural. Also, it helps if she's hot."

Noah was describing exactly our relationship.

Startled, I glanced up at him again, watching him reviewing his cards. We both could be ourselves around each other, and we certainly enjoyed each other's company. Was he hinting at something? Did he want more?

His leg kept brushing mine, and he kept smiling.

"Gin again," I said.

"You're on a roll tonight."

We both reached for the cards, and our hands lightly touched. I looked at him, and he looked at me. Everything seemed to stand still. His eyes brightened, and the touch of his hand felt different tonight, almost electrifying.

"Another glass?" he asked softly.

I nodded as he poured the remaining wine into my glass, but it was only half full.

"Looks like we need another bottle. I'll be right back."

He ran down to his basement and came back with a bottle. He went over to the counter to open it.

"Did you see that video of the cat playing the piano?" he asked me.

"No."

"You've got to see it."

I got up to go to the bathroom, and when I got back, Noah was on his couch, pulling up the clip on his computer.

"Check this out."

I plopped myself next to him and together we watched the video, laughing hard.

As our laughter died down, he stared into my eyes, brushed back my hair, and kissed me. Kissing Noah felt good, it felt like home. It felt like this was supposed to happen, that we were supposed to be together. This was how my story was going to end. We were such good friends. We enjoyed each other's company. Noah was someone that I could be myself around. I didn't have to hide who I was, and I was okay being vulnerable around him.

His hands moved down my body. The warmth of his skin on mine made my heart beat faster. I reached for his shirt and took it off. His tan, sculpted body looked good. In the moment he lifted off my shirt and pressed his lips to my neck.

I kissed him deeper. I felt like I could just melt into him. This felt right. Noah was one of my closet friends. It only made sense that we would take it to the next level. I heard him moaning as his hands made their way down my back.

I looked into his eyes and smiled. He smiled back.

"This feels so right," he said, reaching my top button. All of a sudden, I jerked back. What was I doing? This was Noah. He was one of my best friends. If we did get into some sort of relationship, it shouldn't start from a drunk night after volunteering and cards. And a one-night stand would most likely ruin our friendship. I had just decided that I needed some more time to work on healing and keep the focus on myself, not jump into a relationship. I wasn't even sure that's what I wanted with Noah.

"What?" he said, giving me a puzzled look.

"I think I've had too much to drink. We should call it a night," I replied.

"You're probably right. You should go," his tone quickly changing to cold and distant.

He put on his shirt and turned his back to me. I grabbed my keys and walked toward the door. I looked back and saw him sitting on the couch, not making eye contact.

"I'll call you later," I said as I closed the door.

-12-

JUNE

I laced up my shoes and looked at my phone. With the humidity, Jennifer and I had decided to run at 6:30. It was early, but anything after 8:00 was just too hot to run in.

Last night, I had received another text message from Noah. I hadn't really talked to him much since that night at his place—I wasn't ready. I was embarrassed and didn't really feel the need for a big talk, but I knew that it was inevitable if I wanted to maintain our friendship. I just didn't know what to say.

Jennifer was outside her door waiting for me. "Man, it's early," she said with a big yawn.

"I know! This is dedication," I said, feeling powerful.

"We are bad asses," she said as she gave me a high five.

We set off on our six-mile run.

"So, have you talked to Noah?" she asked.

"Wow, we're just going to start with that?" I inquired.

"I was just curious."

"He's texted me a bunch. Even last night. But we haven't talked about what happened. I'm just really embarrassed and not ready to go down that road and be honest with him."

Noah had texted me a few days after the incident to ask if I was okay. I'd just responded with something simple, saying all was good, just busy. I had heard from him a few times after that, usually sending me a picture of him and Gabe doing something fun, or an update on the Nationals game, but all of the communication on my end had been minimal.

"I do miss him," I said.

"Well, then, talk to him. If you want to salvage your friendship, you might as well just get it all out there."

I was still trying to sort out my feelings for Noah. Something inside of me set off when I was kissing him, and I wasn't sure what it was. While my body was saying go for it, my mind was sounding blaring alarm bells. Noah was great; on paper, we would be perfect. But the breakup with Daniel was still fresh in my mind. Was that the only reason I was hesitant? Was that even a good enough reason? Or was there something else? I didn't even know if I wanted to be more than friends. What would happen if we didn't work out? Would I lose one of my closest friends?

Noah had been a good friend, especially through this past year. He was always there for me, asking me how I was doing, trying to put a smile on my face. He was always there to lend an ear or just goof around with, and, as one of my few divorced friends, he just got it. When I'd told him about Chad getting married, he'd come over with a bottle of wine and a deck of cards. We drank and played gin, and he didn't ask me about Chad. I didn't want to talk it out. I had already talked ad nauseum with everyone else.

"I know we joke about you two becoming a couple, but is that what you want?" Jennifer asked.

"It hadn't crossed my mind before that night. Our relationship was always a clear friendship. But I did like kissing him."

"Did you feel butterflies?"

"I wouldn't say butterflies, it just felt natural. But at the same time, I have no idea what he is thinking. Why he even kissed me in the first place. Was this something he wanted to do for a while?"

"Well if he did, you know want to be more than friends, what would you say?"

"I don't know."

"Well, you two need to figure out what you are. And then you need to figure out if you're okay with that, because not knowing isn't going to be good."

"You're right. I'll talk to him."

"Promise."

"Promise," I said.

After our run, I got home and took a shower. I really thought about my friendship with Noah. Kissing him felt good, but it wasn't the fact that I was kissing Noah, it was that, at that moment, someone wanted me. I had gotten used to that feeling with Daniel, and it felt nice. But dating was still new to me. I had learned a lot about myself with Daniel. Sure, I could be myself around Noah, but maybe that would change if we became intimate. There was a small part that wondered what if, but it would be heartbreaking if we didn't work out and Noah wasn't in my life anymore. It wasn't worth it. I hoped that Noah had the same feelings, but there was only one way to find out. I texted Noah asking if he wanted to meet up.

I went to blow dry my hair and saw there was no response from Noah. Was Noah ignoring me? Was he doing to me what I'd done to him over the past week? I started to get nervous that I had waited too long.

Finally, two hours after I'd sent my initial text, he responded.

Noah: *A walk sounds good. Meet at the park at 2?*
Me: *See you then.*

I got to the park and Noah was with Rusty.

"Hey," I said coming up to him hesitantly.

"Hey," he said back. It was so weird between us. I went in to give him a hug hello, but it felt forced.

We started walking down the path.

"How have you been?" he started.

"Good. Busy with work."

We walked in silence a little more. Someone had to make the first move, and I was tired of the awkwardness.

"So, are we going to talk about it?" I said.

"About what?" he said.

"Don't act like that. You know what I'm talking about."

"You'll have to refresh my memory."

"Don't be cute," I said and gave him a nudge. He gave me a playful smile.

"Okay," he took a deep breath. "That night, we were kind of drunk, and in a moment of, I don't know call it weakness, call it being horny, call it whatever. I kissed you."

"I know, I was there," I said.

"But you just up and left. I was so embarrassed."

"I'm sorry."

"And then you just ignore me? I was worried I had done something terribly wrong."

"I know, I guess I was also a little embarrassed. I didn't know if you wanted to start a relationship or not."

"It was just a kiss."

"Well, it was starting to become more."

"I tried to call you. You wouldn't even let me explain. Not cool, Beth."

"I know. I just didn't know what I wanted," I sighed.

"And what do want?" he asked.

We got to the field, and he threw a ball for Rusty to chase. I stood there, took a deep breath, and looked him directly in the eye.

"This year has been tough, and your friendship has been invaluable. I can talk to you about things that I can't talk to the girls about. You just get it, and you get me. I love spending time with you, I always have. And after Daniel, I realized, that while I've come a long way, I still need more time to work on Beth," I paused. "I just feel like we should be friends."

Noah looked at me as he raked his fingers through his hair. I was so afraid he was going to tell me he wanted more, and our friendship would never go back to pre-kiss. I picked at my nails, waiting for him to answer.

"I totally agree. You are also one of my best friends, and I was so afraid that kissing you would ruin it. It was just a stupid drunken thing, I promise."

A huge wave of relief came over me.

"Well, I know it's hard to resist Beth Bradley 2.0, but you are going to have to try," I joked.

"I'll do my best." He smirked, as he threw the ball again for Rusty to chase.

I was so glad that Noah and I were on the same page. I figured one day, we would be able to look back on this and laugh.

The morning of the Beth Bradley 2.0 party, I bolted out of bed before the alarm clock went off. I was so ready for this day. I was excited to celebrate with all my friends and officially kick off the new me and my new life. There was a lot to get done before the party, and anxiety kept trying to butt in. I had planned out every last detail and even thought of contingencies.

The morning started off with a five-mile run with Jennifer. We usually ran on Sunday, but we figured that we'd probably be pretty hungover on Sunday, so we'd agreed to do the run today. We had signed up for another half marathon, so we needed to keep our long runs going.

After my run, I took a shower and called the bar to confirm the details. The party was starting at 7:00, but the manager told me that I could come at 6:30 to set up. Camila, Jennifer, and Rachel had all agreed to help me. This meant that I needed to stop at the party store by 5:00 to pick up the balloons and banner. I'd decided on blue, gold, and clear balloons with blue and gold confetti in them—six bunches of four balloons tied to two gold Bs for Beth Bradley. I was going to put them around the room. I'd also gotten a banner that said, "Beth Bradley 2.0." I'd finalized the menu two weeks before. It would be open bar with house wine, a few beers on tap, and rail drinks. For food, we had crab dip, mushroom and spinach flatbread pizzas, tater tots, and chicken pot stickers. The final touch was the dessert that Camila was making. She hadn't told me what it was, because she wanted it to be a surprise. I was excited to see what she'd whipped up. Anything Camila made was guaranteed to be delicious.

After confirming with the bar, I went to get a manicure and blowout. Today was my day, and I wanted to look fantastic. It was nice to get pampered. All day, I was bouncing with excitement. I was ready to thank my friends for all that they had done, and I was excited to just celebrate this new me. The last year had had so many ups and downs, but I had come out on top. I was a strong, independent woman. I knew I could face anything, and I was ready for a night full of fun. Today was about moving forward, about all the possibilities of the future for the new Beth Bradley.

I got home and sent Jennifer, Camila, and Rachel a picture of my hair blown out. I was rocking sexy beach waves, and they all approved. I confirmed they would be at the bar at 6:30.

I'd shopped for a new outfit for tonight. After all, this was a party about a fresh start and moving on—I didn't want to wear something that had any tie to Chad. I pulled on my new skinny blue jeans that really made my butt look good, a purple tank top that brought out my eyes, and new zebra-print flats—they'd been a little expensive, but I figured it was good to treat myself. I certainly deserved it.

I got to the bar first and was arranging the tables and putting the balloons together when the rest of the crew showed up. I gave them all a hug.

"We have a surprise for you," Rachel said as she handed me a box.

I looked in, and there were fifty blue buttons that said "B.B. 2.0" in gold. I smiled with delight.

"These are awesome," I said.

"We figured people could put them on, sort of a solidarity thing. And then they also have a little souvenir to remember this awesome party," Jennifer said.

"I love it. What a great idea."

"And here, I made these." Camila handed me another box; this time filled with lemon cream puffs, one of my favorite desserts. She'd made some last summer when we'd gone over for dinner, and I'd nearly eaten all of them. I tried not to cry.

"You all are the best," I said. "Really, I couldn't ask for better friends. Now let's get to work. This banner isn't going to hang itself."

The room came together nicely. People started coming in around 7:00, starting with Kelly and Derek. The food was coming out at 7:30, but the drinks were already flowing. I went over and gave them a hug and some buttons. More and more people trickled in. Just seeing everyone there for me made my heart swell. I was so lucky to have this support.

"So, is Sean coming?" Rachel gave me a little nudge.

"He said he would when I saw him on Thursday," I said.

Since running into him at the bar, Sean and I had started texting every so often. I felt like our relationship had blossomed from quick three- or four-minute conversations into something deeper. I felt more of a connection with him. He was a really good guy and always trying to go out of his way to help, not just with me, but with everyone in the neighborhood. Just yesterday he'd agreed to bring Camila's new TV upstairs for her. It was nice to have another single friend, another person that just got it.

"You two seem to be best buds now."

I gave a little shrug. "We've got a lot in common, and he's easy to talk to."

"Is he replacing Noah?"

"What? No. Noah and I are still good friends."

"So, you're laughing about locking lips now?" Rachel inquired.

"We just don't talk about it."

Just then I spotted Noah across the room and gave him a wave. He came up and gave me hug. It felt nice and wasn't awkward at all.

"Wow, what a party!"

"Yeah, I'm pleased with the turnout." I hadn't been sure how many people would show up. If people would think what I was doing was silly or empowering, but about forty-five had turned out.

"I'm impressed, with everything. This is a great idea. I wish I thought of having a 2.0 party when I get divorced. I love how it's positive, about moving forward."

"Exactly. It's all about focusing more on what I have, who I can be, and less on what I've lost."

"You have a lot," Noah said with a smile.

I continued working the room, saying hi to everyone. My spirits were flying high. People laughed and had a good time, and the food was amazing. It was all very surreal. All the people I loved, from all different parts of my life, were here to celebrate me. There were friends from college, friends from work, neighborhood friends, even my old roommate, all together in one room.

I decided that it was time for my speech. I got up on a chair so everyone could hear me and clinked my glass. The crowd quieted down.

"Wow, this is great," I said.

I heard a whistle and Michael screamed, "Yeah, 2.0!" which was followed by a big cheer.

"So, I just wanted to thank everyone for coming here tonight. You know the last year has not been easy for me. But, when I look back on everything I went through, there was one common thread. It was you all. I am seriously the luckiest person to have all of you in my life. Every one of you has been beyond supportive. You have listened to me excessively, and let my problems take over almost every conversation. You have cheered me up when I needed it. You've made sure I was okay. And I want to thank you. Because your support has helped me get to where I am. A place where I know that when I get knocked down, I get back up. And when I do, I'm even stronger than I was before. I'm excited for this new chapter, the new adventures. I'm thrilled to share it all with you. Thank you!"

Everyone clapped, and Michael led the group in chanting "2.0! 2.0! 2.0!" It was honestly the best feeling I'd had in a while. I pumped my fists in the air with a huge smile on my face. It was a moment that I wanted to define this year. Not the moment when I'd been crying in my bathroom, not the moment when Chad had told me he was leaving, not all of the times that I didn't feel good enough, that I wasn't worth it, that I was a failure. No. I wanted to remember this year as the year when I stood up and said, "I'm Beth Bradley, and I can handle anything that comes my way. When my life got turned upside down, I moved forward and made an even better life than I'd ever imagined."

I knew that Chad getting married wasn't going to be the last blow. There would be more to come—maybe he and Courtney would have a kid. But I knew that, if or when that happened, I was just going to remember this party, and remember that Beth Bradley 2.0 was a warrior.

As I got down from the chair, I spotted Sean arriving.

"Nice speech," he said, winking.

"Thanks! Thanks for coming," I said. I wanted to give him a hug but stopped short. We settled on a fist bump.

"Thanks for inviting me. Wow, this is crazy, I don't think I even know this many people."

"Ha ha, I'm sure you do. You're friends with everyone. But it does feel nice to be loved and supported. I'm a very lucky girl. Do you want a drink? Everything is on me," I said with a smile.

"Works for me," Sean said.

Sean put his hand on the small of my back as we walked through the crowd to the bar. I got a glass of wine and Sean ordered a beer.

"To you, Beth," he said. After we took a sip, there was an awkward pause, and we both just kind of looked at each other.

"I'm glad you came. Did you see Max Flick's 13 strike outs last night?" I asked, breaking the silence with my go-to baseball talk.

We talked a little bit more. Jennifer, Camila, and Rachel came up to say hi to Sean, and I went to talk to some friends from college. After a few minutes, I glanced over at Rachel and Sean. I wasn't sure what Rachel was saying to him, but he looked like he was having a good time.

"Who's that? He keeps looking over here," Noah asked, appearing at my elbow.

"Oh, that's Sean, our UPS guy," I said.

"You're friends with your UPS guy?" he asked, incredulously.

"Yeah, he's friends with everyone in the neighborhood. He's also divorced so we've bonded over that a bit."

"I see." Noah said as he crossed his arms over his chest.

Was that a touch of jealousy in his voice? Was he threatened by Sean? It was clear that Noah and I weren't quite back to pre-kiss.

Just then, Sean came over, and I introduced him and Noah. They shook hands, and it seemed like Noah gave him an awkward look. Noah excused himself to get another drink at the bar.

"Hey, Beth. I've got to get going, but thanks for inviting me."

"I'm so glad you came."

I went in to give Sean a hug. "I'll probably see you Monday."

The night wound down, and it was just the girls and me left at the bar.

"What a night, Beth. You know how to throw a party," Camila said.

"Thanks, ladies. And thanks for everything. Really, this last year has been tough, but I'm really glad you all were there for me."

I grabbed a bottle of wine and poured out four glasses.

"To the best friends and best neighbors," I said.

"Cheers!"
We clinked our glasses and drank.

The next morning there was a knock at my door. I glanced at the clock and saw that it was 8:30. Who could be knocking at this hour? I knew the girls were probably as hung over as I was. We had finished the night dancing and singing, closing down the bar. I had stumbled in around 2:00 am, the latest I had been out in a long time. My head throbbed, and I was in desperate need of some water.

I opened the door and to my surprise, Chad was standing there.

"Is Zoe okay?" I asked, panicked.

"She's fine."

"Then what are you doing here?"

He drew in a long breath.

"Look, Beth. I haven't stopped thinking about you, I made a mistake."

"What the fuck, Chad?" I grumbled.

I could feel my head pulsing. I was too hungover to deal with this.

"I miss you. I miss our family. I want you back."

"Did you forget that you are getting married in two months?" I hissed.

"I know. Courtney isn't for me, you are."

He tried to look deep in my eyes, to make a connection, but I moved my head away. My hands tightened into fists. Did he really have the nerve to stand at my door, and just declare this, as if nothing had happened? I was utterly shocked. After all this time, what did he think? That I would take him back? Sure, last July I would have done anything to hear him say he had made a mistake and he would fight for our marriage. But a lot had happened, I wasn't the same person anymore, and neither was he. I was Beth Bradley 2.0. I was on a journey of self-discovery, re-inventing myself as a divorced single mom. After the roller coaster of a year, I was coming around to this new person, and I liked her. I liked that I knew I could get through anything. That I had come out the other side better and stronger. And Chad would always be the same lying, cheating person who broke my heart. He would never be the Chad that I had fell in love with so many ago.

"You just can't handle that I'm doing fine without you."

"No, that's not it."

"Yes, it is. You saw the pictures on social media from last night, and you couldn't take it. I'm not this heartbroken person. I moved on, and I'm stronger. Stronger than you ever thought I could be."

"I miss you." He tried to reach for my hand, but I pulled it away.

"Well, you can't have me. And besides, I don't want you. I deserve so much better."

He stood there speechless for a few moments. I wasn't sure how he played this out in his mind, but I was sure this wasn't the ending he thought he'd get.

"But," he trailed off.

"But nothing, Chad." I said, softening my tone. "Go home."

He turned around and slowly walked back to his car.

-13-

JULY

The morning of the block party, Zoe and I had three very important jobs. We had to put together the gift basket, make meatballs, and fill the balloons for the water balloon toss. I told Zoe we could do the balloons at 11:30, as she ripped open the package and started sorting by color. First, we had to put together the gift basket.

I went into the office and grabbed everything we needed. This year's gift basket was one of our best yet. I had high hopes for a lot of donations to the raffle. We had four different bottles of wine, designer sunglasses, pineapple earrings, gift cards to Backyard Bistro and La Caverna, squirt guns, sidewalk chalk, an inflatable palm tree sprinkler, and beach towels, all packaged in a Yeti cooler.

"I really want to win the gift basket," Zoe said as she helped me put the wine in. "I really like the squirt guns."

"Yeah, they are cool," I said.

"I could play with Willow and Wyatt with them."

It had taken a year, but I had started getting used to Zoe's obsession with Courtney's kids. She adored playing with them, and it seemed like they were really good to her and always included Zoe in their fun. They didn't act like Zoe was too young, and it made me happy that she had someone to play with. *That* part of the insta-family I was okay with. I still wasn't okay with her soon-to-be stepmom. Now that Chad and Courtney were getting married, I knew that I was going to have to figure out a way to be okay with that. It would take time, but I knew I could get there. Even just yesterday when Zoe was telling me about Courtney taking her for ice cream. I didn't cringe, I didn't feel sick, I didn't even feel all that sad. I just looked at the sweet smile on my daughter's face and knew that she was happy. And I would be okay.

I put the rest of the stuff in the cooler and added some colorful tissue paper to make it pop.

"How does it look, Zoe?"

"Looks great!"

"Now for the cellophane, can you help?"

"Yep!" Zoe said as she grabbed it off the table.

After my fourth gift basket, I still had trouble with the cellophane, but Zoe proved to be a good helper.

"Ta-da," I said when we were done and gave Zoe a high five.

"Can we do the balloons now?"

"Why don't we make the meatballs, and then blow up the balloons."

"Okay!" Zoe said, running to the kitchen.

She pulled out our aprons, and I got the ingredients for the meatballs. I had found a recipe for a pineapple version that I figured would be perfect.

"First we need to make the sauce," I said.

Zoe poured the pineapple juice, teriyaki sauce, and sugar into a bowl and started stirring.

"It smells yummy," she said.

"It does." We put the sauce in the crock pot with the meatballs. "It should be ready just in time for the party."

I heard a buzz on my phone and looked to check it. It was a

message from Scott, another match from Here Comes Love. We had a pleasant date last week and were making plans to meet up for a second one. I still had a little anxiety with putting myself out there and being vulnerable, but I was working through it. I wanted to just have fun with dating. I knew I wasn't ready for something serious, but was enjoying meeting new people, and learning more about myself.

"So now can we do the balloons?" Zoe asked.

"Yes, now it's time to fill up the balloons."

"Yay!" Zoe exclaimed.

We got started, and soon we had quite the system down. Zoe would hand me a balloon, and then I would fill it with water and tie it, and then she would put it in the bucket. First, we started with the purple ones, and then we moved on to the green and yellow. Halfway through the white ones, Zoe said, "Julian said he'd be my partner for the water balloon toss. I think we're going to win."

Julian and Zoe had been partners last year, and they'd lost in the second round, but I loved her enthusiasm. I still hadn't found a partner for corn hole. I'd been planning to ask Noah, but things were still a little awkward. I could always play by myself, but that wouldn't be any fun. It was sad to think that I'd have to sit this year out and not be able to defend my title.

After we blew up all hundred balloons, Zoe and I got dressed. I'd gotten us matching grass skirts, which we paired with white tank tops, purple leis, and yellow flowers clipped in our hair. Rachel had told me to wear the coconut bra, but I'd reminded her that this was a family affair. We sure looked cute. We headed outside, where Camila and Sebastian had already started roasting the pig.

"I can't wait to eat that," I said.

"Not me!" Zoe said making a sour face.

Jennifer and Michael's house usually had the food and drinks. Last week, Michael had made a tiki bar, and Jennifer and the twins were helping to decorate it. Zoe and I brought over our meatballs and plugged in the crock pot.

"Smells good," Michael said, lifting the lid to take a whiff.

Rachel and Avery were decorating the street with flower garlands and palm trees. Highland Avenue looked great. Around 12:50, we put the traffic cones on either side of the block, Travis cued up the music, and we were open for business.

I put on my fanny pack, ready to sell the raffle tickets, and started mingling with the neighbors. David and Susan, who lived behind me, came up to say hi.

"Hi, Beth," Susan said as she gave me a hug.

"Hi, how are you? How is your summer going?" I asked.

"It's good. We just got back from Maine. It was so gorgeous."

"What part?"

"Bar Harbor."

"I love that area."

Chad and I had taken Zoe there two summers ago. It was so nice and peaceful.

"Can I get you any raffle tickets?" I asked. "We've got a great basket this year."

"Sure, I'll take ten dollars' worth," she said.

"So, are we going to meet again in the corn hole finals?" David asked.

Last year, Chad and I beat them in a very intense match.

"I don't know. We'll see. I still need to find a partner," I said.

"I'll be your partner," a voice from behind me said.

I turned around and there was Sean. He had on a green Hawaiian shirt with a yellow lei. I was excited to see him getting in on the fun.

"Sean! You came," I said.

"Yeah, it sounded like fun. I'm glad you all invited me; I didn't have much else going on today. So, what's this I hear about a corn hole tournament?"

"Well, I don't mean to brag, but I'm the defending champion. Unfortunately, my old partner left me."

It didn't sting so much when I said it. I could even joke about it, with the right company.

"Well, it's been a while since I've played, but I'd be happy to play with you."

"Great! I'll let Rachel know. Now, can I interest you in any raffle tickets? It's for the gift basket over there." I pointed to the gift basket sitting next to the food. "The proceeds go to SOAR, the place I tutor at."

"I'd be happy to. But only if you'll drink the wine with me if I win."

"It's a deal."

Sean bought ten dollars' worth of tickets and went over to talk to some of the neighbors.

The block party was off to a huge success. I had already sold $150 worth of raffle tickets, and the water balloon toss was about to start. Zoe and Julian lined up across Camila's yard. They had huge, ear-to-ear smiles on their faces and danced around with excitement. They made it past the second round, but they got out on the fourth round. A huge improvement from last year. Julian missed the balloon and the water splashed all over him.

"Julian!" Zoe exclaimed.

Julian shrugged his shoulders, and then they both grabbed squirt guns and chased each other around, spraying one another and laughing. Their laughter was infectious.

I spotted Noah from across the lawn and waved. He headed my way. We weren't quite laughing about the time we made out, but I had a feeling we would get there.

"Zoe looks like she's having fun."

"Oh, a blast," I said. "I think this is one of her favorite days of the year. Come to think of it, it's probably one of my favorites as well."

"Well, every year it gets better and better," he said. "Caleb took off towards the squirt guns without even saying goodbye. I saw the raffle was for SOAR. That's nice. I've missed going."

During the summer months, the center did camps and stuff for the kids, so there was no volunteering to help with homework.

"Yeah, I'm excited for the school year to start up again so we can go back," I said.

Noah bought thirty dollars' worth of tickets.

"So, did you find a partner for corn hole?" he asked.

"I did, actually."

"Who?"

"Sean."

"The UPS guy?"

"Yep."

"Well, he's probably better than me, so good luck."

At that moment, Gregory came by to get more raffle tickets. I was in a bit of a haze, but we chatted about his oldest son, who was getting married in the fall. He couldn't believe how quickly they grew up. I knew what he was talking about. This year had been crazy, but it also felt like I'd just blinked and Zoe was done with kindergarten.

Rachel finally announced that the corn hole tournament was about to start. Sean joined me.

"I guess that means we're up," he said.

Sean proved to be great at corn hole and a worthy partner. We dominated the first round, knocking out Camila and Sebastian, then we beat Mark and Olivia, neighbors from down the block, in the semi-finals, which meant we were playing against Jennifer and Michael in the finals.

I went to grab another beer and saw Jennifer. "You and Michael are going down," I said.

I took this tournament very seriously.

"I'm glad Sean is here. You two can cry on each other's shoulders after we destroy you," she said. I was glad that we were on the same level of competitiveness.

The game against Jennifer and Michael was very close. All Michael needed to do was get his last beanbag in the hole, and they would win. If he missed, we would win.

"C'mon Michael. Get this in, or you're sleeping on the couch for the rest of the year," Jennifer said.

Michael tossed his bean bag in his hand. "Don't worry, babe. We got this," he said with a sly smile.

Michael went for the throw. The bean bag was in the air, and I felt like time had stopped. We all let out a large gasp and then, *bam*, Michael missed the hole, and the board completely.

Sean and I had won.

Sean picked me up and spun me around.

He set me down and we stared at each other, big smiles on our faces.

"That was intense," he said.

"Yeah, but I'm so glad we won. If we hadn't, I don't think we would be able to be friends anymore," I said with a wink.

"Well, that wouldn't be good then."

Sean went off to chat with some more neighbors, and I grabbed a beer and sat down to Rachel, sighing heavily.

"Man, it's been a year," I said.

"It sure has. But you got through it, I'm impressed."

"Trust me, there are still moments. But I just let myself have five minutes, and then pull myself together. Because if I sit there and feel sorry for myself, or overwhelmed then Chad wins. I'm not going to let being cheated on and left define who I am. I want people to think about how I weathered the storm and came out a better person."

"Well, you certainly did," Rachel said.

Camila and Jennifer came and sat down by us.

"Another successful block party, ladies," Jennifer said as we clinked our beers together.

"Yeah, and we raised $650 so far. Not bad," I added.

"There's still time—when are we doing the raffle?" Camila asked.

"Twenty minutes. I better make a last call."

I stood up on a chair and yelled, "Last call for the raffle! We'll be doing the drawing at 3:30."

As I looked around, I just smiled. I looked at the girls and thought about how grateful I was that we'd all ended up on this street together. How lucky I was that I found neighbors who were like family. I looked at Noah and was glad we had patched things up. I knew he'd always be there when I needed him, and I wasn't going to risk losing that. I looked at Sean and was happy that I had made a new friend, one that was a worthy corn hole partner. And then I looked at Zoe. Sure, Chad didn't turn out to be the person I thought he was, and we wouldn't be sharing our life together, but together we'd created this amazing little human, and, because of that, I couldn't and wouldn't hate him. This wasn't where I'd expected my life was going to take me, but I was happy that I was there.